I Was Told There
Would Be Jetpacks
And Other Stories

By Robert John Jenson

I Was Told There Would Be JetPacks

and other stories

Robert John Jenson

I was Told There Would Be Jetpacks

By Robert John Jenson

First Paperback edition March 2021

Book design and cover art by Robert John Jenson

ISBN 978-0-9600737-1-9 (paperback)

ISBN 978 -0-9600737-3-3 (ebook)

Library of Congress Control Number: 2021905244

https://www.facebook.com/robertjohnjenson

Once again and always,
To my lovely wife and daughters -
Without you, all is lost.

And to my parents, who always
encouraged a good tale…

Table of Contents

Introduction

MY wife gasped, and I was sure I was going to hit a dog or cat - or a small child.

"What?" I asked, alarmed, and hit the brakes.

Then she laughed.

Damn it. That was the problem when she was startled. Drops an earring? Gasp! Shocked at someone's behavior on TV? Gasp! There's a rampaging herd of bison thundering around in the basement? Gasp! There is just no scale to measure them by. They all have the same volume of shocked alarm, and she gets me every time. Over 30 years of marriage, and she gets me. Every. Damned. Time.

This time, she thought she saw a TARDIS in our neighbor's yard. It was actually a blue and white air mattress tipped on end and tied with bungee cords to the street sign on the corner. An honest mistake.

"For a minute there, Lee was cooler than I thought!" she said. She didn't think it was a *real* TARDIS. Don't be silly. Just one of those cardboard facsimiles. Either way, I'm betting the Gasp! would have had the same level of energy.

I wouldn't be a very good husband if I didn't immediately post about this on Facebook. I joked about how she would have leapt out of the car if she thought it was a real TARDIS, and my cousins encouraged her adventures. My brother-in-law Matt made the comment that the blind Ryan women see things that others don't, and then I joked about a story being in there about how they save the universe…and then over two years later my second novel, *All The Stars That Ever Were,* was finished.

Now, I know what you're thinking. Husband of the year - making fun of his blind wife on Facebook and then capitalizing on it by writing a book. Look, when the fire gets lit, this writer has no shame. I had not intended on this being my second novel (a long-suffering ghost story, *Latent Images*, is still pretty pissed at me for not working on it other than an occasional polishing at what's been written so far – this has gone on for about 25 years now). I had wanted to write a multiverse story, but had no focus for it, until the sisters formed in my mind. To say they are copies of my wife and her sisters is only seeing the eyesight problems they have in common (you write what you know), and that they are blond and blue-eyed. There are mannerisms that my wife inevitably shares with the character of Cheryl, but there are also my daughters in there as well (if my daughters ever want to sue over identity theft for the sisters in my first novel, *The October Light Of August*, I more than likely would lose in court).

All The Stars That Ever Were grew organically, the story evolving into its own tale as it went. I knew how I wanted it to end, it's the middle bits that changed – for the better.

You'll get to meet the three sisters again in a short story in this collection, "Epilog for a Mad Bomber". I'll warn you that there is a bit of a spoiler going on if you haven't read *All The Stars That Ever Were*. I'm not done with those set of sisters yet for sure, and they may tie into future novels in an unlikely way. Stay tuned.

I knew I wasn't done with the sisters in *The October Light Of August* either, and they've waited patiently to have their origin stories explored. There are two stories with the zombie sisters here, along with two more set in that world. Again, spoilers if you haven't read *that* novel. Let us remember I am sticking to the distant world of 2012 where it takes place, so if there seem to be anachronisms to our day and age, that is why.

You may very well be thinking what's up with this guy and sisters? I never had a brother (although I have great brothers-in-law), and I am extraordinarily proud of my two daughters, so I guess my inclination when writing about siblings is to stick with the sister dynamic. Plus, I like to write strong female characters, which leads me to my mom and the only fully non-fiction piece in this volume ("In the Dying Days of Photo Labs" is a true story, but a streamlined and fictionalized version). "To Bed: 11:30" is an homage to my mom, a woman who did whatever she wanted, and on her own terms.

The first novel I wanted to write was an epic fantasy. Some of it was actually written, and some of that was cannibalized for other stories since that particular novel will never come to be. I just waited too long, and the grim and gritty fantasy world I envisioned was done so much better by George R.R. Martin. Some of the prose was stolen for "Long Forgotten Blue" – the only story I wrote in one sitting (although I polished it up over a few months, of course). One idea was incorporated into my 'elf with no name' fantasy world in "Cothram Ceartas". That is the only short story where I wrote an immediate sequel, "The Lure of Tall Bridges After Midnight" – perhaps my favorite thing I have written so far. I do hope to kick off that world into a novel, but the ideas for that are still percolating.

I have had a love of the mythology of sasquatch lore ever since I saw *The Legend of Boggy Creek* at a drive-in back in the day. While I think that if they existed one would have wound up on the hood of a logging truck by now, the 11 year-old in me likes to think they are stomping around out there, the last secrets the wild has yet to give away. I have two very different takes on the mythology. One is more of an old fashioned science-fiction tale called "Temporal Footprints"

11

where the bigfoot is more of a vessel for travel. I wrote this for the first volume my writers group put out called *A Roll of the Dice* (we rolled story dice to come up with themes for the stories we wrote). Apparently, my sasquatch was considered transgender, and so our short story collection was unable to be sold in India. While I hadn't thought much about that as a component of the story (I saw the character as having more of a maternal fixation), when the analogy was pointed out to me I liked it very much and made it clear the character's transformation was a happy one. Between that and my friend Eric's lesbian characters in his story, it kept us from the (I like to think, anyway) lucrative Indian market. I feel like I have some sort of street cred. "Banned in India, dude. Controversial as *hell*."

My other sasquatch story – very different in form and mood - was written to try to get in a local short story collection, but wasn't a good fit. It had to be about 1,200 words, so it gave my voice a brevity I usually don't have, but I liked the constraint. Still not sure where the story came from.

"Through a Veil of Moondust" is another story written for my writers group, yet another old-fashioned sci-fi tale, and is an homage to a turtle I found and my favorite childhood toy line.

And then there's the title story, "I Was Told There Would be Jetpacks." It can feel very strange, at times, living in the future that was so far away when I was a kid. I wonder if the future has *ever* lived up to the dreams of a generation in its youth? That we are still dealing with the same problems and prejudices we always have is maddening, and that so many people do not care about the rights and quality of life for others is incomprehensible to me. Realizing that you have been a part of the problem all along is a shameful thing.

If there's any sort of theme to these stories, much of it is about change, I suppose. Some of it is welcomed and embraced, some accepted grudgingly, and some forced upon the characters. I don't have them grouped in sections – while ones tied together in their own universes will be presented chronologically, they all will be spread out in a grab bag of tales.

I wouldn't have the luxury of being able to scribble away at these stories if it weren't for my parents who always encouraged me to be creative. My sister and I grew up with love and were treated as if we were worth listening and talking to. We had parents who cared about what we thought. I don't know if that happens a lot, at least back in the day.

I had an English teacher in college, a man by the name of Homer Lusk, who made an impact on me philosophically, and also opened my eyes to better literature. I probably wouldn't have written anything if it weren't for him.

I also think it is important to thank the authors that lit the fires of imagination over the years. From Lester Dent to Lord Dunsany, Stephen King to John Steinbeck, Raymond Chandler to Patrick O'Brian and so many, many more it's a crime I can't list them all. But they all helped add flavor to the sauce, and were inspirational, making me want to try my hand at telling a tale.

I owe a huge debt to my friends in the Science Fiction, Fantasy and Horror Writers of Spokane. Thanks for the camaraderie, inspiration and feedback. I hope by the time this is published, we have the band back together.

My daughters are hands down my best work. Thank goodness for their momma, who they inherited their brains and work ethic from. They have grown into the young women I had always hoped for, and they make a papa so very proud. You really should envy me.

My wife, Kari, is my muse. Earlier I wrote that she gets me, and she does. In more ways than one. I think creating, and writing, is first and foremost showing off – "Hey, look! Look at this! Look what I can do!" And anything I've ever done since I first met her is to try and show off and impress her. She keeps me grounded, and makes me want to be a better person. She makes me laugh, makes me think, makes me honest and makes me care. I've always said it's not fair that she gets to be the brains and the beauty of the outfit, but there we have it. I am a very, *very* lucky man.

* * *

I had intended this collection to be released into the wild last year. I hadn't finished two stories I wanted in here, and it dawned on me I was dragging my feet until this year. I mean, *honestly* - it was 2020…

Robert John Jenson
03-03-2021

Bobby Jenson

When I was littel adout 6 or 7 I was afrad of the dark. I saw Ugly faces in the dark So my Mother had to give me a floshlight to shine at it so that it was nothing to be ofraid of.

Epilog for a Mad Bomber

The pixie had been picking them off one by one. According to Caleb, anyway. Big, dumb, but living up to his name, Caleb. He may not have been the brightest of the flock, but you could rely on him without fail. Caleb had pure, unadulterated faith in him. Everette, Malachi – they were the ones that stayed near you to feel important, to have a taste of power by proxy. And that was fine, as long as the work was accomplished. But you didn't trust them like you could Caleb.

If Caleb had a daughter of child-bearing age, he would have happily let Isaac take her as another wife. Malachi…wouldn't have been happy if Sarah had been taken. He would have consented, of course – the holding on to power would have been more important than the happiness of his daughter. But there would have been an opening for discontent. And as a leader, you had to know where to draw lines, to keep your desires in check to keep the faithful as one.

The only time he had struck Caleb was when he called the pixie "adorable".

"You would call an agent of The Enemy adorable?" Isaac had snapped, and back-handed the oaf without thinking, and instantly regretted it. *He isn't the brightest, and it isn't his fault*, Isaac thought. Still, he was under a lot of pressure now, and sometimes you *did* need to use the whip.

"I didn't mean it as anything," Caleb had muttered, wounded. "She…it…ain't what you would expect from The Enemy, father."

"The Enemy will disguise himself in unexpected ways, Caleb. This you should know."

Not that Isaac believed in The Enemy one God-damned bit. The only enemy was the rest of the whole wide-world, and if he could make them bow down to kiss his ass without resorting to superstitious nonsense, he would. But, to gather an army, you had to collect the gullible.

"I do know that Father," Caleb had said. "I do. But it was…*disconcerting* to see her in some sort of hippie shirt, those little round hippie sunglasses and sweatpants. She - it - has short blond hair – it looked like Tinkerbell, you know? I guess I would have expected something more…"

Disconcerting?, Isaac had thought, amused. Caleb had been trying to broaden his vocabulary of late. Isaac's first impulse had been to suggest that perhaps Caleb found the Tinkerbell look desirable and had better pray long and hard about that, but he needed no more leverage over the big man, and frankly he didn't have the time right now. They were under siege.

"The Enemy will try to seduce you in unimaginable ways, Caleb," Isaac had responded. "Not all of them dealing with desires of the flesh."

"Yes, father."

Someone else might question Caleb's perception of events. Everette, if he were still here, would have scoffed at the man and declared he had imagined it all. Everette scoffed at everyone else except Isaac, though, and Caleb didn't have the imagination to create the pixie out of thin air. If he had come to Isaac and described a horned-demon of smoking red-leather and forked tail, Caleb would have known the man was lying, or gone over the cliff of insanity. No, Isaac believed Caleb saw what he had – or at least believed he did. It wasn't beyond comprehension that he had hallucinated something, but Isaac didn't buy it. Something as weird and unlikely as a young woman appearing out of thin air, snatching your lieutenants away with a wink and a smile was so utterly fantastic that it more than likely was true. The

Feds had them surrounded, sure. But they weren't at the stage where they felt they had to storm the compound. It had been a long time since Waco, but they didn't want another one of *those*, he was certain. And neither did Isaac, truthfully. He let women and children leave, in fact, he ordered them to go, and any of the men that wanted to. Not many of the men would, and that was fine. Isaac understood misplaced bravado, and liked to take advantage of it. When the time came, he would not sacrifice women and children and be branded a coward like Koresh. He had tended his flock, and be judged merciful. But he would take as many Feds with him as he could.

"She grabbed Malachi, Father," Caleb had said, beginning to repeat himself. "She just kind of blurred into existence out of thin air, grabbed his neck and he stiffened up. I didn't shoot at her because I was afraid of hitting Malachi, and she smiled at me and said, 'Don't worry big guy, your turn's coming.' And she - it - blew me a kiss and they both were *gone*."

Well, evidently she had made good on her promise. He hadn't seen Caleb in several hours.

Isaac wasn't sure if he was the only one left in the compound or not. The Fed's drones roamed around freely now, and no one was taking shots at them anymore, so he very well could be. He was under the assumption this pixie apparition would be coming for him, so he had retreated to the sanctuary to wait. Apparently the Feds had taken out the surveillance cameras, as black monitors reflected his gaunt and stubbled face. No matter. He sat in a desk chair, back to the concrete, within reach of the main detonator.

* * *

When the pixie showed up, things happened fast. She hadn't popped into existence right next to him like Caleb had reported, but across the room by the only door. Isaac was on his feet, the SIG in his hand and nine shots fired right at her – he was fully prepared to

19

empty the clip as she stumbled back into the door – but he felt a prick of pain in his neck, and he felt a rush, as if something was tuning up in him, his nerves thrumming as if a rosined-up bow had dragged across them. He also could not move. The pixie remained on her feet, one arm across her chest, the other flung out behind her as she hit the door.

A voice whispered in his ear, "Always be aware of your surroundings. You never know who will sneak in your six, dude."

Isaac stood, unable to move, the SIG still gripped in his hand, his right arm still extended. He was a statue.

"I think I caught one," the pixie said. There was no blood on her, or anywhere.

"What?" said the voice behind him. Another woman.

"I caught one! A bullet!"

"You liar."

"I did!" The pixie opened her left hand, and blob of metal lay in her palm.

"No way! You picked that up off the floor."

"I did not."

"Well, as many rounds as he got off, you got lucky."

"I actually *tried*, and I *caught* it. Look, you have to let me have this. I caught it, damn it."

"*Fine*. You'll be insufferable now, Kal-El."

"My goodness - we'll make a nerd out of you yet."

The voice behind him snorted, and Isaac could feel panic begin to well up in him. He was hyper-aware of the sensations surrounding him: the warm skin of the woman's strong fingers prying the SIG from his hand, her breath drifting across his cheek, the lingering scent of lilac that flavored the soap she had used to wash herself. But he had no control over any movement except his breathing and blinking.

"Don't hyperventilate on me, buddy," said the woman. "You'll pass out and be fine, but then that makes it hard to explain things to you."

The woman moved into his field of view. She wore a simple green t-shirt, her long blond hair falling to her shoulders. She looked to be in her early thirties, and had light freckles dotting her tanned face. She looked familiar, as did the pixie. Her blue eyes darted slightly back in forth as she gazed him.

"You recognize me?" she asked, then turned her head to the other woman. "You think he knows who we are?"

"Hard to say," the pixie sighed as she moved into view, and slid the sunglasses up to the top of head. She stared at Isaac, and he noticed her eyes matched the movement of the other woman's, and he was certain that they were sisters... And then, of course, he knew them. And in that instant, he could tell that they knew he did, too.

"There it is!" they both said at once, then turned heads to each other and laughed.

"Yeah, you tried to *kill* us. Didn't you, you miserable son of a bitch?" said the older one. The one that had wandered the streets of Las Vegas for months before...coming to her senses, apparently.

"That's okay – honestly, we don't take it personally, do we Dar?"

"Nope. Well, maybe a little."

"Okay yeah, a *little*. But, you weren't aiming for us specifically. And yet you *did* kill an awful lot of other people. And that *really* bugs us."

"More than a little."

"But hey – you missed *us*. Fortunately, I guess, we had bigger issues to deal with. And, when you think about it, you actually did your part to save the universe."

"You know, I hadn't thought about it, but you're *right*," the pixie laughed.

Darla, that was her name. And the other one was Carol. The media had *loved* to shove the three sisters in the face of the masses. Well, Isaac had enjoyed the pain he had dealt every time they did that, imagining the sheep of the world wagging their ignorant heads in sorrow at the deaths of three lovely sisters, and all the other innocent lives that were lost that night. It would never stop tasting so delicious, he was sure of it.

"Yep, we were the pieces that clicked into place and took out a bigger problem than you," Carol said. "But we were picked for the job during your act of terrorism, ultimately, so we'll give you a teeny bit of credit."

Isaac's breathing began to calm, as anger began to overwhelm his fear. As it had always done. Planning revenge always had that effect on him.

"Look," Darla said. "We're at the part where he starts calming down because he's already *plotting our demise*."

"Oh yeah, look at that," Carol replied. "This one's gotten there faster than all the rest, don't you think?"

"Could be. Must mean he's more evil than the other ones?"

"Why sis, could you be projecting our prejudices because he's our very own, *personal* mad bomber?"

"Wow, we'll make a scientist out of you yet."

Isaac blinked, and kept his breathing controlled.

"But," Carol continued, "I imagine we are dealing mostly with fine lines here, right? Mere percentage points of evil? We've seen the ranting and ravers – the true believers – and the con artists, like this creep. I think the devout ones were just bug-fuck nuts. But this guy…he hates everyone equally."

Carol directed her attention fully onto him. "Yet, you don't want credit for your crimes. You tell your *flock* that to make it look like some Islamic jihadists have bombed Vegas will finally tip Americans over the edge and demand the middle-east be turned into a glass parking lot. You claim to want to incite a race war. You want to overthrow the government, and you'll do that by attacking like-minded people such as yourself. But you always want it to look like someone *else* did it. Why is that?"

Let me speak, you filthy whore, and I'll tell you exactly why you'll die like the worthless sack of flesh you are, Isaac thought bitterly.

"And why would I let you speak?" Carol stated. Isaac blinked again, and his breathing stumbled in its even pace.

"No, I can't read your mind. Wouldn't want to climb into *that* rats nest even if I could. See, we've just done this enough times that being called a filthy whore over and over has lost its charm, oddly enough."

Isaac's breath halted and huffed, and he was utterly confused. He had never actually verbally abused a woman like that, aloud, even if the thoughts were always muttering away in his head. *Had* he? "Yeah, I understand you're confused. And I can explain, *yet again*, what's going on, but you know what? I think Darla and I are tired of this phase, and we just want to move on to the endgame."

"Boy howdy, do I ever," Darla remarked.

"So, why do you like to try and pin your dirty work on others?" Carol asked him again. "Because you want to keep doing it. Like a serial killer, if you take credit for it, someone's going to stop you, right? But serial killers do get caught, and now it's the end of the line for you, bub." She leaned in, her wicked smile lost from view as their noses almost touched.

"Let me make it clear, there is *no* escape from where you're going now."

and then he was mashing the detonator but really he was just sweeping the backstock at the hardware store where he worked as his wife reached across the breakfast table to squeeze his hand when his cell mate asked him to light 'em up, light 'em all the fuck up and take out the garbage you little bastard, his mother screamed at him, or you'll get a whipping like

And he was standing in the pre-dawn light, the morning air drastically cooler, the sharp smell of pine in the air, mixed with the pungent smell of other men. Isaac drew in ragged breaths, deeply afraid that he had finally lost his mind. He had always prided himself in his ability to think clearly, but now he wasn't certain that he may have set foot in the outer circle of hell he did not believe in. Carol still stood before him, but she was silhouetted against the pale morning sky.

Darla whooped. "A bit nippy out. Are you cold, sis?"

"Yeah, I'm changing clothes," Carol answered. She stepped away from Isaac, and he saw her clothes shift into warmer garments, a loose hood slipping up and over the top of her head.

"Better get him taken care of before he freezes," Darla suggested.

"I'm getting there," Carol replied, and pulled what looked like a knife out of her coat. Before Isaac could suck in a breath, she was

23

deftly cutting at his tac-vest, his shirt, slicing his belt and holster free, splitting the seams of his Wranglers, and carving at his boots. He squeezed his eyes shut, and could feel the blade hit his skin, yet he was never cut. But his clothes were soon ribbons drifting off of him, and his bare testicles felt like they wanted to crawl up inside him when the cold air gripped them.

What the hell is going on? his mind screamed. He was completely, and utterly lost. As he took pride in clarity of mind, he also considered himself a master chess player, a person who could foresee problems before they developed. But he could never imagine a scenario such as this. Naked and defenseless before a mere woman. It felt as if his body wanted to tremble, both from the cold and fear, but evidently even that sort of involuntary muscle control was denied him.

"Okay, suit him up," Carol barked, and in that instant he felt something crawl all over his body in a flash. It may have originated from his neck, but he couldn't be sure. Soon, though, he was warmer. Oh yes, that was better. Much warmer...

"Alright," Carol said, somewhere to his left, "now let's shut them down. For good."

That hyper-aware, tuned-up and highly-strung feeling he had begun to accept as a constant, vanished. He gave a quiet, astonished grunt, and he heard a chorus of them surrounding him. In the gloom, he could see at least three shadowy figures directly in front of him, and perhaps more behind those. Ah...is this where the pixie had been taking his men?

"We all comfy?" Darla asked. "No complaints? Goody." Her sister snorted.

"Not like we give a damn how y'all are feeling right now," Carol stated. "And we sure as shit aren't going to give you your voices back to start cursing and condemning us. We'll let you save it for yourselves."

Isaac's nerves were calming again. He had his men, he was sure of it. And if he had people to control, things were looking up. He didn't know where they were, but his confidence in escaping this situation rose ever higher. These women would *pay*...

"I suppose you're wondering why we've brought you here," Carol said loudly.

Darla groaned. "Go for the obvious opening statement, sis. Geeze."

"Shut up. Good a place as any to start." Carol raised her voice again, as if addressing a larger group. "Some of you may have enough imagination to wonder where 'here' is."

Isaac wished he could take a look around, see what his environment was. Outside, obviously, open space – cold and arid, the smell of pine and mesquite and dust. The figures in front of him were as motionless as he, enveloped in the same form-fitting garb he must be wearing. There was a familiarity of their silhouettes, but they all had the same height so he could not judge who they were for size. There was no giant in view indicating Caleb was there.

"Gentlemen, you are very far from home, and there will be no going back. There will be no one to check up on you, so no one to try and ambush for escape. The quicker you accept this is where you are now, the better off your chances of survival. The node we installed in your neck is now collapsing in on itself – we couldn't take you back now even if we wanted to. Your protective suit may last about a month, but eventually it will be gone. Look on the bright side – you get to indulge that survival fetish you've stroked to all your life, because you are really going to have to pull out all the stops to survive here."

Carol began a slow walk through the group, and she passed out of his sight to the right.

"Gentlemen, you are in the late…plasticine."

"Oh, so close!" Darla laughed.

"Damn it," Carol muttered. "Plast…plaster – *ply!* Let's try that again. You are in the late *Pleistocene* era, roughly 10,000 years ago, at the end of the last ice age.

Oh, bullshit, Isaac thought. He knew a con when he heard one. He had no clue how he had been maneuvered into this position, but he was beginning to suspect he had been drugged somehow.

"Now, I know a lot of you just flat out don't believe the universe is any older than 6,000 years. Honestly, I can't help you there, and you're on your own. If you want to keep your faith in counted be-gats, then be my guest. Pretend you're in hell, and have a ball. Now, maybe a few forward-thinking souls can accept the notion of time travel, and, sorry to say, you're off the mark as well. We can't travel through time – but we can jump into other universes."

Isaac let out a sharp scoff of a breath, and heard others echo the same.

"I know, I know," Carol continued. "I don't blame you. I was right there with you once. I still haven't embraced nerd level with open arms, but I accept the worlds we live in. And the simple fact is we have a multiverse that is real, and you are on an Earth not of your own. As it gets easier to see, you might find yourself accepting the notion quicker than you think."

"And if not," Darla offered, "a sabertooth cat on your ass may make your mind up for you."

"Yep," Carol agreed. "That'll do it too. *Anyway*, you are in the same geographic location you came from, and that is in the incredi-bly awesome Great Basin of North America. Any horses that may still be here are too small to tame and ride, sorry. Good luck with the mastodons and rhinos, and don't fuck with the giant sloths, even if they are slow."

Isaac closed his eyes, willing a bolt of thunder to crackle out of the sky to shut the mouthy bitch up and free him from his paralysis.

"Just a little info here, we will leave you absolutely no weapons. You are, of course, more than welcome to fashion any out of the rocks and sticks you come across. I would think if you all cooperat-ed, life would be that much easier. But honestly? I don't see that happening. You all will be so busy trying to dominate each other I expect a bloodbath by tomorrow morning. Maybe I'm wrong – hell, *maybe* you'll love each other so much it'll be one big orgy five minutes after we're gone."

"That would be *awesome!*" Darla laughed.

"I'd recommend leaving a few on watch if y'all go that route," Carol advised. "Honestly, guys, I'm afraid you aren't taking the sa-bertooth cat threat seriously. Darla's actually tussled with one. Let me tell you, it was one tenacious beast."

"I wore it out, though," Darla remarked. "I think it ended up kind of depressed, actually."

"Anyway, there are plenty of animals here that would love to eat you, and ones you'll piss off royally if you try and eat them. Good luck with that."

The only things getting eaten will be your souls when I'm through with you, Isaac thought, and opened his eyes. It was much lighter now, the sun behind him yet, but not quite over the horizon. But the even lighting gave much more detail to his surroundings, and his spirits were lifting. Until he realized the man across from him was himself. All three of them were.

Isaac drew in a surprised breath, and a chorus of gasps surrounded him.

"Ah," Carol said. "I think they've noticed what's going on."

"Yay!" Darla replied.

"I've been trying to tell you, we have left you with *nothing.* No one else to help you. No one else to try and dominate. Just your one true love, and your own worst enemy. You've met him, and he is yourself."

"You tell 'em, Pogo."

This is just another trick, Isaac thought bleakly. *Another illusion – a hallucination brought on by some drug. It has to be. A multiverse. Worthless, comic book nonsense!* But...he could see the same thoughts in the eyes across from him.

"I will keep stressing, the quicker you accept this, the better off you'll be. You are stuck here with exactly sixty-three other versions of yourself. Yes, Darla and I have been busy. It's a hobby, what can I say. Some people travel while on vacation, I collect mad bombers."

"Personally, I have a lot of free time," Darla quipped.

"You have essentially vanished from your world – your minions were left to be collected by law enforcement to pay for their crimes. We may or may not have suggested to them that you were dragged off by an angel of retribution and tossed down to hell. Since Darla was effectively back from the dead and taking them out, perhaps it's not far from the truth."

"Aw, thank you sis. Fist time you ever called me an angel."

"Don't let it go to your head."

I am in hell, Isaac thought. *Women who will not shut up.* The eyes across from him said much the same.

"So we're going to wrap it up here, and let you guys get on with trying to survive. I'll remind you, your suit is already decaying. It will keep you warm, protect you from blows and cuts and any attack…for now. In about a month, it will be gone. It will not keep you from getting sick if you eat the wrong thing. From suffocating, drowning. If it were up to me, you would be freezing your asses off until you found a way to stay warm. I was outvoted, and so be it. There are no other humans on the continent, no – ah, hell, I'll let Darla fill you in. I'll just butcher it all."

"She's right," Darla informed them. "There are no archaic Homo Sapiens on this Earth. There are Neanderthals in Europe, and a few Homo heidelbergensis in Africa, but nothing to evolve into modern humans. We don't know why, but that's how things worked out here. *If* you somehow manage to organize and thrive, thinking you'll march north and cross the Bering land bridge to conquer the Neanderthals in Europe…good fucking luck with that."

"Odds are you'll die here in at least a few weeks,' Carol said. "Those are much better odds than you gave all the people you murdered in Vegas. All our…*alternate* sisters that died at your hands. You missed *us*, but we will show you an ounce of mercy you withheld from your victims, and give you a chance at survival. But, for a few *special* cases…you're going to get a *little* bit more."

Isaac heard the woman's feet crunch in the dry ground as she began to make a circuit around them again.

"For the worst of the worst – and honestly, that is not saying much – those that did what you did because you just liked doing it, you get some special attention. We know that there are some of you that actually *believed* in what you were doing. You're sick puppies too, don't get me wrong, but we will let honest conviction be its own reward. I have a feeling you'll get some clarity when you realize the direwolf chowing down on you can't be banished back to the hell it never came from."

Isaac heard her feet stop several yards away from him.

"You few who are getting this 'extra attention' are getting a gift you don't deserve. It will be a handicap, I'm afraid. Your brethren here will not appreciate your new perspective."

Isaac heard a sharp intake of breath, and a grunt that was as close to a sob as could be without paralyzed vocal cords to give it weight behind the sorrow. But he recognized it for what it was, because, after all he could very well have issued it himself, as much as he would have denied it. He was becoming uneasy again.

The woman's feet moved closer to him, they stopped, and again the miserable breathy gasp, a personification of grief and anguish.

"Who knew a little bit of empathy could be so painful?" Carol said, as her footsteps moved closer yet, and then she stopped before him, and turned her back. "This one's personal," she whispered. "Say hello to our *other* sister." She had pulled down her hood, her blonde head shining in the morning sunlight. She parted her hair, exposing her neck and two sets of eyes staring back at him. One was a simple tattoo, an artful representation of the younger sister's eyes – the pixie. But the other set...

He gasped. The eyes were less than two feet away from him - sharp and clear, with clean detailed lines - yet they were further away than anything he had ever seen in life. The most distant star could have shared his bed compared to this set of eyes. And yet they saw him, and saw through him, and then far past him. They saw him for what he was, and they saw him for what he could have been. They had sorrow for what he wasn't, and forgiveness for what he had done. And they showed him an honest love, something he felt he had never received, and so had never given. Those eyes held fear that measured his and found it small in comparison, and they were happy for it. Those eyes held courage he could never live up to, yet declared him brave. And those eyes wished for a contact they would never have, yet would not trade places with him because they would not wish their predicament on anyone. *Anyone.*

So he mourned for someone for the first time in his life, and wished he could take back every evil thing he had done, and then of course he mourned for all his victims, which was a crushing thing.

29

Carol's blonde hair fell back across her neck, curtains closing to signify the show was over, and his heart pounded in his chest and he wanted to cry out to let him see her again – he wasn't ready to let her go! He needed her strength, and her love, and her forgiveness.

Carol turned to him, and looked in his eyes, and she could see he wasn't what he had once been. She gave him a tired smile. "I can forgive you now," she whispered, and kissed his forehead. "But you have a *lot* to pay for."

I know, he thought wildly. *I know, I know, I know, I know! But please – let me see her again – let her show me how to pay!*

But she walked away, and he heard her say to her sister, "You ready to go?" He never heard a reply, and he imagined a quiet nod of the pixie's head. And then he knew they were gone.

The freedom of movement wasn't the liberation it should have been, and he almost dropped to his knees, almost began sobbing uncontrollably. But a lifetime of control was still hardwired into him. He did not look for the other two that had fallen and began crying, but he could see the look of horrified disgust on the faces of the rest. It was obvious that they wanted to rush in and start beating them mercilessly – up until mere seconds ago, he would have been one of them.

But they were afraid, because in their hearts they knew the ones that lost control were the same as they were, and they didn't understand, and were fearful of catching...something. So they turned to Isaac, a mirror of each of them, and they recognized his struggle for control, and would leave him be, judged not to be a threat. For now. So they turned to each other, and already the calculating and measuring had begun, each one certain they would dominate, to be the one to take charge and control and conquer.

I'm sorry, he thought. *I am so* sorry. *Please - let me see her again. Let me feel her love.*

It was not to be, and he knew this, and it was devastating.

"I'm sorry," he said aloud, to the universe, and continued to repeat it, until his voice was as raw as his sorrow.

Temporal Footprints

The beetle didn't know he was the only one of his kind left in the world. Since he also didn't know he had time-traveled 420 years into the future, he could be forgiven for this. True, the little bug didn't know very much at all, except that he was hungry, and could stubbornly cling to the hair of the creature he had hitched a ride on, until he grew tired of the commotion around him. Up had turned down, and a lot of other noisy monsters had swarmed around his host until the beetle grew alarmed at the nonsense and decided he would seek shelter elsewhere.

He wasn't supposed to be able to leave the temporal chamber. And, yes, he *was* very tiny, but he should have been killed in the decontamination phase. That he *wasn't* killed made him one tough little bastard.

Naturally, he did not know this.

Axel studied the little man through the data scrolling across his field of view. Slight build, glasses, bald little dome of a head. *Take some follicle stimulators, moron*, thought Axel. *Probably thinks ocular implants are an insult to mother nature.* The man's wispy-neat mustache irritated the hell out of Axel. Why would you even bother maintaining something so pathetic? Axel absently stroked his full beard. It wasn't something he would ordinarily keep if it wasn't for the job, but Wildman Enterprises had a certain image it was trying to sell, and Axel understood that - even if he didn't personally endorse the philosophy of facial hair.

Jesus, the little guy had one of those names that were popular so many years ago, one that incorporated extinct trees into it. Thankfully that nonsense had become unfashionable, and Axel was proud that his parents were of a more pragmatic stock.

Hold on.... Axel's eyes flicked up, scrolling back to the box marked for gender. *This can't be right.*

He stared passively at the man for a moment. "Elmer, it says here that you would like a *female* body?" Axel asked. "That correct?"

The little man bunched his shoulders up in a nervous shrug.

Axel leaned forward slightly, laced his fingers together, and rested his chin on a shelf of thumbs. Insignificant little guys like *this*, they always wanted a huge eight or nine-foot tall male body to inhabit. *Always.*

"I was told this wouldn't be a problem," the little man said, in an almost defensive tone. "I was told...." But he trailed off, and quietly stared down at his feet.

Axel tipped his head left, then right, studying the man as he tried to keep a quizzical frown from forming. Elmer wasn't the first guy to want a female body to vacation in – it happened occasionally, and usually Axel didn't give it a second thought. But this time, it made no *sense*. Guys like Elmer always wanted a massively-endowed nine-footer. No doubt hoping that they would get a chance – even though they knew better, *knew* they were being monitored – to pull a beauty and the beast shtick on some lovely young backpacker in denim shorts. And that was the polite way of putting it, of course.

Clients (and the rest of the world, for that matter) didn't know about a disturbing incident when Wildman Enterprises had first opened for business. No one who worked in the rookery would forget the Danish longhouse debacle years ago. *That* had certainly been nothing to joke about. Secretly, though, Axel was sure everyone was just a *little* bit proud that they had fixed the situation with no major temporal shocks, and time didn't have to sort itself out. And a damned fine epic poem had been created. Sure, people had been killed, and of course their descendants had been erased. But life went on, the present time held, and some legendary literature had arisen from it. *I mean, come on - that's kind of badass.*

Still, a time stricture of no longer than 450 years had been adopted, with a constant monitoring of the subject and the environment. The little men in their new, environmentally designed bodies mostly wandered the forests or mountain ranges eating and pleasuring themselves. *Probably not a lot different than their life currently,* Axel thought. Well, except for the hiking in nature part. Those days were long gone.

Axel leaned back and spread his arms open, palms out.

"Well, of course it's not a problem," he said with a smile. A reassuring, *non-judgmental* smile. "I just wanted to double check, is all." Elmer tipped his head up, and smiled tightly. "We have just the body for you, and I'm sure she'll be a perfect fit." The little guy's smile warmed into an honest one.

"Okay, then," Axel added with enthusiasm. "Shall we get the legal stuff out of the way?"

The little man nodded vigorously.

The tablet formed on the tabletop, and Axel began the long list of legal dos and don'ts, all basically designed to protect the company and absolve them from any mishaps that might occur in the course of the client's time-travelling. Like the forests of yesterday, gone was the legalese of who-to-fors and first and second parties designed to confuse anyone but a lawyer. It was language simple and to the point, especially the point that they would not hesitate to terminate the client in his or her host body, whether they had successfully transferred consciousness back into their bodies in present time or not.

WE MAY HAVE TO KILL YOU could not be stressed enough. Significant deviation from allowed activities could cause severe temporal distortion and alter history. This *has* happened, and *cannot* happen again. That usually gave them something to think about – most of them, at least. Axel suspected some clients wanted to try and cause a temporal paradox of some sort, not knowing any sort sophisticated scheming like that would be wasted once they joined with their host body. The body had been genetically engineered to live off the land without clothing, defend itself from apex predators and, by and large, kill anything it wanted to eat. Certain safeguards were hardwired into the brain, like an aversion to people, towns and major roadways. Complex forms of thought weren't capable with the primitive mind provided.

"And if you can read and then thumbprint the paragraph about possible brain damage or psyche contamination," Axel asked, and Elmer dutifully planted his thumb on the screen, which flashed green momentarily. "Thank you."

Axel then made a recording of Elmer in the little man's own words, a stammering declaration of how he, Elmer, was doing this of his own free will and with no coercion from anyone else, no one talked him into it, he has had a fascination with the nature of days past and would like to experience it as it was meant to be, wild and free and with nothing to rely on but one's own body and that it was a shame mankind had done this to mother Earth and he didn't understand why anyone could enjoy living in such a sterile world and he would have gone on longer but Axel nodded and rolled his hand in the air, and the man's rambling verse wandered to a stop.

"I'd say that about covers it," Axel said brightly, and Elmer straightened, finally showing an indication of excitement. Usually these guys could barely sit still.

"So," Axel asked, "do you want to see her?"

The beetle had been crawling in a determined direction for quite some time, stubborn in his desire to find food. And there was *nothing*. Naturally, the beetle couldn't ponder this oddity, wondering at the complete scarcity of any sustenance. He could only crawl and crawl, until the sterile surface he had been wandering across changed abruptly, and here now was a forest of hair that he was used to. If there was any excitement generated by the tiny bug, it only manifested itself in a quickening of his pace. Warm, moist air was blowing dead ahead.

Warm and moist was a good thing.

She was only seven feet tall, but Axel could tell that Elmer was in love. *What in the world is up with you, little guy?* wondered Axel. *Seriously, I cannot get a handle on you. Must be some sort of 'Mother Earth' fetish thing...*

Elmer couldn't reach out and touch her – she was behind the transparent blocks of the transfer vessel – but his eyes roamed across her brutish, conical head, lingering on her thick brow ridge and blunt, wide nose, until they darted to her broad shoulders and muscular arms, then positively doted on her heavy, hairy breasts. His gaze continued down across her massive thighs until it rested on her tremendous feet; wide stable platforms, calloused tough and dependable.

Axel let Elmer admire his vessel for a few minutes. Disgusting as it was to him, this was probably the least stomach-churning moment of the whole process. Having to monitor people as they traipsed across an ancient landscape, killing, eating, crapping, and generally wallowing in their primitiveness... Well, it paid handsomely, didn't it? And he had become inured to it, for the most part.

Axel felt a tickling in his left nostril, and he gave a startled little snort. Then another. He resisted the urge to jam a finger up in there and dig around. Nose picking was for the undignified monster Elmer would soon become. He brought a knuckle up to his right nostril, blocking it, and snorted quietly once again. The tickling stopped.

"I bet you must have done this many times," Elmer murmured.

"What?" Axel asked.

"Gone back and experienced what it was like. Must be a perk of the job, getting to do this?"

"Oh. Well, actually *no*, I haven't. Not even once."

Elmer frowned. "Really? I would have thought..."

"I'm afraid I'm not brave enough to take the chance," Axel said gravely. "Just don't have what it takes, I suppose."

The little man nodded his head, as if this made perfect sense. Axel was not above shameless flattery, even if at his own expense. The truth of the matter was he had absolutely no desire to climb into some dirty, hairy monster's body and stomp around a landscape that, as far as he was concerned, was gone for a reason, and good riddance to it. Axel enjoyed a society that had no disease, no nature, and no surprises. Life was good. The thought of going back and experiencing such a filthy world was revolting. But Elmer was incapable of understanding that, so it was best to let him think Axel was too afraid to make the journey.

A timer blinked in his right eye, warning Axel to get a move on. They were alone in the rookery, as was the procedure, but they liked to get the others loaded in so the chamber could be put in vacuum. Then all the happy travelers could be on their way. There was a woman already loaded in the rooks to their right, but Elmer hadn't noticed.

"Well, Elmer, it's time," Axel said.

"Oh," the diminutive man said. "Oh, yes. Of course."

Axel indicated the empty castle tower-like vessel that mirrored the one holding Elmer's host.

"Do I need to…take my clothes off, or anything?" Elmer asked shyly.

"What? No." Axel again gestured that Elmer step inside the empty rook, and the little man did so, then turned back to face Axel.

"Just relax, let the rook embrace you. Good. Let the fool's cap drop down over your head."

"The what?" asked Elmer, as a soft cap with wires and tubes dangling from it draped itself across his bald little head.

"Fool's cap," Axel said. "Just a nickname – kind of going with the medieval theme." He gestured around the chamber. "The castle rooks, a jester's cap." He shrugged. "Not the technical names, just our way of making it friendlier, I guess."

"Oh," Elmer said, frowning. "That's why it's called the rookery? Because that's not the definition of –"

"Fascinating," Axel said. "You can explain it to me when you get back."

Elmer gasped as the rook hugged him tightly and the fool's cap snugged itself up.

"Comfortable?" asked Axel. Elmer nodded his head. "You'll be asleep soon. When you awake, you'll be in your host body, in the rugged hills of California in the late nineteen-sixties. Sound good?" Elmer nodded, and Axel grinned. "See you in a month." Then Axel slid the rook's heavy door into place, listening for the hollow thump of a secure seal, and watched the thin crack of the door's shape disappear as it melded into the rook.

Axel's nose itched again, and he grabbed it and squeezed, twisting it left and right until the urge to sneeze went away. He would have to look into who was controlling the climate in here these days, and have a word with him.

He watched Elmer through the crystalline block pattern of the vessel. The man's eyes wandered around the chamber, until they became heavy, and then finally closed in sleep. Axel then swung Elmer's rook up and back, until the crenellations mated and locked together with the rook holding the host.

TRANSFER INITIATING blinked in his right eye. Great. It would be a few hours, and he had two other clients to prep and load. The 1907 and 1940 were already loaded and transferred. On to his 1958…

The beetle was not in very good shape. One tiny leg had been broken off when he had been crushed into the mucus of the nose he had crawled into. He had bitten into the soft flesh in an involuntary response to the perceived attack, and then had vomited and defecated. One missing leg would not have been a death sentence, of course. He was tough, and as long as he could struggle free from a predicament, he could soldier on. But he was doomed to die, struggling in a glob of congealing snot, as trapped as an ancient insect in amber. All in all, not a very nice welcome for the world's first time-travelling beetle.

All five of the clients had been loaded and transferred, and the rookery's chamber had been emptied of air. Axel climbed into his temporal control station. Here he would spend the next month, monitoring two of the clients. Two other stations had monitors as well. Axel monitored the 1967 and 1958 clients, another person monitored the 1940 and 1931 ones, and a single monitor observed the 1907 client.

While the dates might appear oddly random, they were calculated to be the least susceptible to paradoxical shenanigans. Axel had no idea how this was accomplished, but as it seemed to work he accepted it without further thought.

While Elmer didn't need to disrobe, Axel and the other monitors didn't have that luxury. He dropped his suit and shoes into the recycle chute, slipped into his suspension rig and let the waste reclaimer envelop his hips, grunting as it forced its way between his buttocks. A small price to pay for the month of zero-gravity he would enjoy. While he may have not cared how specific years were selected to travel to, he was still annoyed that he had to monitor the clients in real time. Couldn't that part be accelerated? They were dealing with time travel, after all. Hell, accelerate the clients time too – how would they ever know? Apparently, they could not. Observing them, the monitors had to be outside the timestream itself, mindful of potential paradoxes. If they were in the present timestream and a paradox was created, the timestream would self-adjust and they would not know it. *Outside* of it, they could control it. Or so the theory went, anyways. They knew the truth behind *Beowulf*, and the rest of the world didn't, so the theory appeared sound.

"TCS 58 and 67 secured," Axel said.

"TCS 40 and 31 secured," came a voice out of thin air. It was Sawyer. He was a competent monitor. Not Axel's favorite to have on his team, but he would do.

"TCS 07 secured," said another voice. Female. Willow? Ah hell, she was pretty good, hippy-dippy name notwithstanding.

"We ready to spin them up?" Axel asked, and was answered with two affirmatives.

The five locked vessels in the rookery chamber began to turn, slowly rotating at first, their occupants visible through the segmented crystal, looking not unlike victims on a spit roast. The rooks spun ever faster, until they were five blazing white lines of light in the chamber. A rippling mirror formed between the rooks of the clients and the hosts, and Axel felt the queasy feeling in his stomach as his control station left the time stream and he was now weightless. Lightning danced and flicked around the host's rooks, and then they were gone. In Axel's left eye, 1967 came online. In his right, 1958 did as well.

The hosts were now in the past, while the clients still occupied the present. Axel and the other two monitors were now in a place where past and present didn't mean anything. Time to get to work.

Axel watched as his rooks dropped their hosts out into to the dark and down to the cold ground. If someone was there to observe this – and that was a real possibility – it would look like a blue ball of lightning descending from above, and then a massive hairy figure would slip out of the bottom of it and stand, staring stupidly for several minutes. He could make the host bellow out vocally or in infrasound. Either way, that would scare the hell out of anyone and they would run off, with a wild tale to tell. Once the client took over completely, they could do this on their own. The rook would phase in and out quickly, essentially not existing anywhere until it was needed for the return trip.

This time, no one was around to see the hosts arrive. The only casualty was a moth crushed beneath the left foot of the 1967 host. Axel checked the 'dox display. Less than half a percent of temporal distortion. It would have died soon anyway. Excellent.

Axel scanned the immediate area in both times, and found nothing more intelligent than bears, one of which was running away as fast as it could in 1958. Ah, the pheromones were a wonderful thing. Kept dogs away as well.

"We all good?" Axel asked. Sawyer and Willow both replied with a "Yes."

"Alright. Let them get their feet under them, and then we can turn them loose, having *so* much fun walking around in mother nature." The other two monitors laughed. It was going to be one boring month. But damn, the pay was good.

He could smell the trees first.

Elmer stood in the crisp night air, breathing in the myriad scents that rushed into his wide, sensitive nostrils. He had never smelled a tree before, and he was almost lightheaded with the delight of it. *So many* different ones! He didn't know which scent belonged to which tree, but he relished the sharper, pungent odor of the pine, contrasted against the deeper, almost sour, scent of the oaks and other deciduous trees, their leaves just now beginning the transformation from sunlight-soaking green into the celebration of colors announcing their death. He tipped his head back and opened his mouth, drawing in the air, shivering as it flowed through his nose, across his tongue. He could taste the scents. He wanted to swallow and consume them in every way possible. He emptied his lungs and filled them again and again, each time discovering something new. The grass and weeds at his feet. The dead wood – bleached logs as dry as his mother's wit, and also the wet and rotten wood, sleepily decaying into the mulch floor of the forest. The bugs. My goodness, *all* of the bugs! Rodents of all shapes and sizes, and the skunk and racoon and badger – none of these he knew by name, but all distinct. His heart knew them, and that was all that mattered.

As he stood and smelled, he listened. Of course, it was the wind in the trees that entranced him, a sound created out of a symbiotic relationship between air and tree, one that could whisper and mutter for long stretches and then shout with a sudden fury, but Elmer couldn't grasp what the anger was for, because really the wind didn't ignore you so much as that it didn't even believe in your existence. Yet it was proof positive that the Earth breathed. And of course, the bugs. All the bugs, crawling and scurrying through the grass, ground and air. Whirring wings buzzing in flight, and grinding together to chirp out intentions of lust. Clicking mandibles and ratcheting limbs, and the pulse of contracting muscles pushing earth out of the way as they wormed their way through the world. And there were the fast beats of tiny little hearts, of birds and mice and deer, and the soft breaths that they took, very aware of him as he was of them.

When he opened his eyes, it was almost a disappointment. He could see very well by the starlight, but it was dim and almost colorless. Most definitely the sight of the surrounding trees made his heart thump loudly, causing a mad dash away from him in the undergrowth. But…it gave him less information than his other senses. He had seen images of trees from days past, but they had been vibrant and lush. He knew *why* they were not as beautiful now, but his brain didn't have the patience for this and he growled. But the trees were not easily frightened into color, and the sky was similarly unimpressed and remained black. The stars – my God, the *stars* – now *they* more than made up for the lack of color. They were the reason you wanted to look up. If anyone cared to dwell on the past, it wasn't so much as to pine for what had been lost, but to point the finger of blame or to jeer and mock. Most people seemed content to navel gaze, and they no longer cared to look up or out. And, truthfully, it wasn't worth the effort when nothing could be seen through light-polluted skies. The burning of distant suns could no longer fire the imagination. But now, here they were, and glorious seemed a shabby adjective of their description. Several hours ago, Elmer could have comprehended their scale and why he knew that he was a part of them. But right now, he wanted to wade his fingers through them, scoop up a handful and let them spill out of his palm so he could dance under a celestial shower. He made a half-hearted swipe over his head, and in doing so realized he could finally move his limbs.

He wasn't really aware that he had been unable to move until now, but there was a moment of *at last*, and Elmer bent a knee and took a solid step forward. His foot planted itself down with a decisive *whump*, something so natural it was woven as law into the fabric of the universe. His feet were the bedrock of his existence, and they would carry him on a journey he would never comprehend, and he would soon reach a point where he could not wonder at it. He only knew that he was designed to move, and his compliant gait took him across the meadow he had dropped into. His mighty footfalls drove the insects and animals away from him, and he relished the feel of the grass and earth pushing up between his thick toes, the shock of his muscles anchored on his bones, the bounce and sway of his

41

breasts as he strode across the world. There was a faint part of him that was amused that he still thought of himself as a male, but that would soon fade in the harsh glare of who he was now.

There would be plenty he would be ignorant of in the weeks, and even years, ahead.

It was quite a while into the job when Axel realized that he must be ill. *Seriously*. Actually *sick*. He had never been sick, and had never known anyone else who had been. Sure, it still happened. To *other* people, in places he could not give a damn about - places where they still needed the body's own defenses to try and fight off invading pathogens. Those places were dwindling cesspools of the past, and Axel would toast to their demise someday. Or at least, he would have.

It began as a thickening at the back of his throat, something he wasn't aware of, except that he sipped more from the hydration tube near his lips. The thickening turned into an irritating tickle, and his nose felt heavier, and that was when he took notice, checking the temperature of the temporal control center. A standard 75 degrees. Still, not knowing what being ill *felt* like, he couldn't conceive of the possibility of some sort of infection. Existing nowhere in time could make you feel a bit weird, and it was different on each run. This was just another aspect of it.

Axel busied himself with the tasks of containing temporal shocks. In 1958, the client seemed to be obsessed with a roadwork construction site, and was leaving massive footprints all over the damned place. There already was a mythology in place for such artifacts, but holy cow - the owner of the construction company seemed to be helping them out by faking tracks as well. Axel checked for temporal distortions and found they were negligible. If their time-traveling clients could be turned into a world-wide joke, that would make things a lot easier. Until they could control the host completely, but make the client *think* that they had some sort of free will, this job would take almost all his concentration.

The 1967 client, Elmer, seemed content to wander blissfully through the forest, eating bugs and berries for the most part. He had killed a deer with seeming reluctance, and hadn't roared and beat the carcass with his huge fists like most clients would, didn't gorge himself silly, leaving a substantial amount for other animals to feed from. Temporal distortion to the present date of about two percent. *What a weird little man*, Axel thought, and then sneezed.

Elmer wandered down the hillside to the creek. Some years before a flood had torn through here, and shipwrecks of uprooted trees made the sandy bed a weary battlefield, a magnificent no man's land of twisted stumps and logs. Trees, still barely standing, were bleached and dry, a dead protest of the overbearing fall colors of the hillside.

She sat on the sandbar and let the cold liquid rush over her legs and feet. Such unrestrained and feral flowing of water was still such a novel experience to her that she hooted and chuckled in joy. No, it was not a river, the minute, tame, part of her brain admonished. Certainly no *ocean*. But even the barely civilized section of her mind couldn't help but be impressed by such a free and exuberant rushing of the water cutting through the sandy wash.

There was a small town nearby, and while she had no interest in trying to interact with people of the time, she would rummage in trashcans in the early hours of the morning, growling at barking dogs and wondering why. More often than not, they would cower and slink away to try and hide. She felt a guttural satisfaction in knowing that she always knew where they were, their rapid heartbeats accompanying the aroma of their terror. Sometimes the odor would make her sad, depressed that she would frighten an animal like that. Hadn't she wanted a dog, once? Which was strange – why would she *want* a dog? Was it to eat? She was confused. But the feelings of sympathy lessened with each encounter.

She tipped her head back and drew in a mighty lungful of air through her nose. It was cold and sharp, and full of so many stories! Her hair, deep black with reddish highlights, stirred in the breeze that traveled up the creek bed, a wind gifted with even more aromas, never stopping for a proper greeting, yet carrying her *own* scent away on its journey, the cool air pushing into her and past, pulling her hairs and odors along with it like an eager child tugging on the hand of a parent. She felt a sense of being everywhere at once, a wholeness that could only be felt and not described. She had found what she wanted, and life was incredibly, deliciously *good*.

So good, in fact, that she missed hearing the rhythmic thumping of hooves, and the nicker of a horse.

The first temporal transgression set the stage for those that followed, and had the unusual property of actually affecting the past as well, which, of course, would then transform the future yet again. Most transgressions were like a shotgun blast, if one could actually see the event, except that as it fanned out it grew more powerful the farther out it traveled in time. The 1958 transgression seemed harmless at first, but its effect was that of creating an obsession that would infect many, many people in the years ahead.

If Axel had been on top of his game, he would have easily orchestrated the exposure of the fraudulent footprints being pressed into the earth by the owner of the construction company. He could have directed his client into scaring the bejeezus out of the hoaxer, exposing him with a wild, laughable tale. Instead, his client would end up lending a nickname to an industry that followed.

An irritating alarm bell, along with alarmed voices, woke Axel out of his delirium. He had been so very hot, but every time he moved his body convulsed with shivering. Mucus seemed to flow nonstop from his nose and throat - even his eyes seemed to weep sticky tears that glued his eyelashes together. Axel hacked out a lung-scorching gob of phlegm, and thrashed out blindly, trying to silence the alarm.

"Axel, what's happening?" Willow's urgent voice competed with the screeching bell noise.

"What?" Axel answered. "I...what?"

"Axel – Jesus!" Sawyer. It was Sawyer "Oh man, we are so screwed. *Screwed!*"

"Don't say that," Willow said. "You can't say that! It has to be fixed. Axel, *God damnit!* What happened?"

"I don't," Axel muttered, reaching up with a snot-coated finger to dig at his eyes. "I can't see. What happened?"

"Jesus, that's what *we* want to know," Willow barked, panic dancing on the edge of her voice.

"We have a one-hundred percent temporal transgression. That's a *complete* temporal transgression!" Sawyer yelled. "It was going fine, then bam! Thirty percent and then the full Monty. We are so very screwed."

"No! Axel can still fix it!" Willow cried. "Think! Turn this around. Review what has happened, and get your client in damage mode and fix this cluster – "

"He should have aborted at thirty," Sawyer whined. "Just hit abort and taken us home right then. We are so screwed. Shit, we can't even vaporize the clients now – the 'dox inhibitor won't let us until the transgression is fixed!"

"Abort?" Axel asked. He knew how to do that. He could do that so damned easy…

"No!" screamed Willow. "Don't you abort the mission! That will kill us for sure – there's no vacuum chamber to return to! There is no Wildman Enterprises. If you abort without fixing this, it will only get worse!"

Axel's finger picked and scratched at the cover plate over the mission abort controller.

"Axel, listen," Willow pleaded. "I'm ignoring my client right now and trying to review your '58." She was silent as she reviewed the data. Sawyer's sobs and the sound of Axel's finger worrying the abort plate were as constant as the alarm still ringing away.

"Okay," Willow said, "It looks…it looks like we have some very visible interactions with locals. Jesus, Axel – why did you let your client hang around there for so long? God *damn* it – you had so many chances…"

She breathed in ragged little gasps as she continued to review. "Okay, here – it looks like one of our illustrious founder's ancestors…got hit by *a logging truck* while out hunting for a 'bigfoot'. Well, isn't that so freakin' cute. 'Bigfoot'. How amazingly clever. Christ. *Okay*, so with no one to invent temporal travel pods, there is no rookery for us to return to. If we try to return to the timestream in anything other than a vacuum – "

"Space?" Sawyer offered. "Outer space? Could we pop into the timestream in orbit and be rescued?"

"How?" Willow laughed. "The TCS pods aren't freaking spaceships, Sawyer!"

His only response was crying.

"Axel," Willow prompted. "Only you can fix this. You *have* to. We abort, and return to the present, we will be as fragile as a soap bubble."

Axel's finger finally succeeded in prying up the cover plate. He sighed in triumph, and curled his fingers around the abort handle.

"Axel," Willow continued, with a patience that was ready to shatter into panic. "Axel, you need to fix this transgression. If we don't have time to re-form into the timestream, we will implode instantly under the barest of atmospheres and that will be all she wrote. Axel. *Talk* to me!"

"Mission aborted!" Axel crowed, then yanked on the handle.

They didn't even have time to protest.

And now, of course, they never existed.

It all happened so fast.

When she finally registered the appearance of the men on horseback, her engineered shyness caused her to immediately lumber to her feet and begin a steady retreat across the sandbar, heading into the tree line and back up the hillside. But there was a lot of ground to cover, and she could hear and smell the panic of one of the horses. The animal reared up and dumped its rider, who was busy trying to grab something from his saddlebag. She ignored this person for the moment, and out of the corner of her eye saw the other one, still on his horse, rifle in hand. She knew what a rifle was - at least what it was *intended* for - and she picked up her pace. But she refused to run. She could feel the racing heartbeats of all of them, the horse running off, the astounded men, and of course her own. There was a part of her that knew this was something very wrong, something she would get in trouble for, but she didn't understand why.

She risked a look back, turning at her hips, bringing her chin up to look over her shoulder. The man who was off his horse was holding something in front of his face, pointed right at her. There was a moment of irritation, contempt, and the desire to show this little man what she could do to him, but she was hard-wired to avoid any confrontation, and she turned back and continued her steady pace towards the trees. She could hear footfalls and ragged gasps behind her as the man trotted to follow her, but she knew he would not get too close. She could smell his fear, but also his excitement.

Her feet pounded into the sand as she marched away from them, and finally reached the cover of the trees. She ascended the hillside, allowing herself to slow a bit. She would find a concealed spot to wait. And watch.

The 1958 transgression helped fuel an obsession, and in turn helped the 1967 transgression come about. Its temporal meddling drove a logging truck to wipe out of one of the most astonishing scientific achievements of mankind, that of the ability to travel back in time. All clients were stuck in their host bodies, never to remember what had brought them there. The temporal change began in 1958, effected events up to 1967, but the clients in 1940, 1931 and 1907 in turn made their own changes – which reverberated back up through time again. The future didn't stand a chance.

Once, it had been debated whether the laws of the universe would allow such a thing as time travel. Now, no one would ever know that, while time travel *had* been possible, the universe had decidedly put her foot down on such nonsense.

47

She had observed the men for quite some time as she squatted in the trees on the hillside, far above them. They had ran around gesticulating with wild excitement, and then finally poured some white substance into her footprints. Her mind tried to wrap itself around such foolishness. It dawned on her that her footprints were important to these men. She comprehended the ability to track her that way, but then, why weren't they? Their stupidity began to bore her, and she stood with a grunt. She thought about moving back to the easier trek of the game trail, thought of her beautiful, sturdy feet betraying her, and waded through the brush farther up the hillside.

She had been programed to return to the meadow where she had dropped in one night, and had dutifully wandered back to it. As the hour she was supposed to return to the future came and went, she no longer felt compelled to stay and eventually moved on. She had now forgotten what her name used to be, that she had once been a shy, timid little man from the future. She would never know she would become a celebrity of sorts, and be given a nickname. That was just as well. She was tremendously happy just as she was.

The beetle didn't know he had been given a second chance, his journey to the future having been wiped out by the temporal shake-up. As he crawled steadily across a branch rotting itself back into the ecosystem, he didn't sense the massive foot come smashing down from above until he was violently pressed into the groundcover, the mulched wood mixing itself with the wet earth.

He lay motionless for quite some time, and then began the patient struggle of extricating himself from the footprint. He was a very tiny beetle, hardly the size of a seed. But he was a tough little bastard.

Naturally, he did not know this.

Syd And Andy

Andrew waved the phone around, trying desperately to pick up civilization. He squinted at the black slab of plastic in his hand, and tried to *will* a signal bar into existence. If he could do one, then he could do another. Right? He held his breath and concentrated at the top right corner of the phone. *Come on. Come on. Comeoncomeoncomeon. Come. The. Hell. On!* The rational part of his brain – the part he was certain was always in control – was appalled at him.

But these were desperate times… And so his head shook, his eyes bulged, a steady grunt building in his throat as his heart pounded in his ears. *Come on. Come. On. One freakin' bar. Just one….Come on!*

He didn't register the footfalls in the sand behind him until a weight slammed onto his back, tan legs wrapping themselves around him and teeth nipping at his earlobe. He stumbled towards the stream and the phone sailed out of his hand, bounced on a rock with the saddest splintering sound he had ever heard and then it dropped into the rushing water. He yelled – a noise somewhere between a startled squawk and an expletive. Syd giggled in his ear.

"Aw. Did I scare you?" she breathed.

Andrew stood still, trying to maintain his balance with Syd on his back, and stared at the point where his phone had entered the water.

Well, crap.

"What are you doing down here?" asked Syd.

Andrew opened his mouth, and then gestured vaguely towards the stream.

"Really," added Syd. "What's up? Sounded like you were trying to make a load in your pants. Thought you might be having a stroke…"

Suddenly she was off him, hiking boots dropping to crunch in the sand. "Oh, shit," she said. "You're not, are you? Having a stroke?" She grabbed his shoulders and turned him to her, her bright blue eyes studying his face, and then down his shoulder to his arm pointing towards the water.

"My phone," Andrew mumbled, then darted into the stream after the device.

Andrew groped blindly in the water by the rock, until his fingertips felt something smooth that didn't feel coated in algae, then grabbed the phone and plucked it out of the stream. An angry buzzing issued from it as it appeared to be in constant vibration mode.

"Oh, shit… Did I make you drop it in there?" she asked quietly.

"Kinda flew in there, I think," he muttered as he splashed back out of the water.

"I am *so* sorry, Andrew," said Syd. "Sorry, sorry, *sorry* – I didn't know you were…" She trailed off, and then frowned, looking at him sharply.

"Hey, *screw* sorry – what the hell, dude?"

Andrew glanced up from the array of cracks across the face of his phone, and studied Syd's face.

Ah, shit. *Shit.* How to play this? Her eyes seemed a shade darker, more vivid. Best to just take it, he reasoned. The phone's buzzing became feebler, and he pried absently at the back cover. *Should get the battery out*, he thought wanly.

Syd's eyes blinked rapidly, her breath coming in sharp bursts out of her freckled nostrils.

"Well?" she asked. "I thought this was supposed to be a *technology free camping trip*." Her fingers curled into the shape of air quotes on the last four words.

Andrew opened his mouth, shut it, and gave a limp shrug of his shoulders. Syd reached out and hit him in the upper arm.

"What the *hell?*" she continued. "Oh, *Syd*, I bet you can't go three hours without checking your phone, let alone three weeks. Oh *Syd*, do you ever put that phone down? Jesus, you sound like my mother." She stepped closer, and stared up into him, her jaw jutting out. "It's been two and a half Goddamned *weeks* asshole and I haven't even got my phone out the glove box!" She waved her arm vaguely in the direction of camp and his ancient '71 Ranger.

"I know," Andrew muttered weakly.

"What were you doing? 'Oh-emm-geeing it' with your bros on Facebook?"

Andrew winced. The things you say that come back to bite you in the ass...

"What's the latest *gossip*, huh? Who's *butt-hurt* over his girl-friend not paying any *attention* to him now?"

"I was just trying to –"

Syd punched him in the arm again, then leveled a finger in his face. "You're a hypocrite."

"Yeah..."

"Yeah? *Yeah?*" Syd continued to glare at him. "So what was the burning need for you to climb down from Mt. High Horse and slum it in the evil valley of the *social vacuum*, huh?"

Those air quotes again. You never know how much of an insufferable prick you could sound like until your words were thrown back in your face.

"I can't get the air-mattress to deflate," he mumbled.

51

Syd's upper lip twitched into a sneer, and she cocked her head. "What?" she laughed skeptically.

"The mattress...it won't. The pump won't suck out the air like it's supposed to..."

Syd furrowed her brow. "You just turn the little knob-thingy back the other way," she said. "Right? The opposite way from when you're filling it up? And you turn the pump around so it sucks instead of blowing?"

"That's what I thought," Andrew said, somewhat relieved she was distracted for the moment from berating him. "I can't find the instructions for the pump or the mattress –"

"Oh, I don't need to be told how to fill up a big plastic bag of air," Syd intoned, her head wagging from side to side. "I'm Mr. Nature boy! I only brought this thing along because my frail girlfriend can't sleep on the ground with only pine needles for a blanket – "

"Alright," Andrew muttered. So much for her being distracted...

"So what were you doing with the phone? Trying to call Triple-A to come help?"

"Just...trying to Google instructions," he said sheepishly.

Syd laughed brutally, and slipped the multi-tool from her belt and waved it in front of his face.

"Bet I can get the air out really quick," she said.

"Hey! Not on your life," Andrew barked.

"Aw. Nature boy getting soft?"

"You wish," he mumbled, then tried a coy, sheepish tone. "I've had a lot of fun on that mattress the last few weeks. Kind of attached to it now..."

Syd rolled her eyes. "Don't even try, 'kay? You're going to be attached to your hand for the foreseeable future."

Andrew winced.

Syd sighed, glanced down at the dead phone dripping in his hand and gave a light snort of a laugh.

"Serves you right, you hipster jackass," she muttered.

"Hey," Andrew replied, wounded, but just didn't have the desire to go down that particular road right now.

Syd sighed again, louder, then tipped her head up to stare at him, shook her head condescendingly.

"Well, I bet there's a good old fashioned plug to pull. Roll around on it to force the air out," she suggested.

"You bet we can roll around –"

"What'd I say?"

"Yep," was all he could really answer, and then followed her as she turned and began to march up the stream bank and towards the camp they were breaking.

* * *

The truck shook and bounced along the washboard that was Granite Creek Road, trailing clouds of dust. Syd sat scrunched in the passenger side, knees up by her head, and buds happily jammed in her ears. They still had no service, but she was enjoying her music for the first time in three weeks. Andrew couldn't make out the tinny pop tune over the rush of air and gravel past the truck. Probably Taylor, or Katy or some gawdawful… Christ. He *was* a hipster jackass. Who fucking cares what music she liked? Syd was adorable. Not just superficially. Her personality was infectious. She was probably the most innocent and sincere person he had ever met. She was genuinely shocked at the injustices of the world, as if she expected everyone to be as honest and caring as she was.

Andrew stole glances at her from the corner of his eyes. Her heels twisted on the seat, her head bopping along as she mouthed the lyrics to the tunes on her iPhone. Her blond hair was tangled up in a rough ponytail, which danced simultaneously to her rhythm and the truck's.

She caught him looking at her, and defiantly pushed her face towards him and audibly sang, "Shake, shake, shake, shake, shake!" and then stuck her tongue out at him.

It's not often when someone can point to a moment in time of an actual epiphany. Dawning realization usually takes some time to grow, but there it was: he realized he loved her deeply. He broke into a silly grin, but she had already retreated back to her own private performance.

Jesus, he thought. The idea that he was actually *in love* startled him. *And I may have fucking blown it today.* No – *today* wasn't the problem. Being an insufferable *prick* was the problem. He couldn't imagine Syd holding one hypocritical act against him, but she could weigh his attitude towards her all the months they had been dating and decide that maybe her time with him was over. And the thought of a life without her hollowed out his stomach and made him gasp. Jesus – could he imagine that they might actually…marry?

And he could.

He glanced at her again, filthy socks coated with the dust of their camping trip, assorted stains randomly dotting her shorts and t-shirt like the world's worst camouflage, scratches and bug bites on her lean legs, makeup scrubbed from her face but those *eyes* that were so electric they were unreal.

She was willing to do this – disappear for three weeks and not once complain about no music, no phone, no connection, he marveled. He sincerely hoped that it might actually be for the love of him, and not just to prove she wasn't as shallow as he thought she might be. The idea that she thought that he might not have that high of an opinion of her, that – at best – he was condescending to her, hit him hard and he flinched – then jerked the wheel to the right causing Syd to yelp as she tried to brace her feet up onto the dash. They narrowly missed the ranger's truck as it pulled to its right, and they both skidded to a roaring stop, the world turned into pale, gritty clouds stirred up from the road.

Syd stared at him, not accusingly, but unreadable nonetheless. Andrew let out a shaky breath, and looked in the driver's side mirror. The ranger's truck sat still for a moment, then the reverse lights flared white in the dust and the vehicle slowly backed up until the driver doors paralleled each other. Andrew rolled his window down further. This was not his fucking day.

The ranger stared at him calmly, as if trying to measure up what sort of idiot he was dealing with. The man looked tired, though, and Andrew was wondering if the calm was just plain weariness. He could hear a sudden blast of music as Syd removed her ear buds, and then it cut off as she paused the playback. Silence stretched out to be nearly unbearable.

"Sorry," was all he could think to say, and offer no further explanation as to why he hadn't been paying attention.

The ranger gazed at him a moment longer, then asked quietly, "How long have you two been out here?"

Andrew wasn't sure he heard the man correctly, and he turned to Syd. She raised her eyebrows at him, but leaned forward and offered, "Almost three weeks?" Andrew turned back to the ranger. The man scratched thoughtfully at his sandy-colored beard – a neat, sensible length and not the old-timey monstrosity Andrew sported.

"You've been unplugged for that long?" he asked.

"*Yeesssssssss*," Syd drawled, and Andrew winced.

"So, you have any idea what's…what's been going on?" the ranger asked.

"Going on?" Andrew said.

"Out in town. In the world, actually."

"Um…no?"

The ranger stared at them thoughtfully, then looked longingly up the road from where they came, and shook his head.

"You may not want to go back," he said simply.

"Why?" asked Syd.

"Some sort of...infection going around," the ranger mumbled. "*Really* easy to catch." He turned to stare at Andrew, and then flicked his gaze to Syd. "Some real... *biblical* shit going down if you ask me."

"Biblical?" Syd and Andrew both asked.

"I... I don't know what the hell's going on." The ranger turned his head to face back up the road again. "I have to head on up and check for folks like you – people who may have been out of touch for a while." He paused thoughtfully. "And then I am gone – taking the family for an extended camping trip."

Andrew turned to look at Syd, but she was staring at the ranger, hypnotized.

"Hey," the ranger said shortly, and Andrew turned back to see the man staring steadily at him.

"Yeah?"

"Do not – *and I mean this* – do *not* stop to help anyone you think looks sick, or drunk or passed out dead. Stay in your truck, and avoid anyone wandering around. Got it?"

"Um," muttered Andrew.

"Do you fucking understand?"

"Yeah, yeah."

The ranger held his gaze, then looked down at his hands on the steering wheel.

"No you don't. There's no way you do." He stared at the backs of his calloused hands gripping the wheel, perhaps trying to decode the map of veins twisting through his skin and find a route away from a horror he could not comprehend. He looked up. "But you will soon enough. And you'll wish you stayed in camp." The man shook his head and said, "Good luck to both of you," and punched the accelerator to the floor, stirring up the dust again.

Syd touched him lightly on the arm, and Andrew turned to her, not sure what had just happened. He could tell that she was as confused as he was.

"Andy... what the hell?" she asked.

He shook his head.

You may not want to go back, the man had said.

But they did anyway.

* * *

They sat on a mattress in Andrew's old apartment on Mayfair, the morning light filtered to a dim wash by the boards that had been hastily nailed up by someone almost a year ago. Presumably by the same someone who had dragged his mattress out to the living room.

Syd leaned into his back, her legs wrapped around his waist, jaw tucked into his neck. Warm puffs of breath from her nostrils tickled his beard, and their hands clasped together in a tight ball over his growling belly. They could sit like that for hours, it seemed; a sort of meditation of shared body heat and listening. Andrew would insist on taking a turn on the outside, but Syd could only stand that for a short time, it seemed. She preferred to be against his back. Andrew didn't feel very protective that way, but had long since accepted the seating arrangement.

They didn't talk much when they were like this – they didn't talk much *period*, really. The art of conversation had dwindled to a hushed whisper these days. Syd would usually be the one to break their trance – a long, sharp intake of breath and then a whisper rush of words that asked questions or posited theories or suggestions for the day. Andrew felt that if you hooked his brain up to an EKG during their meditation sessions the result would be one long flat line. But Syd was always thinking, he knew. She could be as quiet as a cat walking on clouds, sure. But the wheels were always turning under that blonde hair.

Syd drew in air, charging her lungs. Andrew waited, but she said nothing, and eventually let out a long warm sigh against his cheek.

Yeah. Things were getting that bad.

* * *

They had returned from camping to find Syd's mom missing, and Andrew's family dead. His mother and father were pathetically twitching animated corpses – only able to snap their teeth ineffectually at you if you got close. Apparently his brother had gotten infected at the skate park and had had one hell of an appetite afterwards.

Syd's mother was just gone. No note. Her dad lived in Los Angeles, and there was no way of knowing what was up with him.

They were able to replenish supplies and head out to camp once more, this time with the intention of living off of fish for the most part. Andrew wasn't much of a hunter. In fact, did not own any firearms. The lone pistol Syd's mom had was gone from her house. The rest of the spring and most of the summer they spent quietly north of Spokane. They encountered very few dead, and had their first run-in with one of the living out near the Little Spokane river.

Andrew had assumed out of the city meant out of trouble – not that easy, surely, but there just didn't seem to be the chaos out here that ruled in Spokane. He could never look back on those days as idyllic – that had been when camping was for fun, not survival. They were always hungry, and there was never enough fish. But the pandemic was still rather new to them, they hadn't seen a lot of the horror of the dead coming to life, and perhaps their lack of vigilance could be forgiven for not seeing pure, sustained existence as something that was to be hard and bitterly fought for.

Andrew had been frying up a decent-sized rainbow, and both of them huddled around the fire, giddy with the prospect of maybe quieting their stomachs for the evening.

"That sure smells good," the man had said as he stepped out of the brush. Both of them had jumped, reaching for their knives, but froze as the man levelled a gun at Andrew.

"I bet *she* smells better," the stranger added, his lips twitching as he tried not to smirk – trying to be cool as could be, but failing. Anyone with that much control these days would certainly have the patience to wait until at least one of them was sleeping.

He was as ragged and weary as most survivors were, the gaunt disbelief at the situation he was now in painted in thick strokes across his face – like most of the faces they had seen, and more than likely now adorned their own stretched too-tight canvases. But this guy had a meanness that has always been recognizable. Perhaps back in more civilized times, he could have lived out his life as simply being thought of as "that asshole" everyone seemed to know, never understanding the reason his life sucked was solely and squarely upon him, and him alone. Now, though…it was his time to shine. Or so he thought, anyway.

Andrew gripped his Buck knife and began to draw it loose.

"Nah, nah, nah," the guy drawled. "I will drop you if you move another inch."

Andrew froze, but continued to grasp the blade.

The man darted his gaze back to Syd, and he grinned.

"Ain't you *gorgeous*," he said. "You don't see 'em too pretty these days, but I'll be damned if you ain't a sight for a sore dick."

Andrew felt his anger build, and he knew he had better not let it control his actions – whatever they might end up being… He flicked his eyes over to Syd, and she had a cool smile on her face.

Please don't say something smart-assed, he thought. *We need to outwit this guy…*

59

She licked her lips, startling Andrew.

"My, that's a big gun," Syd drawled.

"Don't be flirtin' with me darlin'," the guy said. "I don't buy it."

But Andrew could tell the guy *wanted* to. Would spend everything he had to believe it, that someone like Syd could finally – finally! – show him his due.

"Oh, you aren't much to look at," Syd breathed. "But what does that get me these days?" She tipped her head towards Andrew. "This pretty little hipster has got us nowhere." Her head shook in slow, contemptuous jerks. "I'm looking for someone to take me somewhere."

She leveled her gaze at the man. "You that guy?"

Pungent smoke crawled up from the pan, as the fish sizzled and popped, blackened and annoyed at the lack of attention being paid to it.

"Why don't I just shoot him for you?" the loner asked.

"Why don't you then?" Syd answered. "Seriously, what's stopping you? *Jesus*."

And Andrew felt *himself* buying it, of all things. All of his crippling self-doubts reached up from the pit of his empty stomach, and dragged his resolve - his determination, his *desire* to keep Syd safe - pulled and tugged at all of it, deflating all he had left until he didn't even feel hollow, just shrunken and emaciated like the dead that littered the land around them. He slumped, and lost the grip on his knife.

"Just let me get the hell out of the way, okay?" Syd asked. "I mean, *I* don't know how good of a shot you are."

Syd began to creep away from Andrew, and the guy darted his gun towards her for a second, and she stopped, offered a tiny shrug. "Seriously?" she asked.

The gun twitched back to Andrew, and the guy's breathing became pants of anticipation, and then Syd lunged, her knife buried in the man's throat as the gun roared, the bullet banging off the frying pan as the fish and Andrew both jumped. Blood jetted from the man's neck as he and Syd thrashed in the grass, but Syd was always stronger than she looked, and the man weakened quickly as she twisted the knife.

"Shh," she whispered gently. "Shh. It's over now. Just let go, okay? It's over. I'm sorry it had to end this way for you, but... it's *over*." She continued to whisper quietly, Andrew unable to hear what she was saying to him. But he figured it was probably better than he deserved. He let his breath out, shaky and tired.

"Jesus, Syd," he finally managed.

She looked at him through the smoke. "Flip that fish, would you?" she asked. "I mean, we're eating it no matter how charred it gets, but there's no reason to turn it into a briquet, right?" Her voice tried to be light and gently chiding, but Andrew could hear the tremor in it.

Andrew dutifully complied, and Syd finally disentangled herself from the guy's lifeless body.

"I swear to God, I was sure he was bluffing," Syd said. "I didn't think he had any ammo, really! I mean...why didn't he just shoot you right off the bat?" She wiped her blade in the grass, then noticed the blood all over her shirt, and wrinkled her nose. "Guess I better wander down to the river." She stood, and grinned down at him.

"But some sweet acting there, Andy! Really, I think he bought it! You looked *so* bummed! And hey, we've got a gun now!"

Andrew was able to generate a laugh. "Just following your lead."

She smiled, and turned to the river. "I expect that fish to be waiting for me when I get back," she called over her shoulder.

Andrew shook his head. That was the thing about Syd – she couldn't comprehend the notion that Andrew actually could have felt that she would betray him. That realization fought to wrestle the guilt away from the fact that his inaction had forced Syd to take a life, and

61

claim the number one spot on the list of things that kept him from sleeping at night.

He stared at the pathetic crumple of a body across from him. *You got way more of an honorable death than you know, shithead*, he thought.

Syd had stayed down at the water for far longer than she had needed to wash the blood from her clothes. Andrew suspected she was trying to rinse out more than just her shirt, but he knew she would have stains now that could never be cleaned. And the guilt just piled up, and up, and up.

They moved camp again, and were even more careful of fires.

* * *

It was winter that proved too much for them.

A dumping of snow for the new year, and then an astonishingly brutal freeze made camping unbearable. Andrew knew that Syd would gamely tough it out, but he was certain they would die. There were indications that the city may have settled down – they hadn't seen any vehicles moving along Highway 2 since early fall. Once a shy, skinny horse with an empty saddle wandered close to their camp, and Andy's stomach told him to kill and butcher it, but Syd's wondrous cooing kept the notion from ever being said aloud.

The almost incessant gunfire they heard whenever they ventured close to the city had also stopped. They had crept up as far as the Y where 2 split off from 395, but the sight of the dead roaming the streets scared the hell out of them and they headed back north. Still, they stayed closer to town where they could fish from the Little Spo-kane, forage from abandoned houses – being careful to insure they truly *were* abandoned. Being shot at several times had taught them this lesson.

If the winter had been mild, they may have been able to make it. But crisp, sub-zero temperatures brought a startling dose of reality, and Andy realized he wasn't as outdoorsy as he thought he was.

* * *

A thin cry from outside made both of them stiffen and lift their heads. Perhaps some months back they both would have whispered excitedly, "Did you *hear* that?" But by now they knew both of them *had* heard it, and were waiting for…whatever would inevitably come next. Andy could feel Syd's heart hammering against his back, and his nerves and muscles tingled with the anticipation of sudden action.

The cry, a child's wail, came again, and Syd flew off his back and the mattress, and stood trembling at the apartment door, her hand hovering over the locks.

"Syd!" Andy hissed.

She turned to look at him, eyes wide, and the child's cry came again and grew louder, stretching out in its terror and then Syd was snatching at the knob and deadbolt and the door was open and she flew out onto the walkway.

"Shit! Jesus – *Syd*," Andy snapped, but he was off the mattress and out the door too, saw Syd was leaning against the balcony's railing and looking into the dead grass of the courtyard below. He was happy to see she had her Buck knife in her hand, and he swiveled his head up and down the walkway to see if anything was coming their way, then scanned across to the other balcony and out onto Mayfair. No gangs – living or dead – seemed to be waiting for them, but he felt naked and exposed out here so suddenly. The early spring weather was finally giving the rain a break. It was gloomy and overcast, but he felt soon that the sun would drive the clouds away.

63

The crying child caught his attention, and he leaned against the railing, then peered in the direction Syd was looking. Under a tree, a woman lay curled around a toddler, who was grasping her tightly as one of the dead strained to reach them through the wrought-iron bars that surrounded the courtyard. Its fingers twitched and plucked at the fabric of the woman's pants, but she made no effort to move. The child wailed again, but with less effort, and his head lolled as if sleepy.

Jesus, how long have they been out here? wondered Andy.

The gate at the far end of the courtyard rattled, and Andy saw another of the dead straining against the bars of the fence – no, there were *two* down there - and a whimper tried to build up in his throat, but Syd was in his face, urging him to go down and take them out while she helped the woman and child. Andy glanced at the only set of stairs at the other end of the walkway, turned back to Syd as she sheathed her knife and then was up on the railing and then launching herself out into space and then into the branches of the lone tree below. He instinctively reached out to grab her and then gasped as she tumbled through the branches. The tree seemed dry and lifeless, but it pulled at Syd's blond hair and clothes and Andy was certain she would land hard and maybe break an ankle, but her coat snagged on a branch and yanked her to a stop. Then he bolted down the walkway to the stairs, pulling a hammer out of his jacket as he ran. He slowed at the top of the staircase, made sure there were only the two dead down below, then pounded down the steps and hung a left towards the fence. He spared a glance and could see Syd struggling to get out of her coat, one arm free and sawing at the fabric of the other with her knife as she spun in a lazy circle. And then she dropped. *Shit!* But then she was up, and limping over to the mother and child.

One of the dead had turned to him, a man who had half of his face missing, and began to advance. Andy had lost most of his fear of the dead a while ago – at least when they were in small numbers – but the revulsion would never leave him, he suspected. He swung the hammer in a mighty arc, his desperation the driving force, and the dead man dropped for the last time. The second of the dead was still enamored with the gate, its latch still seemingly a mystery, but Andy knew that the dead still had the instinct to turn doorknobs and if there were any problem-solving neurons that were still firing then it might figure out the latch soon enough. He brought his hammer down into the back of its greasy head, hit it again twice, then pulled it out of the way, fumbled for the gate latch and then yanked it open and sprinted towards Syd.

Andy was distressed to find Syd daring, coaxing, the dead guy on the other side of the fence to try and bite at her through the bars. The hoodie she wore under her coat was half off – probably yanked up from her dash through the treetop – and under that was a white tank top with an exposed left arm she taunted the dead guy with.

"Yeah? You want some?" she asked in a tone that may as well have been asking, "Who's a good boy?"

"Syd…"

"You want it don't you? Yeah you do. Come on, try for a taste. Put that stinky face right up against the bars – "

"Syd, come on, let me just –"

She snapped her head around and eyed him sharply. "I got this," she stated, then turned and waited until, at last, the dead man pressed his face up against the bars, and then she shoved her knife blade into an eye socket with a twist and a crunch, then let go as the thing slid down and stopped, it's jaw caught between the bars causing the dead man's remaining eye to stare sightlessly up into the gray morning sky. She waited a moment, snapped her fingers in front of its face, then delicately grabbed the knife low on the hilt and carefully worked it loose.

"Careful with the blood," Andy mumbled. "You don't want to…"

She eyed him coolly for a bit, then smiled.

"Yeah Andy, I know. Don't get any on me."

She wiped the blade thoroughly on the grass, and Andy made a mental note to douse it with some alcohol later.

"You want to see how they're doing?" Syd asked, and Andy was baffled for a moment until he looked down and remembered the woman and child literally at his feet.

The boy looked up at him, a tangled head of curly black hair, wide dark eyes with lashes gummed up with tears. Andy knelt, and the boy grasped the woman tighter and let out a whimper.

"Hey," Andy breathed, trying to sound comforting. "Hey, buddy. Is this your mommy? Can I check on her, maybe?" Andy reached out to stroke the woman's long dark hair from her cheek and neck, and the boy let out a tiny shriek. Andy jumped and snatched his hand back, and automatically scanned the area for dead and anyone else who might be attracted by the noise.

"Hey," he repeated, "it's okay. I won't hurt her. Really." He felt Syd kneel next to him.

"Hey big guy," she said softly. "Want to come see me?" She held her arms out, then shook off her hoodie, the flesh on her arms goose-pimpled in the cold air. She clapped her hands quietly together. "Come on. Want to come see me? Are you cold? I bet you are." The boy looked down to the woman he clung to, up to Syd, leaned to-wards her, then tightened his grip on the woman. Syd reached out to stroke his hair. The boy made no sound, only stared at her with wide, wet eyes.

"Oh, Jesus Andy – he is burning up!"

Andy took advantage of the boy's distraction and felt the wom-an's cheek, then slid his fingers down to her neck.

"She is ice-cold, Syd," he whispered.

"Ok," Syd muttered, "Enough fooling around kiddo. Up we go." She slid her hands under the boy's armpits and lifted so quickly that the child's fists were plucked from the woman's black and white checkered coat with little resistance. He strained to reach back to the woman, but Syd turned him away and began to bounce and sway with him, shushing and cooing.

Andy grabbed the woman's left shoulder and pulled it towards him, pressing her torso down and her back into the dried grass. Her left leg flopped down as well, and Andy didn't like her laying with her legs sprawled open, so he modestly pulled her right one over on to the left. That was when he saw the ragged, bloody hole in the denim over her thigh, and he sat back abruptly on his heels, his spine stiffening.

"Yeah, I'm thinking she's gone, Syd."

"Could you hand me up my hoodie?" was her reply. Andy grabbed the heavy fleece jacket, and lifted it up to her, where she took it and wrapped it around the boy.

Andy shook his head. "You are going to freeze, my dear," he mumbled, but smiled to himself.

"Not yet, I think," she replied softly.

The boy was staring silently at him, sucking on a thumb, his head bobbing gently to the rhythm of Syd's swaying. Andy didn't know what to do, afraid any smile, wink, or friendly gesture would cause the kid to start crying.

Syd began humming one of her pop tunes, and the boy turned to her, eyes glassy and blinking. Syd smiled and hummed a little louder, the dips in her bounce a little deeper, the sways a little broader. The boy took his thumb out of his mouth as if to attempt a smile, and then sneezed full-on in her face.

"Oh," Syd gasped in shock. The boy sneezed again. "Oh!" Syd, repeated, blinking rapidly as wet mucus ran down her face.

Andy felt as if a rock dropped in his gut.

"Shit. Jesus. *Shit*. Syd you have to – Syd, wipe that shit off you *now*. Wipe it off now," Andy hissed. Syd looked down at him with stunned horror in her eyes. Andy reached down to push himself up, and then the dead woman grabbed hold of his arm and bit deeply into his right hand.

"Hey!" Andy yelped, and tried to yank his hand away. Then the true nature of what was happening sunk in, and he began to pummel the woman's head desperately as she began to chew.

"Fuck! Jesus Christ oh fuck fuck *fuck*!"

The boy began to cry, and as Andy twisted around to grab his hammer he saw the child reaching down for the woman.

"Jesus Syd – get him out of here," he said, rising panic making his voice tremble. "Fuck – go up and wipe your face down – *please!*"

And then he began to hammer in the woman's head.

* * *

Syd sat on the mattress, the boy sleeping against her chest. Her hoodie still swaddled him, and his dark curls were wet and plastered to his forehead. *The fever*, Andy thought. *Well, shit.*

Syd looked up and stared at him as he stood in the doorway. She was breathing in irregular bursts, like a child trying to catch her breath after throwing a fit. But there were no tears and her face was impassive. Her eyes darted to his bleeding hand and stared at that as he shuffled into the apartment, stood over them for a moment, and then sat quietly next to her. His right hand throbbed with his pulse, his left hand clutching it tight. Blood oozed between his fingers, but there were no jets of it squirting between them or whatever so he probably wasn't going to bleed to death. The fever would take him before any infection would kill him. And then... Well, he hoped there wouldn't be a *then*. But if there were, he just hoped he would be mindless, and it was only some reptile brain function with no notion of pain and misery.

He was so tired right now, and he flopped onto his back and stared up at the moldy ceiling. His eyes shifted to Syd, the white tank still stood in contrast against her faded tan. He let go of his right hand and reached out to touch her back, she stiffened and then re-laxed and as he brought his hand away he realized he had left a bloody handprint on the cotton material.

Shit.

He started to apologize, and found he didn't have the will to start talking.

So, this is finally it, he thought. *All of the mobs we outran – both dead and alive. The sneaky, hidden ones – both dead and alive – that waited for us to wander into their grasp. Starvation. Thirst. Exposure. And what did us in? Not the meanness of the world, but our own compassion. Well, Syd's, mostly. I would have probably been wringing my hands at what to do if she hadn't leapt into it...*

Andy marveled at it, the subtle betrayal of mere compassion. *Well, shit. Not a bad way to go out, I guess. We weren't dicks. We only killed those that tried to kill us.*

He was surprised that he wasn't panicking anymore, that the certain knowledge of his imminent death did not cripple him with paralytic fear. And really, what was there left to rage about? The drama of a tantrum was too draining to even entertain. And it wouldn't do to pull something like that in front of Syd. His heart gave a quiet thump and shudder.

Syd.

Why did she have to go down, too? There was no doubt the boy had the fever, considering his mother. Andy's heart wanted to hope that the child merely had a cold, or pneumonia, or something pre-apocalyptic, but there was no room in there for fiction anymore. Well, small comfort knowing she didn't die ripped to pieces, lying in the useless belly of the dead.

Had he ever told her that he loved her? Yes, of course he did. But did he ever really *tell* her? Let her know the true depth of his affection, that it was the engine that drove him, and if one of the dead were to rip him open right now, to bare his heart to the world, then surely her name would be tattooed boldly across that wildly pumping muscle.

He wanted to let her know that. His hand hovered again over her back, but the blood gluing his fingers together made him lower it to his thigh. He wanted to apologize for any ill-tempered word he spoke to her, any derisive slight he had surely made. She had deserved better than him, she had deserved someone with the will to live life as brightly as she had. To delight in the beauty of small things, and to be shocked at the meanness of people, even after all they had seen in the last year. He wanted to tell her that he wished he could have been as courageous as she was – not just in dangerous times, but also in not caring what people thought of her, and of sticking to her principles – *especially* in dangerous times. He realized he was propping her up on a pedestal she would find uncomfortable, but he didn't care. She should know she was special, and good.

But he was so *tired*, and formulating the thoughts were far easier than articulating them.

"You've made me a better person, I think," was all he could manage, in a harsh whisper.

Her breathing had calmed, and the boy's had the quick rhythms of a fevered sleep. He listened to them for quite a while, and then felt one of her hands reach down and give his leg a long, warm squeeze.

Oh, that's nice, that's nice, he thought.

He closed his eyes, and decided he could afford to sleep for a bit.

* * *

She of course couldn't bear the thought of bashing either of their heads in. She felt like a coward, but ended up locking the boy in the bathroom and barricading Andy in the bedroom, locking the door and pushing the mattress up against it. They had been quiet for a very long time.

A very long time.

And so she never ended up hearing – or at least caring about – the random thumps and rattles of the door handles. The dead knew each other, after all.

She had been so hot at the end, not feeling the cold of spring, just the shivers of the fever. In her delirium, she felt the need to keep the front door open. She surely would have locked herself in if her mind had been in a better place.

When her time came, she rose with uncertainty until she could find her way out the door and into the world, a bloody palm-print on her white tank-top seemingly propelling her forward. She had decided she would die in her favorite sweatpants, the ones that had a single word stitched across the fleece on her bottom: Pink.

Through A Veil of Moondust

T he turtle tapped on Mason's visor. "Hey," it said. "Hey dude."

Mason stirred, his eyes fluttering open.

"Hey dude," the turtle repeated. "You remember me?"

Mason licked his lips - or tried to. All he really did was succeed in pushing his tongue through and parting them, whereupon they all stuck together in a gummy paste.

"What's my name?" the turtle asked.

Mason groaned, and tried to conjure up some spit to work his tongue free.

"Are you trying to tell me it's on the tip of your tongue?" the turtle laughed, then added, "You don't remember, do you? You had me for all of a year, and you don't remember what you named me."

Mason coughed, tearing his lips apart, spittle stippling the inside of his visor. He was able to work more saliva around in his mouth, and this time licked his lips properly.

"Go away," he croaked. "Busy dying."

"I can see that," the turtle sneered. "And you're going to die without remembering my name."

"What the hell do you care?" Mason replied. "You left me."

"I did," the amphibian said. "You didn't seem too cut up about it. Don't recall you looking very hard for me."

"You weren't exactly the friendliest of pets," Mason grunted. "Anytime I came near, you hissed and shut your box up tight. Every. God. Damned. Time."

"I don't remember wanting to be anyone's pet."

"What were you doing in our driveway, then? Seriously, one morning there you are, right in the middle of a sea of concrete. Not exactly your ideal habitat, I'd say."

"Chickens gotta cross roads, I had to cross your driveway. I was resting." It waved it's clawed foot around. "Jesus, look at these little things. I'm not exactly designed to *sprint*, genius."

"I think you were designed to be an annoying piece of –"

"Whoa, really? That's how you want to spend your remaining minutes? Being hateful? That's just sad."

"You're the one bothering me you little son of a –"

"Again with the name calling! *Maybe* you should be asking *why* I'm bothering you."

Mason closed his eyes, trying to control his breathing again. Shallow, even breaths – don't get worked up. He would run out of air before he froze, that was certain. His suit would keep him warm as he lay in shadow, inside the slope of Fra Mauro T. No doubt he would be a warm and toasty corpse by the time he was found. The tiny nuke powering his life support would see to that. But it could not generate oxygen for him, and could not bring his comm system back online, or fix his broken back. He could only stare up at a beautiful full Earth and through the sheer, stubborn force of willpower, try and get the good people of Australia to notice him.

But that damned turtle was in the way.

"Hey!" the turtle snapped. "I asked you *why* do you *think* I'm *bothering* you?"

"Why are you bothering me?" Mason asked, disinterested.

"Because I want you to tell me my *name!*"

If Mason could have moved, he would have swatted the little bastard into orbit. He was virtually certain he could have done it, too. One healthy smack, and the mouthy little jerk would have been spinning through vacuum like that Japanese monster – *kaiju* – what the hell was its name? Oh yeah.

"Gamera," he said aloud, feeling proud of himself.

"Oh, you did *not* just call me that," the turtle said, indignation dripping from each word. "You can remember the name of some cheesy monster, but not someone you spent a whole *year* with?"

"I got way more enjoyment from those cheesy monster movies than I ever did from you," Mason whispered.

"Then why keep me around? Huh? Why bother feeding me? Building me a pen? And wasn't *that* a marvel of engineering! A plywood and chicken wire gulag – not exactly Barbie's dream house, I can tell you that."

"Sister wouldn't let me use that, sorry," Mason laughed. Crap – he bet his sister could remember the damned turtle's name...

"So if I sucked so bad as a pet, why did you keep me around?"

"You are not going to let this go, are you?" Mason groaned.

"Why should I?" the turtle asked. "You didn't let *me* go."

"And yet you left anyway."

"Ever think you sucked as an owner?"

"I was ten. Ask my dog if I sucked."

"Oh, please. Dogs, man. They fall in love with anyone – and how easy is it to fall in love with a dog? I mean, it's a cliché, really. Wouldn't you feel better if you really had to earn that love, that loyalty?"

"I've seen cats with more loyalty than you, I can tell you that."

"Don't get me started on cats. 'Oh, they're so independent!' Bullshit. *I* was independent. Until I got picked up and tossed in a cage."

"Where you were sheltered and fed."

"Oh, yum. Lettuce. Day in. Day out. Lettuce."

"I'm tired," Mason muttered. "Leave me alone."

"What's my name?"

"Shit..."

* * *

He didn't know how the fire had started. At this point, he couldn't even work up a respectable hypothesis of the cause. The crawler had been traversing the lunar plain, it's rhythmic thumping hypnotic even as it jarred and shook your body. It was one of the bigger crew transports, with an enclosed cabin. Luckily enough, safety protocols dictated that helmets were to be on and secured at all times, with emergency oxygen units tethered to you. Well, at least one of those had stayed with him...

It had been a long week working on the new sub-station. It would soon be a lonely outpost, designed for secure transfer of telemetry to...well, it was none of his business - or any of the rest of the work crew's, for that matter. Just build the station, pick up a hazard bonus for the travel and shitty 'bunk house' quarters on site, and come back with a week's rest at Fra Mauro base. Rumor had it that their next project would be building a visitor's station at the Apollo 14 site, making a park out of it. Of course, that was more of a running joke than a rumor. The trick was to come up with the most outlandish provenance of such a project.

His buddy Jeff had been citing evidence of turnstiles and velvet ropes when the fire had blossomed at the back of the crew cabin, transforming into a furious inferno in seconds. The emergency airlocks had vented and popped, and Mason had been shot out of crawler in a mighty arc, his airline trailing behind him. As he reached the apex of his journey, he was able to disconnect the hose and plug in his emergency supply as he began his descent. *This is gonna hurt*, he thought, as Fra Mauro T loomed larger in his visor. He could see patches of black under the fluttering strips of the ragged and ripped white outer covering of his suit. Various alarms flashed on his heads-up, but no loss of pressure was indicated. The crater grew bigger and bigger, a round O of surprise, as if it was as shocked as he was at the turn of events.

Not likely, were his last thoughts before he hit the inside of the rim and bounced once before blacking out.

* * *

He didn't know how long he had been out. The moondust had set-tled, a thin haze across his visor, but that had probably not taken very long at all – it fell with the same alacrity as a feather or hammer. His chronometer gave him the current time, but he was a bit hazy on when the explosion happened so his best guess was around five minutes. He was astonished that he was alive. But he was certain that wouldn't be for very much longer if he couldn't get up and out of the crater.

He tried to give a verbal command to run a system check, but all he could get was a flashing cursor on his heads-up. His emergency beacon seemed doubtful, then.

"Well, swell," he muttered.

His back hurt something fierce, and he could not move any limbs. *That makes it a little difficult to climb out of this crater*, he thought grimly. A bluish smudge dead center in his visor worried him – he was afraid it might be a micro crack with ice building up in it, until he realized he was seeing Earth obscured through moondust. He was able to lift his head and drop it a few times to try and knock the dust free, and was rewarded with a better view of Earth, looking glorious as the moondust slipped aside like parting curtains in a theater.

So, more than likely paralyzed below the neck, low on air, no way to communicate my position – can't even wave a friendly howdy-do to the good people of Earth, Mason thought. He stared at the marbled hues of his home planet, and thought that there were probably worse views you could have when you were going to die. His eyelids drooped, and he decided a nap was in order.

And then that damned turtle showed up.

* * *

Tap-tap-tap…
Mason groaned.
Tap-tap-tap…
"What?" he growled.

76

"Oh, am I bothering you?" the turtle asked innocently, releasing a flurry of taps on his visor. "Is that irritating? Kind of like all the times you tapped on my shell? *Tappity-tap-tap-tap.* "We're not done here, buddy."

Mason swore. A long, steady stream of soul-satisfying curses that would blister eardrums and trigger nightmares in those with a more delicate constitution.

"My," the turtle remarked. "And to think you kissed your mother with that mouth."

"Who do you think I learned my vocabulary from?"

The turtle actually laughed. "Yeah, she was not a shy one, was she?"

Mason chuckled.

"Remember my name yet?"

"No."

The turtle sighed. "You know what pisses me off the most?"

"I'm sure you'll tell me," Mason rumbled.

"Remember that parakeet you found?"

"Yeah?"

"What was his name?"

Mason remained silent.

"Come on, you remember that."

"Caesar," Mason finally replied.

"Yeah. You had him for what – two whole weeks?"

Mason said nothing.

"Two. Weeks. You bought a cage for him – put out an ad trying to find his owner, and then he up and died on you but you can re-member *that* little bastard's name but not mine."

"He was friendly, hopped right up onto my finger, and never bit me."

"Two weeks!"

"Well, maybe if you had died in two weeks I would have felt bad and remembered your name too – regretful that we didn't have more time together."

The turtle snorted. "You had hamsters longer than that parakeet. One even seemed to like you. What were *their* names?"

77

Shit, Mason thought. *Is a hamster going to show up to haunt me now?*

"Well I guess I shouldn't feel too bad if you can't remember a cuddly little ball of fluff's name."

"Oh!' Mason said brightly, remembering the hamster's name. "Alexander!"

"Screw you," muttered the turtle.

"See?" Mason asked. "Maybe if you were friendlier I would remember your name."

"And I'm going to ask you again, if I sucked so *bad* as a pet, why did you keep me?"

"Because a kid just doesn't give up on something like that!" Mason blurted.

"Bingo," the turtle said quietly.

"What's that supposed to mean?"

"A *kid* doesn't give up. So why should you?"

"Really?" Mason groaned. "Is that what this is all about? A motivational badgering of tough-love bullshit? I have a broken back, no comms, and no more air. What precisely can I do about that?"

"Well, that does sound dire. But I have to ask – *is* your back actually broken?"

"Well, genius, it hurts like hell and I can't move. What do you think?"

"I'm going out on a limb here, but let me ask you – if your back is actually broken, would it *hurt?*"

"I...don't know."

"I'm going to guess if you can't move your arms and legs, that would indeed be serious trauma to your back. But let me ask you this – can you *feel* your arms and legs?"

"I'm kind of numb, so –"

"Oh for God's sake, wiggle a toe in your boot, then!"

Mason concentrated, and was able to twitch a big toe.

"I'm going to let you catch up with me on this," the turtle said.

Suit lock-up, Mason thought. *The shock of the impacting the surface, or explosion itself, may have put it into...shit, am I in safe mode?*

"Suit: system reboot," Mason whispered. "Password: Alexander, Bonnie…"

"What's my *name?*" screamed the turtle.

"*Cornelius,*" Mason finished.

"Easy as one-two-three," the turtle said.

The heads-up cursor winked out. *Shit,* he thought. *I should have noticed that I was in safe mode.* The suit was quiet for several seconds, and then the cursor returned, blinked, then transformed into a data stream in the heads-up. Soon the familiar thrum of power coursed through the suit.

"Warning," a woman's voice stated in his ear with irritating calmness. "You are disconnected from an oxygen source. Please connect immediately. Dangerous levels of carbon dioxide are detected. Warning. You are disconnected from –"

"Hush," Mason replied, and the alarm shut off. But a red warning light continued to flash. *Okay, so I never had air to begin with. No wonder I'm not thinking clearly…*

He struggled to sit, and his back screamed in agony. *Screw this shit,* he thought, and relaxed his muscles.

"Suit: powered assist. Sitting position."

The suit dutifully bent at the waist, levering him up and he gasped as pain spasmed in his back. *Probably not the brightest move to make right now,* he thought. *But time is running out…*

He tried to take a deep breath, but it was a thin, wheezing intake and he coughed. He tried an experimental twist of his neck, and was able to swivel his head. Ah. There it was. His emergency oxygen supply. The turtle sat on the flat, dust covered tank, and waved at him.

"Better plug it back in, buddy."

Mason managed a tired smile. "Guess I didn't forget your name after all."

"So I guess I never did leave you, then."

Mason managed to roll his eyes. "Don't get sappy on me now, you little shit." If a turtle could grin, then Cornelius managed it.

Mason bent, ignoring the pain, and grabbed the braided-metal hose, banged the connector against the heel of his left hand, watching moondust drop out of it. He actually brought it up to try and blow on it, until it clacked against his visor.

"Shit," he breathed.

"Tick-tock," chided the turtle.

Mason jammed the connector against the one protruding from his suit, and waited for the cool rush of air. There was a moment of trepidation as nothing happened, and he worried that dust was blocking the airflow. Or, possibly worse, of it getting inside his suit. He did not need to inhale those dangerously course particles... Nothing to be done about it, though. He needed air more than anything right now, hoping the filtration unit would take care of any particulates. And then a comforting hiss echoed in his helmet, and soon he was able to take the deepest, most wonderful breath in the history of mankind.

And then many more. He hadn't realized how stale and close the inside of his helmet had been.

"Suit," he commanded. "Powered assist. Stand." He felt himself rise, a toy being lifted, his legs straightening as if on their own. Mason stood carefully for a few minutes, letting the suit's gyros stabilize him. He didn't need to take a header and tumble further into the crater.

He twisted at the waist, and felt his back protest. *But not too much, methinks*, Mason decided, and tried a tentative step. Soon he was taking many more, his hands grasping at the slope to assist, as he began the arduous task of climbing out of the crater.

He had been at it awhile when he noticed the turtle was curiously silent. He automatically took deep breaths, an instinct to help clear his oxygen-deprived mind, and looked around. Cornelius was nowhere to be found.

"Well, he's done it again," Mason grumbled.

The alarm signal flashing on his visor winked out.

* * *

80

The lunar plain was littered with debris. Tangles of twisted Dura-hull for the most part, but much of it was recognizable objects: tools, food stuffs...suit parts. And there were many, many emergency oxygen packs. *So this is where they grow*, Mason thought without humor. He picked up the ones he came across and strapped them to his suit.

The crawler was still upright, amazingly enough, but the back end of the cabin was blown open, along with the airlocks. The cockpit looked dark, silent, and dead. He didn't want to investigate, but knew it was his duty.

He spotted the familiar blue suit of his friend, and did his best to hurry over to him - his bounding shuffle turning into a bouncing trot. "Long!" he shouted. "Hey Jeff!" And then remembered his comm was out. His friend lay face down in the moondust, and as Mason turned him over, a rock was jammed fully into the man's visor, bits of sharp plastic surrounding it like teeth.

Mason sighed, too worn out to let it sink in. He spotted a bit of red on the far side of the crawler. Another body − probably Storm. And then a yellow suit jammed in the shredded opening of the crawler. Davis.

An indicator flashed in his helmet − he was receiving the distress signal of the crawler. Hopefully his suit was sending out its own. He turned north, hoping to see the purple flash of Fra Mauro Station's navigational array, but it was far over the lunar horizon. That was the thing about working on the Moon − when going home, every landmark and way station always seemed to be over the horizon, until you just came upon it. He flipped up the cover of his comm unit on the back of his hand, but there was still no indication it was in working order. The suit could pick up distress signals, but his VOX appeared to be dead. He stared up into the airlock openings, and could not reach them. He was too tired to pull himself up, and his back would not allow him to jump so high. He decided he would check to see if the body on the far side of the crawler was...not a body. *Hell, if I made it, someone else could*, he thought. The realization that his coworker might be going through an ordeal like he had just gone through made Mason hustle again, despite the twinging muscles in his back.

He gave the blasted-open end of the crawler a wide berth. His suit was tough, but maybe not so tough it couldn't be torn open. He continued on towards Storm, who appeared to have been tossed aside with a casual indifference. As he closed in on the figure, he could see the suit breach, all twisted and ragged strips, frosty with blood. It was just as well the suit was red.

Mason stood, indecisive and overwhelmed.

"Not to be indelicate," a familiar voice whispered, "but *his* comm unit might be working…"

Before Mason could make any decision about salvaging equipment from the dead, a crawler hove into view, moving at an astonishing clip, the pads at the end of each spoke churning up lunar soil in furious grey geysers.

* * *

His rescuer wore an armored suit – the first of its kind really. Lazhar was a big guy – *very* big. The wreckage of the crawler didn't make a scratch in his suit as he investigated its interior. *Future of suit tech*, Mason mused.

Lazhar had been out surveying with ground penetrating radar for hidden lava tubes, when he had picked up the crawler's signal. He had immediately dropped what he was doing, and set out to help. He had accessed satellite surveillance footage of the accident, remarkably enough, and had watched in fascination as Mason had been blown into the crater. A salvage mission was already on its way from the station.

As Lazhar investigated the interior of the crawler, Mason busied himself switching out his comm unit from the spares located on his rescuer's vehicle. He had pantomimed that his communications were out, and the big man nodded as he dropped down from the cockpit, a fist gripping a comm toolkit. The metal kit looked like a child's lunchbox in the man's hand. Once Mason swapped out the comm unit – hoping the antenna embedded in his suit was still viable – he called out to Lazhar.

"Superintendent, this is Mason. Do you copy?"

"This is superintendent. I copy."

Awesome, Mason thought. He didn't know what else to say, but felt he had started a conversation he didn't really want to pursue, so he settled for asking about the state of the crawler.

"Unsalvageable," came Lazhar's terse reply. "And no survivors."

"Ah," Mason replied. And left it at that.

Lazhar linked together several sleds from the destroyed crawler to load the bodies on, eleven in total. He used deflated emergency shelters as tarps, their bright-blue color reminding Mason of camping trips when he was a kid. Tied to the crawler's winch at the back, the sleds made a much merrier-looking train behind them than could be expected, considering their cargo.

Lazhar's crawler was a two-seater, open to vacuum, and it was a tight squeeze sitting next to the giant of a man. Mason watched the horizon rock back and forth as they got under way. It would be another hour to the station. Lazhar was a man of few words, which right now was fine with Mason. I mean, the guy was fiercely smart, seemed to know *everything* – a good guy – but he never seemed to warm to anyone. Jeff had sworn the guy was an alien...

Mason pushed that memory away for now. He let them ride in silence for a while, but eventually that got boring.

"Hey, Cap?" he asked, and Lazhar grunted in response. The guy never liked the nickname he'd been stuck with, and Mason decided he would start using the man's first name – difficult as it was to pronounce.

"You know anything about turtles?"

"Turtles?" Lazhar replied.

Holy cow, was that a hint of surprise in the guy's voice? A day of miracles, Mason thought.

"Yeah. I had a box turtle when I was a kid. Just found him in our driveway one morning. Had him for about a year, and one day he escaped. Moved on, I guess."

Lazhar grunted again, but more of a prompt than irritation.

"I was just wondering; do you know how long they live?"

Lazhar pondered the question, and then his lecturing tone crackled over the speaker in Mason's ear – a tone that was usually the most animated the guy ever got, as if sharing knowledge was the most exciting thing you could do.

"Well, if I recall, a common box turtle can live up to 50 years, but it wouldn't be unheard of for them to live longer, under the right conditions. It would depend on the environment, I suppose."

"Huh," Mason replied. He liked the idea of the little guy wandering the hillsides of his youth, free as could be – probably not lonely, since he wasn't very friendly to begin with.

"What made you think of this turtle?" Lazhar asked, and Mason was startled by the question. *Well, that is positively* prying *by Cap's standards*, he thought, and then he realized the man was probably trying to assess his mental state.

"Ah, who knows? Brain bouncing around, weird things you think of when you assume you're dying. Happens to all of us at some time or another, right?" Mason answered.

Lazhar gave a low chuckle. "Yeah, I suppose," he said. "We'll get you to the station, have Doc check you out."

Wow. An open expression of humor served with a side of sympathy, Mason marveled. *A day of miracles indeed.*

The rode on in silence, the crawler maintaining its stately pace.

The Zombie Sisters

*T*rouble can brew at a Starbucks more often than anyone would believe, Gavin thought. *The nonsense that can go down in the cafe...*

Gavin watched the man swaying outside the doors, as if it were a mystery on how they opened. Well, they would be closing soon – should he just lock up now? All he needed was this guy to wander off to the bathroom. It would be a nightmare getting him out of there...

The man would reach out, paw at the handle, then stop as if forgetting what he wanted, then repeat the process. He was in his forties probably, and dressed like he had just crawled out of bed. He didn't *look* like he had been released – or escaped – from the hospital across the street, or was homeless, but he was definitely on *something*. Hell, it was a miracle he had clothes on at all.

Gavin was about to tell him to move along, that he was blocking the doors, when a young man approached, head down, buds planted firmly in his ears, the cord snaking down to the phone in his hand. Before Gavin could call out a warning, the student pulled up short with a, "Whoa," his backpack sliding off his shoulder and down to the crook of his arm.

"Dude, what?" the student asked. "Shit, are they closed?" His eyes flicked back to his phone, no doubt checking the time. "That's bullshit – they have ten minutes yet." He tipped his head up, his eyes meeting Gavin's. "Hey, you guys closed?" he yelled. The older man's head swung around in a drunken jerk to direct his attention to the student.

"We're not closed," Gavin replied, raising his voice. "This gentleman seems to be having some sort of problem, and is blocking our doors."

The student darted his eyes to the older man, and then took a step back. He lifted his backpack and clutched it like a shield. "Yo, man, this guy is *sick* – he's got that thing that's going around – I would bet on it. Call the cops, dude." And then he turned and was gone. Gavin couldn't help but feel a little abandoned, and the betrayal made him angry. He tapped on the glass door.

"Sir," he said, voice firm, "I'm afraid you're going to have to move along."

Damn it, where was Lori? She was always best at handling this type of situation. She could charm the homeless and the addicts into leaving, but also get tough when she had to. Ah yes – Gavin had made her quit bar and go clean back of house after she had sassed him, commenting that she wished the stick up his ass would at least go all the way up to give him a spine. Gavin was new to being a shift supervisor, and didn't want to have to talk to the manager about it. Frustrations were running high these days with a lot of the partners out ill, so he ordered her to grab a mop as Aaron and Lance snickered. Gavin was sure their humor was directed at him, and he also realized he had given Lori the exact punishment she had wanted...

The door rattled and thumped as the guy experimented with the mechanics of pushing it open. He lifted his eyes, unblinking and rimmed in red pain, a pale film of yellow dimming the blue irises. Gavin took a step back.

Oh, Jesus, he is *sick*, Gavin thought. *He's got that fever that's going around. Lock up, just lock the door!* He fumbled for his key ring, and the door jerked towards him as the infected man finally maneuvered his way into the store. Gavin gave an astonished bleat of surprise, and took more than one step back this time.

"You need to stop right there, sir," he managed, his voice high and shaky. "You need to go seek some medical attention. There's a hospital right across the street. Now, go on. Get out of here."

"The guy's not feeling good, G," Aaron said from behind him. "Quit trying to run him off like he's a dog. That's not cool."

Gavin's fists clenched involuntarily as a detonation of frightened anger burned through him, and he tamped down the urge to scream at Aaron, to tell him that what was *really* not cool was his stupid, stringy manbun and the pathetic wisps of hair that was his beard. *That's not cool, Aaron, you half-assed hippie wannabe!* But he was sure it would only come out as a series of inarticulate vowels, his stretched nerves - virtually thrumming like a plucked bass string now - would not let him form a coherent sentence.

The man had stopped again, propping the door open with his body as he stared at Gavin, letting in a breath of the cool spring air outside. Gavin tried to stare him down, to radiate firm authority, that he wasn't the type of person who would put up with shenanigans such as this, but then the man's jaw began popping and jerking, his chin describing irregular orbits, as if it had finally broken the bonds imposed by tetanus.

Or rigor mortis? Nonsense – those rumors are impossible! But Gavin discovered that he most definitely could accept those rumors as cold, hard, certifiable *facts* right now.

The man's mouth opened wider, tongue writhing and darting, and Gavin could hear quiet gasps from the back of the guy's throat.

"Oh, man – that dude is fucked *up*."

Apparently Lance had joined the party. Three of them now –

87

three! Facing down *one* man, and none of them felt compelled to do more than… just be in his way, it seemed. Gavin was afraid to move, to turn his head to talk to the two behind him, to reach into his pocket for his phone, to do anything other than stare back into the man's barren eyes. His own jaw began to work, and finally he managed to whisper, "Could one of you please call – "

And then the man was moving, stumbling towards them, and Gavin shrieked, his black Sketchers trying to find traction on the tiles, but he bumped into both Aaron and Lance, screamed again, and a chorus of *Dudes!* and *Fuck, mans!* issued from the other partners as they scrambled out of his way, then Gavin's feet tangled themselves up and he went down, flat on his back with the man lurching forward and then falling onto Gavin.

Gavin had no screams left in him, his body only capable of working his legs to try and scoot himself out from under the man, his arms rigid braces propping up the dead weight lying on him, to keep the rancid smell of the guy's mouth away from his face – to keep those teeth, gnashing together in arrhythmic spasms, the hell away from him.

And then the man's face was gone as a blast of cold water, smelling heavily of bleach, exploded over Gavin's chest. Grey tendrils dragged across his neck as the mop was pulled back and slammed into the side of the man, knocking him off of Gavin. The mop retreated and then thrust into the guy yet again, shoving him further from Gavin, and Lori stepped over him, straining to push the guy into a corner.

"What the hell are you two good for?" Lori yelled. "Seriously – help Gavin up and let's keep this guy away from us. Can't you see he's got that fever that's going around?"

Hands gripped Gavin under his shoulders, and he felt himself being lifted to his feet, low murmurs reassuring him that he was fine, that he would be fine.

But the guy didn't bite you, did he?

Gavin shivered, the cold water seeping through his shirt and trickling down his stomach. He didn't even know how to respond, wasn't sure he could. The adrenaline that had flooded through him had left, and all he felt was hollow and weak.

Lori had succeeded in scooting the man into the front corner, pinned against the plate glass and metal framework. If she released pressure to give her arms a rest, the infected man would try to push up from the floor, and she would shove him down again, muttering, "Nope, uh-huh."

She shouldn't have to keep that up, Gavin thought listlessly. Aaron and Lance stood by, watching as if they were being trained on task. *Typical.* Gavin cleared his throat, and finally found his vice.

"Hey guys?" he asked quietly. They turned to him, eyes round. "Maybe get some of the smaller tables moved over to pen him in, so she doesn't have to keep knocking him down? We can maintain some more distance that way."

They both scrambled into action, dragging some three by threes over, tipping them on end to make a modern shield wall. Lori stepped back and let her co-workers construct the trap. She turned to Gavin, her lungs still heaving, trying to give her the extra oxygen she needed after the exertion and excitement.

"You okay there, G?" she asked him, then blew a lock of auburn hair out of her face. "He bite you at all?" Her eyes flicked down to his waist, an eyebrow raised. Under the smell of bleach, Gavin could smell the faint whiff of urine. Blue and red lights began flashing outside. "Yeah, I called the cops," she added.

Gavin closed his eyes. *Wonderful. I get to talk to the police with a big piss-stain on my pants.*

He opened his eyes, watching as Lance and Aaron were occupied with pinning the guy against the windows, deep in conversation about the strategy of it, as if it were a complex military campaign.

Lori casually lifted the mop, and swiped it across his crotch and right thigh, and smiled gently.

"Looks like I nailed you with the mop. Sorry. Didn't know what else to do."

He was too spent to have a wave of relief wash over him, but the gesture of covering up some embarrassment for him touched him deeply. That was the thing about Lori – she could be maddingly frustrating, hard-headed and sometimes mean. Yet she usually made the workday better when she was in a good mood, and she was a damn hard worker.

Gavin swallowed around the lump in his throat, thought about making a joke about sending her his laundry bill, but couldn't muster up the tone to pull it off. Instead, he managed a smile and said, "I really appreciate you helping me out."

"Oh, sure! No Problem," she replied, in that surprised-that-you-would-think-that-was-a-big-deal tone the millennials used these days when you thanked them for something. Gavin wasn't much older than his co-workers, really, but never felt in tune with his generation. Or, for that matter, even his parent's generation - and maybe even his grandparent's. Whatever generation was last to revere manners and respect authority, *that* was one he could identify with. Naturally, that didn't work well for him as a shift lead...

The front door swung open, and Officer Taylor poked his head in. "Everybody okay in here?"

"We got him pinned down over here," Aaron informed him.

Not what he asked, Gavin thought, as the cop flicked his eyes briefly over to the corner, then back to Gavin.

"Yeah, we're fine officer," he said. "Just a little wounded ego." The cop's eyes trailed up and down Gavin's chest and legs, then glanced over to Lori and her mop.

"The guy knocked Gavin down and was on top of him," Lori offered. Officer Taylor's dark eyes snapped back to Gavin.

"He bite you?" the cop asked.

"No, I don't think he really even touched me. Lori knocked him off me with the mop."

The cop's eyes moved back to Lori, and he gave an amused grin.

"Nice," he said. "Keeping your distance."

"Hey, I'm all about that," Lori replied.

Officer Taylor chuckled, and moved into the lobby, letting the door swing shut behind him. Three easy steps, and he was over to the corner, standing over Aaron and Lance.

"He's not like the average tweaker, Mist – uh, *Officer* T," Aaron offered.

Yeah, I told you calling him that behind his back would be too much of a habit, Gavin thought. *The fool we would be pitying would be you, Aaron.*

The cop leaned over the two baristas, and gingerly peeked over the tables. His head nodded a few times as he sniffed.

"Yeah, I think we've got a relatively new one," the cop declared. "He stinks, but not on the reeking level yet. Doesn't seem too active. He seem more confused than aggressive?"

"Pretty much," Gavin said, and the others murmured their agreement.

"Well, he won't stay that way much longer." Officer Taylor sighed. "Alright, Ay-ay-ron, and Vince, I'm going to need to get in there." Lori gave a short bark of a laugh, and Aaron scowled. Lance just looked confused.

Looks like Officer Taylor can give out nicknames too, Aaron, Gavin thought with a touch of glee.

The radio on Officer Taylor's shoulder crackled in incomprehensible cop-talk, some 10-something whatever at the pottery shop over on Olive. The cop replied in more advisable 10-who-knows-whats, explaining his situation and something about needing an ambulance.

91

"I'm sorry," Lori piped up, dropping the mop. "Did they just say something about You're Kiln It, over on Olive?"

"Uh, yeah," Officer Taylor replied. "Another disturbance down there, sounds like."

"Fuck," Lori said, and yanked her apron off and moved towards the door.

"Hey, Lori – I need you to make a statement…"

But she was out the door, and Gavin watched as she ran west on 13th.

Officer Taylor looked at Gavin as if he wasn't sure if he had really seen her bolt and run. Gavin just shrugged. *I mean, it's Lori. Who can tell what she's going to do next?*

"Doesn't her sister work there?" Aaron asked. "At the pottery place?"

"Ashley?"

"Yeah."

"Shit…" Gavin breathed.

"That's a pottery store?" Lance asked. "Dude, I thought it was a funeral home or something. You know, kilns?"

Both Gavin and Officer Taylor closed their eyes and sighed.

"You're thinking of crematoriums, genius," Aaron snorted.

"Okay then," Officer Taylor said. "I have no backup, yet have to cuff this guy and keep him restrained, and I need you two out of my way. Thank you for corralling him."

"Let us help you," Gavin said impulsively.

"Yeah!" Aaron and Lance said simultaneously.

"No, I can't have – "

"Officer Taylor, we don't want you to get bit, and the chances are slimmer if we help." Gavin picked up the mop from the floor. "Maybe I can pin him at the back of his neck?"

"Really, guys – "

"Times are fucked up, dude – *officer*," Lance said. "Things are getting weird out there, and I'm thinking we all need to work together to get through it, yeah?"

"I can't believe I'm saying this, but he makes sense," Aaron suggested.

Officer Taylor stared at each of them in turn, bobbed his head neatly and said, "Yeah, let's do this. Just stay the hell away from his mouth."

* * *

I am in hell, Ashley thought. *Literal hell. Forty year-old women in designer t-shirts with 'Mommy Needs Her Wine' written across them, with obnoxious laughter and bad jokes on endless repeat.* At least this wasn't a children's party with the *Frozen* soundtrack playing over and over.

Ashley closed her eyes and took a deep breath. *Don't be so negative. They're just out to enjoy a little creativity and friendship. Put up with the Bublé blaring on the stereo, and smile. It's almost time to close – half an hour, and they have to go.*

She almost convinced herself that it wasn't so bad, until the Enforcer got up again and headed her way. *Shit. What now?* Ashley was running out of kind euphemisms for, "I'm not your maid or waitress, I'm here to help you paint your fucking pottery."

The Enforcer was the professional mom. Every sporting event involving children had them, the ones that would stand on the sideline screaming at the refs, thinking they were supporting their child. They roared up in their giant SUVs, spilling out kids and barking orders. Even a simple trip to the store was a managed event. Nothing was ever right with anything in their world – life was an endless task to be put in its place, and if ever there was a smile to be had, it was a grim one. The Enforcers always had a gaudy rock on the ring finger, and the outfit of the day was cropped denim and flip-flops. Their skin was richly tanned from their natural habitat of soccer field sidelines and bleachers.

The Enforcer didn't seem to fit in with the rest of the ladies, but every damned group seemed to have one. The older the group, the more the Enforcer was thought of as a 'hoot'. Ashley suspected that they very well knew what their role in the group was, and it was to get shit *fixed*. That way the rest of them could keep up appearances.

"We're out of red."

"Excuse me?" Ashley asked.

"We. Are *out*. Of *red*," the Enforcer repeated.

Ashley scanned their worktable, and on the three lazy Susans filled with paint bottles, there were innumerable shades of red among them.

"It's actually called 'Crimson Tide'," offered one of the women.

Oh. No wonder. The woman had been painting an enormous pot – one of the more expensive pieces of ceramic in the shop. That particular shade had been discontinued, probably due to some sort of copyright violation. She would have suggested 'King Crimson', but… same thing. Less of that left, probably.

The owner of You're Kiln It should of have had them tossed out, but she wasn't one to waste a damn thing, even if someone would run out of it on a project – just like this.

"Unfortunately," Ashley said with as much empathy as she could muster, "that is the last bottle of that particular color. They've discontinued it."

The woman took a swig from her wine glass, and gave a sorrowful frown, gazing at her pot as if it were a bird dropping on her Lexus. Then she mustered up her courage with a smile, and sighed. "Well, I guess I'll have to change colors, then."

Aaaaand, three, two, one….

"Can't you see if you have some more in the basement?" the Enforcer asked, eyes blinking. "Marcie's husband went to Alabama, that's why she liked that color. It's important to her."

And there we are, the you-should-look-elsewhere demand, because clearly you can't do your job because you're a clueless kid.

"We don't keep paint down there with the kilns," Ashley said. *And I have a shit ton of pottery to glaze too, but* please, *let me go look for non-existent paint for you.* Ah hell, it was partly her fault for not making sure the woman didn't use the two colors in the whole shop they were running out of.

As the Enforcer vented her breath through her nostrils, Ashley pointedly ignored her and directed her attention to Marcie and her pot. "Like I said, that color has been discontinued and I know for a fact that's the last of it. What I might do, ma'am, is find the last bit of 'King Crimson' and mix it with over half as much of 'Blood of my Enemies'."

The women laughed at the name, and Marcie was clearly delighted with it, looking forward to reciting the names to her husband, Ashley supposed. *What the hell was her husband going to do with the fucking pot, anyway? Probably park it in the corner of an office, where it will house a dead plant, and then trash.*

She stepped around from the counter and walked over to the worktable, and spun a lazy Susan until she found the shade of red she was looking for. "Here you go," she offered.

"Here's 'King's Crimson'!" another woman offered, wine slurring her words a bit.

"Awesome," Ashley said. "What are you going to paint the shamrocks with?"

"Clover," corrected Marcie.

"Over and *over!*" all of the women sang.

"She probably doesn't know that song, do you dear?" Marcie asked.

95

"Sure do," Ashley replied. "Tommy James and the Shondells. My mom loves that song. I prefer 'Draggin' the Line', personally."

"I think it was Joan Jett, dear," Marcie corrected.

"Sure, she did a cover of it."

"Well, Nick thinks it's a Joan Jett song."

"I won't tell if you don't," Ashley suggested, and the women laughed. The Enforcer quietly sat back down in her seat.

Ashley spun the lazy Susan again, as red lights and a siren whipped past the shop.

"My goodness, they are out in *force* tonight," Marcie commented, and her friends murmured in agreement.

Ashley found the color she was looking for. "This might be good for the clover – we have plenty." She handed over a bottle labeled, 'Roll Me Over.'

Marcie laughed at the title, and showed it to the rest of the women, who all giggled, except the Enforcer, who smiled grimly.

"I bet she doesn't know *that* song," the tipsy friend stated.

"That's a song title?" Ashley asked, innocently. *I mean, sometimes you just had to give them one…*

The women laughed, the Enforcer rolled her eyes as if Ashley had to be the dumbest creature in God's green universe, and Ashley moved back behind the front counter where she continued to send out emails of 'gentle reminders' for customers who still hadn't picked up their pottery.

The Bublé CD ended, and apparently there wasn't another one in the carrousel. The sound of paint brushes dragging across pottery filled the silence, and random comments of "Cute!" and "You're Kiln it!" were announced as pieces in progress were displayed to the group for comments. Ashely flicked through her phone for the Old Lady Playlist, ready to plug it into the sound system before the Enforcer felt it was her duty to inform Ashley that the music had stopped, but one of the women starting humming "Roll Me Over in the Clover" and then the rest of them joined in. Ashley knew better than to ruin their fun with music right now.

The women would sing random snatches of the song, mostly just the chorus. Ashley preferred the wine-drunk women singing an ancient, bawdy ditty than hearing them complain about their husbands, or their ex, or bragging about their children and what university they had their sights on, which usually wasn't U of O. That would be too...common. She felt comfortable enough to leave them out of her sight for a few minutes to catch up on some glazing, when the front door rattled open.

The woman who stood there clearly lived on the streets. In fact, she looked familiar to Ashley. The owner of You're Kiln It had long ago made the shop an unfriendly place for the homeless so they were rarely bothered by them. Ashley felt a pang of guilt of thinking of the homeless as *bothersome*, but in truth one of the reasons she had quit the 'bux – after the entitled students - was the constant battle with them and having to clean up the bathrooms after they had been in there. *It's a complicated world we live in*, she thought. *And it's been getting weirder the last week or so...*

Ashley's gut knotted, and she knew trouble had just opened the door. The Enforcer knew it too, and stood, reaching into her purse. *Oh, shit, please don't be a gun...* The rest of the women looked confused, muttering about shutting the door, since it was chilly out now.

The homeless woman's yellowed-eyes roamed across the room. *They look coated in 'Bombadil Boots'*, Ashley thought. *Another color we're running low on...* She shook her head. She's infected with that *crap* that's sprung up. Ashely began searching the bottom shelf of the counter for the hammer and goggles that were used to enforce the mandate posted that 'All pottery will be DESTROYED after 6 months if not picked up' – a sign that Ashely interpreted as, "We have your money already, so screw you." The goggles were there, but not the hammer. Shit.

The Enforcer's movement caught the attention of the infected woman, and her mouth worked soundlessly, like a fish gulping for air at the surface of a pond. She staggered towards the Enforcer, who produced a cannister of pepper spray and aimed it at the woman.

"I would stop right there, *honey*, unless you want a face full of *this*," the Enforcer declared triumphantly.

Oh, no, Ashley thought. *Please don't spray that in here... Shit, I would rather she had a fucking gun!*

The homeless woman did *not* stop, and the Enforcer let fly with the pepper spray. The rest of the women screeched and began to get out of their chairs, some scrambling over the worktable to get out of the line of fire. The infected woman *still* did not stop. *Didn't even bat an eye!* Ashley thought wildly, and then bent down to reach for the goggles on the lower shelf. All of a sudden, those just came in *very* handy, along with the bandana that was used to cover the pottery as it was smashed. She stood in time to see the woman lunge across the table and grapple with the Enforcer, who apparently thought it was a good idea to keep firing off the pepper spray, even if it was useless.

Just get the hell away from her, Ashley wanted to scream, but held her breath as she slipped the goggles across her eyes and tightened the elastic straps as much as she could – they were far too big for her face, but would have to do. She watched in horror as the homeless woman bit into the Enforcer's ear, and bright red began running from her mouth.

By golly, that really does *look like 'Blood of my Enemies' after it's been fired...* Ashley quickly tied the bandanna over her nose and mouth, and moved out from behind the counter. The Enforcer yelled in fury, more from the audacity of her orders being defied than from being bitten, Ashley bet. You just didn't refuse the will of the Enforcer...

Ashley scanned the room, looking desperately for the hammer –

where in the hell did it go? The Enforcer began coughing and
retching, having inhaled her own pepper spray, and tried to push the
woman off of her without having her ear go as well. Ashley spied the
big pot Marcie had been working on, and scooped it up. Her first
impulse was to smash it down over the blonde head of the infected
woman, but hesitated – she didn't want to hit the Enforcer as well.
She maneuvered herself around the edge of the table, raised the pot
over her head and brought it down as hard as she could on the back
of the infected woman's blonde head. The pot cracked and shattered
into pieces of pale, un-fired crimson and clover, and the woman was
knocked loose from the Enforcer, who then fell forward across the
table towards Ashley.

Oh, no fucking way, Ashley thought, and back peddled away from
her. *I'm not getting anywhere near you after you've been bit.* She
covered her revulsion by turning to the counter and snatching keys
hanging off of a hook under the first shelf. She turned to the rest of
the women, who were huddled against the cases of pottery. She
swept her arm in an arc towards the door. "Come on, ladies, let's get
out of here." They stared at her with wide eyes that darted between
her and the infected woman, who lay twitching across the table, still
chewing on a piece of the Enforcer's ear. Presently, they began
coughing and rubbing their eyes as the cloud of pepper spray wafted
over to them.

"Now!" Ashley barked, and the women bolted to the front of the
shop, making a wide berth between them and the homeless woman,
Marcie stopping to help the Enforcer up and out the door. Ashley
paused for a mental check – yes, the back door was locked. She kept
an eye on the woman sprawled across the table, as her hands groped
for some clean towels and a six-pack of bottled water under the
counter. Her own eyes began to tear up as the pepper spray seeped
around the edges of the goggles.

We are so getting sued, she thought. *Or I am. I don't know. I mean, I busted a customer's pot, and another lost an ear. That is* not *a way you want the night to end. Shit, even the infected woman might sue me. Well, that wasn't likely. Or, for that matter, the Enforcer won't either. She's probably infected now…*

Ashley calmed a little at that thought. The so-called 'fever' or 'infection' had only in the last few days been seen as some sort of virus as opposed to some drug the homeless or addicts were taking. Not many of the general population were taking it seriously. Well, Ashley bet they would now…

She backed out the door, towels and water tucked up under her left arm as she locked up. She dropped the keys into her apron pocket, and then set the bottled water down. The women were bunched together in a group, supporting the Enforcer, who was loudly complaining, "The fucker *bit* me!"

Ashely tossed a towel at them. "It's clean," she said. "Tuck it up against her wound, maybe?" She unscrewed a cap off of a bottle of water, then handed it over while trying to maintain some distance. "Flush her eyes out?" she suggested. "All of you – flush your eyes out." She pried more bottles loose from the shrink-wrapping that held them together. She handed over more towels, keeping one for herself and a bottle.

"I called the cops," the now ex-tipsy woman offered. Funny how a rush of adrenaline can sober you up some. Ashley gave her a thumbs-up, removed the goggles and bandanna, and began to wash her own eyes out.

The cops arrived to find a huddled mass of women with mascara running down their faces, looking nervously into the shop as the infected woman wandered around looking for a way out. *Guess I didn't hit her hard enough*, Ashley thought glumly. She had kept her distance from the women, and tried to text Lori to see if she was off work yet, but hadn't got a reply. She was in the middle of texting her boyfriend when the cops rolled up with a whoop-whoop of a siren and spinning lights.

"And here's where I get blamed for everything," she sighed under breath. But, surprisingly, the women had nothing but praise for her, describing her "Like this tiny little superhero, who just jumped into action."

Well, hell. That was nice of them. Still, they had to take a shot at her height, didn't they?

More cops showed, and began to cordon off the area in front of the shop. Ashley squatted against the block wall of the shop, finishing her text to her boyfriend, and then one to her parents, letting them know that there had been some drama at work, but she was fine and would fill them in later. She felt overwhelmingly tired now.

"Ashley – *Ash!*" Lori's voice called out to her. Ashley looked up, and saw her sister standing behind a line of cops. She looked out of breath and agitated. She couldn't help but grin. Typical Lori.

"Hey," she said, and stood up. She could hear low arguing, the cops calm and reasoning, Lori worked up and angry. *Please don't swear at them and give them a reason to bust you…*

An officer strolled up to her. "That your sister?" she asked.

"Yeah," Ashley sighed. "Honestly, I would just let her come over, or she will make your life a living hell."

The cop smiled tightly. "Actually, we've been forewarned. Been expecting her to show up."

Ashley frowned. What now? The cop motioned for her to be let through. Lori darted around the other cops and in for a hug. "You okay?" she asked Ashley, then stepped back for a visual confirmation. "You get bit at all?"

"No, I'm fine," Ashley replied with a small chuckle. "Boy, you got here fast. How did you manage that?"

"Heard it from Officer Taylor's radio."

"Officer Taylor? He doesn't get coffee this late."

"He responded when a sick guy attacked Gavin."

"*What?*"

"Yeah."

"Jesus…"

The sisters stared at each other, then turned to look at the officer next to them. "Between you and me," she said quietly, "there's been three other attacks tonight as well." An ambulance rolled up, and she flicked her gaze over to it, then back to them. "It's going to be a very long night, ladies. Let's see if we can get you two comfortable."

In the Dying Days of Photo Labs

P hotons," I heard him mumble under his breath. I pretended not to hear, absorbed in pushing pixels around in Photoshop.

A sharp intake of air into his lungs, and a long exhalation. "Photons," he repeated reverently. "Photons…"

Man, those pixels were astounding in their ability to fascinate me. I could look at nothing else. It was me, and the pixels. Select, click, clone and the kid's zits were zapped into nothingness. I was better than any miracle cure on late night TV. This kid's yearbook pic would have skin clearer than a junk-food-shunning Mormon.

His fist banged down onto the light table, making the loupe, a ball point pen, and *me* jump. In my darkened room, I looked up sharply. From where I was sitting, I could see no cracks on the glass of the table. Working for decades in the photo lab industry, you did your best to ignore some of the customer's preoccupations. For the most part, it was the same random vacation shots, sunsets, family snapshots. The pro end of the spectrum had the portraits and commercial work. But we had the reputation of printing almost anything that could go on between consenting adults, with no judging. Openly, anyways. Whether lack of eye contact could be interpreted as condemnation was up to them to decide.

I could *not* ignore any damage to our property, though. I stared at the back of his head, feeling like a troll under the bridge, and waited to see if there would be another outburst. This guy had never really talked much. Only gave his first name - "Gary" - and paid in cash. Always. Normally he shot slides, and would spend up to an hour pouring over his transparencies at the light table late in the day. Usually we had to inform him we were closing, and that we opened up at 8:30. He would scowl, continue to look at his slides just long enough to let us know we weren't kicking him out that easily, and then gather them up in a rush, jam them into his backpack and bolt out the door. Never *once* did he turn off the light table.

This time, he had shot on print film. Yet for some reason he felt compelled to pour over the 4x6 glossy prints at the light table. A habit, I guess. But looking at photos backlit didn't make much sense with the printing information and paper watermarks.

I watched as he grabbed the loupe, dropped his head like an eagle diving on a fish and pressed his eye up against the small cube of clear plastic. Several short, astonished-sounding gasps hissed out from between his teeth, and his left fist rose, paused, rose higher and then *I* was rising out of my seat as his fist dropped sharply only to halt inches above the glass surface.

I stood in a half-crouch, waiting, bathed in the glow of my monitor and Ott-Lite, and then slowly eased back into the office chair. I kept my eye on him for a moment, and when I was feeling confident I could ignore him again he stood abruptly, his chair shooting out behind him. But its back legs could not overcome the friction from the carpet and tipped over backwards with a muffled thump. He turned, looked absently down at it, and then shot a look at me.

Shit...

"Photons," he barked. "Those are *photons*!"

Shit.

"Huh," I offered, trying to find the right balance between "Well ain't that interesting" and "I'm really busy here."

He grabbed the tufts of hair above his ears and pulled – a dangerous maneuver since they seemed to be the only ones left on his head – and turned back to the light table, then quickly back to me. One hand let go of his hair and dipped to gesture frantically behind him.

"*That* isn't reflected light! Those are photons being emitted!"

"Cool," I offered noncommittally. I smiled tightly, still under the delusion that I would be allowed to continue working on my digital dermatology.

But he wouldn't have it. "Look. *Look* at it," he sputtered, and turned back to snatch up the 4x6. I suppressed a sigh and stood, stepped through the doorway and out around the front counter. Once he had my full attention, he was chattering away at light speed. He was more animated and communicative this one evening than in all the years he had been bringing us work. I bent over and set the chair on all four of its feet.

"There is no *way* that's just reflective light," he continued. "Just no way. Wait until they see this. It's proof! Honest-to-God *proof*!"

Instead of handing me the print, he turned and placed it with a deliberate flourish onto the table. I thought about switching the light off – a sort of passive aggressive show that it wasn't necessary, but decided to let it go. It was probably important for him as a ritual to look at his photographic escapades, and it didn't matter whether it was transparencies or prints.

To be honest, I didn't quite know what to expect his photos to be *of*. I didn't run the E6 film processor, never mounted slides. I was a custom printer, and in recent years introduced the digital aspect into the lab - a turn of technology that would soon kill off a majority of photo labs, and also put a lot of professional photographers out of business. It would be years before the selfie would be a fixture in school's yearbooks, but I could stand back and sniff what the future of photography would be, and the smell of developer and fixer was not there.

"Look," Gary offered again. "Look at it. Those are *photons*. They are being *emitted*, not *reflected*."

I have to say I was surprised at the subject of the photo. I expected a night-shot, possible time-exposure with an indistinct blob of light that was, indeed, a bunch of photons. Over the years I had seen a fair amount of UFO enthusiasts, usually with less than inconclusive results. We had a regular customer near Valleyford who did have an honest mystery on his hands as far as I was concerned, but he was convinced his lights in the sky were of the military experiment origin. I had seen tracks in the snow that were supposed to be from a sasquatch, and blobs of light that were supposed to be ghosts. A lot of the customers were sincere in their beliefs, some just seeing how much bullshit you would swallow, and others just plain loony. I had pegged Gary as a loon.

So I was surprised to see that his photo was of the standard scenic variety. It was a pretty lake with mountains shot, around dusk with a little overcast sky. The lake could have been Priest, but I wasn't sure. Nothing stood out to me as unusual to the shot, and I wondered if he had picked the wrong photo to show me.

"I don't -"

"Look," he instructed, and pointed to a patch of vacant sky. "Right there." He crossed his arms and beamed triumphantly.

I bent over to peer closer at the photo, and my heart sank. I knew what it was immediately. A tiny speck of white was indeed in the sky. I dutifully placed the loupe over it to confirm what it was - a small, somewhat twisted fleck in the sky, hard-edged and not fading off into surrounding film grain. Photons, yes, but a lack thereof.

"Gary, this is just a dust spot," I said quietly, and straightened.

He immediately frowned, all goodwill and humor gone.

"What do you mean 'dust spot'?" he shot back, instantly on the defensive. I imagined this happened to him often – open, naked disbelief in a lot of what he had to say, so I decided to tread carefully and not come across as hostile or mocking.

"This is just a bit of dust that fell on the negative when it was being printed," I said. He shook his head.

"I've never seen anything like *that* before," he replied. "*Never.*" He jabbed his finger towards the print. "Never anything like that."

I nodded, but reached down and searched for his negatives in the kangaroo pouch they were stored in.

"That's because you shoot slides for the most part, right?"

He nodded with a curt dip of his head.

"Well," I continued, "You could see this in your slides if your camera were dirty, only it would be a dark speck in the picture. You make sure the inside of your camera is clean, right?" I figured it couldn't hurt to praise him a little, and I got another clipped nod.

"Okay," I added, and pulled out the set of negatives. The plastic sleeves rustled as they dropped down like a limp accordion bellows. "What happens when you make a print from negatives is that a small dust speck can fall onto the film as it is being printed, and that blocks light from that spot reaching the paper's emulsion-"

"No," he interrupted. "Don't give me -"

"Gary," I said patiently, and held my hand up to stop him. "Let's look at the negatives. Okay? If that is truly *in* your picture, it should be visible *in* the film, right? A dark speck in the sky?"

Another grudging nod.

I produced white cotton gloves from my shirt pocket and put them on. I was exceedingly careful with film – it was an ingrained habit after all, but I didn't need him whining later that I got my grubby little mitts all over his film and possibly destroyed any photographic evidence of extraterrestrials – or worse; misreading fingerprints as weird signatures that proved inter-dimensional beings were among

107

us. I flipped the print over, found the frame number and pulled the corresponding strip of film out of the sleeve and placed it carefully on the light table.

I bent over the film, placed the loupe over the appropriate frame and bent to study the image. I scanned it quickly, from side to side, top sprocket holes to bottom, but saw nothing in the amber-hued sky to suggest something alien. The dust speck that had caused the problem had long since fallen off the film.

I straightened, moved out of the way and motioned to him to take a look. He bent over, and squeezed his left eye shut as he examined the frame of film.

"See?" I asked, but received no indication he had heard me. "We're not supposed to let that happen," I continued. "We do have quality control, but sometimes these things slip past us."

Silence.

"Sometimes the dust can settle on the film before it's dry and can be tough to remove and we don't want to damage the film," I added. *Or not take the time to rewash*, I thought. *Heaven forbid if you guys don't get your precious photos as soon as possible....*

"So in that case we do what we call 'spotting' of the print," I said, filling the stony silence as he studied every square millimeter of the film frame. "That's where we take a small brush, find the exact shade of ink needed to fill in the white spot of the print and, uh, spot it out...."

He lifted his head from the loupe, and then reached behind himself to grope for the chair. I moved it up closer to him, and he eased on to it then scooted it in closer to the table.

"So, do you understand?" I asked as he slipped the film strip back into its protective sleeve.

He gave a noncommittal twitch of his head, refusing to look at me. I wasn't sure if it was because of embarrassment for himself or disgust in me. For all I knew, he was already formulating theories of men in black suits, their evil reach stretching all the way to humble photo labs in Spokane.

"I'm sorry," I offered. "Again, that's not supposed get by us, and I feel bad about it." And I truly did. Customer service was a point of pride in the lab. No matter that the sales were dwindling. Give them the best product we can. Even the weirdoes.

"Do you want me to spot it out?" I asked. "Only take me a minute. Honest."

He gave a dismissive jerk of his head. He was done with me.

I wanted to ask if he truly thought that if it actually was in the picture, why didn't he notice it at the time he shot it? Had he expected to see it, or was he just *hoping* to? Why in the world would someone get so excited if you weren't expecting it? Did he take pictures hoping to see weird shit? Did stuff like this occur often to him? In short, what the *hell*?

I gave an anemic, "Okay then," and turned to look at the clock. Closing time. Wonderful. I debated if I should mention it, thought about moving to the door to flip the open sign around to the closed side and give a subtle hint that way, but I knew he wouldn't pick up on it. I decided I would wait until the owner would come down, give me a puzzled look and ask why I hadn't rang out the till yet – it was past time to close! And get Gary out of here.

That would happen soon enough, and as I turned back I heard, "Photons." Barely a whisper and grunted so low that I could have imagined it. It was in such a defiant tone, much like I imagine Galileo was reported to have said, "Still, it moves."

I didn't know if I should admire him or roll my eyes. I settled for turning my back on him and moving towards my room and the computer. I still had work to do.

Umatilla

They hit the road early that morning. Lori couldn't remember what day it was supposed to be. The second? The third? It *was* June now, right? She was reasonably certain it was. Time had ground to a halt and became meaningless. When the network went down and you couldn't get online or even call anyone, you just didn't check your phone anymore. It was amazing power was still flowing. But she was certain it wouldn't be for long.

This is not the temporary quarantine we all thought it would be, she thought. *This is so much worse than anyone dreamed...*

Dreamed. Jesus. A fucking *nightmare*. Dead people were trying to *eat* you. I mean, that had finally been established. People got sick, they *died*. Not mostly dead, all the way dead. Ten toes up, little x's over their eyes and tongue lolling out *dead*. And then they rose again with an unhealthy appetite.

Lori gripped the steering wheel of the ancient Forester, and shook her head. This was *insane*. And yet, here they were. She wished she had the tiniest urge to turn the car around – just off-road it over the median and head south back to Eugene. She was convinced she would do it if there was the barest of sparks to ignite the desire. What they were doing was foolhardy and desperate. But if they didn't take the chance now, then they would never make it to Spokane. She knew it would get so much worse. And then it wouldn't be the dead who were the big danger...

Her boyfriend had tried to talk her out of leaving, of course. He hadn't pleaded, hadn't begged. He knew better than to try and order her not to go. He had tried pure, rock-solid reason, and she had agreed with every point he had made. She invited him to come with them as her rebuttal, each and every time. When he began to repeat his arguments, she accused him of just going through the motions. She was going. Ashley was going, along with her boyfriend Gabriel, and their roommate Kenzie. Kenzie's boyfriend had gotten the fever, and well...they had never seen him again after they dropped him off at the Peace Health emergency room. Ages ago. Lori wondered if he now wandered Eugene, mindlessly hoping for a bit of warm flesh to satiate a hunger that seemed...endless. Hell, they were lucky they hadn't caught it from him. Especially Kenzie.

Her boyfriend had left before dark last night, silently handing over his .30-06 and a box of ammo. No "good luck", and no goodbye. And she had no tears, just a desire to finish packing. Not much sleep, and what there was of it was anxious and fretful. Up by 4:00, out on the road soon after with the sound of doves cooing blending into the drone of the tires on the surface of 105, and then 5.

Let's just see how 205 is, she thought. Let's make it up to 205. *If it's not too bad, we can see how 84 looks. Then 82,and then we will cross that bridge when we come to it. Ha.*

"205, 84, 82," she whispered under her breath. "205, 84, 82. 205,

84, 82."

"What?" Kenzie muttered sleepily.

"Shh," Lori lectured. "Gabe and Ash are trying to sleep."

"Oh. Sorry."

Lori flicked her eyes into the rearview, and saw her sister's dark blue eyes watching her. Ashley's eyebrow arched to mimic the tart curve of her smile. Lori returned the gesture, then shook her head. *There is no one else on the road. Jesus, no one! Never has a freeway been so empty,* she thought with wonder. *This would be amazing if it weren't so chilling. I mean, they're plenty of cars abandoned along the side.* And why? Where did they come from, and where were they going? It's not like they were in the middle of nowhere. Yet. She didn't allow her eyes to linger on the motionless vehicles when she saw them – she wanted to concentrate on the road ahead. She had seen too many movies where the driver gets complacent, distracted, then wham! Shit hits the fan. Not this girl.

"205, 84, 82."

"What?" Kenzie mumbled.

"Seriously, Kenzie, hush – you're being rude."

"Sorry, sorry."

* * *

She saw the worst wreck in her whole life where 5 and 205 merged. A minivan looked like it had exploded in the grassy area between the ramps, and the area was littered with debris. Figures stumbled and lurched through the wreckage, as if searching for answers. But the way to 205 was clear, and she drove on, eyes flicking to the gas gauge. *Fine, you ninny. Still above the ¾ mark.* Her nose could catch the faint whiff from the two gas cans in the back, and the aroma always took her back to summer Saturdays, mom, daddy and yardwork, the mower and then the weedwhacker belching angry fumes...

Her heart lurched in a spasm of worry, and she gripped the steering wheel tighter, twisting the leather cover as if wringing a neck.

They're fine, she thought. *They. Are. Fine.* Her brain ordered it, willed it, commanded the universe to make it a solid reality. *They probably headed over to Idaho to stay with gramps and grammy, and it's well armed over there. Unless they stayed put expecting us to show up. Or headed this way...* The thought made her heart clench again, and she almost swore, but Kenzie's gentle snoring made her press her lips together in a grimace. Her eyes flicked up to the rearview, and she saw Ashley and Gabe kissing softly in the morning light, her sister's pale skin contrasting against the darker complexion of Gabe's, looking like the dualism and wholeness of true love. An irrational flame of anger leapt up in her, fanned by the memory of who she left behind, and she swung the wheel savagely left, and then back right, the Forester's tires barking in surprise. Ashley and her boyfriend's heads separated, then joined again with their foreheads knocking together with a hollow clunk.

"Ow – Jesus!" Ashley yelped. "What the fuck?"

Kenzie started, wide awake now, her hands gripping the seat to push herself up. "What?" she shouted. "What? What is it?"

"A...dog. Ran out... It ran in front of us."

She could see Ashley scowl in the mirror. "A *dog?* Really? Just ran across the wide open freeway in time to play dodge the Subaru?" Her dark eyes flicked to Gabriel then back to Lori. "Jesus, why you gotta be such a bitch?"

Lori's head waggled as her lips curled in a small display of disgust, but said nothing. Gabriel turned from searching out the back window to see if he could spot the dog, rubbing his forehead

113

absently. "So, was it like…a zombie dog?"

All three of the women gave a shout of laughter. "Animals don't get it, silly," Ashley chided.

Gabriel frowned. "Yet," he answered. "We don't know that they're immune *yet*."

Kenzie ran a freckle-covered hand through her copper hair, and twisted in the seat to roll her eyes at him. "Okay, but then the dead don't exactly run, do they?" She turned back and scoffed, "Zombie dog. Good lord. And that's not what a zombie is anyways."

"More like 'phantom dog' if you ask me," Ashley muttered. Lori snorted, but said nothing.

"The one that got Sam moved pretty damned fast," Gabe said softly, and the hum of the tires was his only answer for some time.

Lori cleared her throat and said, "Comparatively, I guess. I wouldn't say that one *ran*. Still, yeah, some of them… Some of them can really move when they want to." *Sam was a moron*, she thought. *Noisy, uncaring and thinking it all was some hoax, even when Ash and I told our stories, he was sure we had been played or something. That fucking smirk on his face… Well, we all get our wake up calls one way or another.*

She shuddered. Sure, Sam was an idiot. But man, that had been the most gruesome thing she had ever seen. Pale arms darting out from the gap in the hedge like an ancient sea-creature's tentacles, and even as the woman began gnawing at his neck he still wore that 'this is bullshit' look on his face as his arterial blood began to jet out as they screamed and jumped back, that look accusing them of being a bunch of pussies falling for another elaborate joke, that look that soon transformed into puzzled concern and then maybe a hint of terror as his arms raised to try and grab the woman by her hair and pull her face away from his neck. But she just continued to chew as if she was trying to take his head clean off. She just seemed so *hungry*… And they had stood back and just *watched*, not knowing what to do. You weren't supposed to get close to them! And then Lori's boyfriend came out of the apartment, shot the dead woman right in the head, and she dropped, pulling Sam down with her. They watched Sam gurgle and gasp, his hands slipping and sliding on his neck, until another shot rapped out and Sam lay still.

That was their world now, constructed out of practical and no-nonsense decisions. Except when you decided to drive about 500 miles without any idea what lies between you and home...

"We on 205, yeah?" Kenzie asked.

Lori bobbed her head. "Really bad accident back there. Hard to say what happened."

"Kinda nervous about going past Portland."

Lori nodded again. "Yep. But - *like we talked about* – this may be the last chance we get to make it through unchallenged. Last we heard people are still sheltering in place. Power still appears to be flowing, and the dead can be dealt with easily. Kinda. But I think we all agree the numbers are heading in the wrong direction as far as infection rates, and I think it's going to be very ugly, very soon."

Kenzie sighed, and Lori felt her irritation flare up. This was pure Kenzie, wasn't it? "Hell, yeah I'm coming with. Let's do this!" And then once wheels were in motion, the reluctant jabs of doubt would start to punch it up, and soon she would be bitching and moaning about how she got talked into such nonsense. Lori shook her head in short, ratcheted bursts.

"Kenzie," she growled between clenched teeth, "we are *doing* this. It's been settled. I swear to God, if you want out, I will let you out, but I will not take you back to Eugene."

"I wasn't even – "

"*Kenzie*. This is what you do. You second-guess every God-damned decision you make."

"Jesus! All I was – "

"Ken. *Zee*. We *all* are scared. But this is happening, and I just

115

can't take you complaining about it. I really can't." Lori took her eyes from the road and focused them on Kenzie. "We on the same page?"

Kenzie shot air through her nose, nodded, then snorted again.

Lori resisted the urge to slap her, and instead sighed and returned her gaze back to the empty freeway. *Don't let a mean streak take over*, she thought. *That is not going to help us right now. There will be people out there that will be plenty mean to us, I just know it. Don't turn into them. We are friends, we are family, and we love each other, and we need to be there for each other.* She knew for certain that this would not be a simple seven-hour drive home. The odds of them making it there were probably very low. But how good were they by just staying put? A moving target is harder to hit, right? She sighed, long and loud, trying to release her anger.

"Look, if there's some sort of sign saying that we're screwed – a massive pile-up, barricades across the road, a hoard of the dead marching towards us – I will turn tail and run back to Eugene, okay?" She raised her voice. "We all in agreement on this? Any…overwhelming odds, and we bail, yeah?"

"Sounds good," Ashley said, and Gabe grunted his affirmation. Kenzie just nodded once more, and leaned her head against the passenger window.

But there were no pile-ups, nor gangs of living or dead. Just a clear and empty freeway all the way up to 84.

* * *

This would probably be the first time that they never stopped at Multnomah Falls on the way up. It was always a treat to visit early in the day. Usually just a short hike up to the bridge, but sometimes they would go all the way to the top if the day were long and the morning beautiful. Of course this was not that kind of day, and they rocketed on past without a glance – it would be heartbreaking to see it falling gentle, normal and sane while the world was going mad.

Something was burning in Hood River, a massive column of smoke poking the sky as if trying to impress the volcano to the south. *Jesus, that's all we need*, Lori thought. *Volcanoes going off...*

They made their first detour in The Dalles. It looked like there might have been some attempt at blocking the freeway, and they all were on edge as they shot through the city for a while until they got back on 84. Seriously, why there? Not like any gas stations were open. Food, gas, take a leak. That was what The Dalles was there for, right? She imagined the dead hungry for their cash and to fill 'er up rather than a taste for their flesh. *Unfair to the people of The Dalles, I guess. But I ain't stopping – even if just to try and find a car we can siphon some gas out of.* She had the feeling they would be shot at if they tried that.

And so they hurtled on, the Columbia rolling along in the opposite direction. No boats bobbing on or skating across the surface. No wind surfers. Just the bleak sides of the gorge, which was always sort of a drag after the lush beauty back west. It was kind of barren all the way up through the Palouse, until the pines started to pop up the closer you got to Spokane. Your heart started lifting after Ritzville – close, oh so close to home – and then you got positively giddy at Fishtrap, where many cold nights had been spent with their telescope and the astronomical society. But there were so many miles of scablands and farmlands between here and there. And the Tri-Cities. Jesus. What insane fuckery awaited them there? She was tempted to cross that bridge in…what the hell was that little junction coming up? Just bypass the Tri-Cities and head up towards Yakima. That would eventually take them to 90, yeah? More out of the way, but…she was unfamiliar with the route. She liked the idea of missing the interchange contortions of Kennewick and Pasco, but it was a territory that was well known, and if something were

Robert John Jenson

screwed up there, well, you knew it was wrong and you could try to adapt, right? But the unknown…

"Ash," Lori called out.

"What?" her sister replied.

"Do you think we should cross over before we get to Umatilla?"

A pause. "At that one bridge coming up soon?"

"Yeah."

A longer pause, but Lori knew her sister was weighing the options, and waited patiently. "Maybe?" Ashely finally said.

"Thing is, we haven't gone that way…well, since we were kids," Lori offered.

That long ago… Lori sighed. Easier times. She would gladly trade today for the inflated drama of middle and high school. The innocent days of a five year old, though… Magic. Where the major decision in your life would be what Disney Princess adorned your backpack as you stepped through the doors of your kindergarten classroom for the first time. She smiled. Who was she kidding? Like there would have been any choice other than Ariel.

"The thing is," Ashley said, "is that we really hate the Tri-Cities."

"Yup."

"But do we want to spend extra time in a detour that we can't be sure is any better than what we already know?"

"There's that."

"I vote no. Keep going the way we always go."

"Yeah. Me too."

"Do *we* even get a say in it?" asked Kenzie.

"Well, sure Kenz. Do enlighten us with your opinion on a trip you've never taken," Lori said sweetly. "But let's consider this – say you and Gabe decide that heading towards Yakima is the better way. That's a 50-50 split, whatever shall we do? Oh, I know. I'm the owner of this car and the one driving. I get an extra vote - the freakin' cherry on top. Not looking good for your side, Kenz."

118

Gabe gave one of his chuckles from the depths of his gut, and Kenzie sighed acidly. "Heaven forbid anyone should dare to disagree with the *sisters*," she muttered.

"Kenzie," Lori said quietly, "I wanted you to come along because I was worried what would happen to you in Eugene. You haven't heard from your family in how long? At least two weeks? Southern California is a lot farther away than Spokane, and no way for you to get there. Gabe gives two shits about his family, so there was no question he was coming home with us. My parents like him too. Our grampa will make it awkward, probably, but he means well most of the time."

"Hey, I love gramps," Gabe said. "He cracks me up. Old people say stupid shit, but without intending to sound mean, you know? They can't help it."

"My point, Kenzie," Lori continued, "is that I wanted you to come with us, and you agreed. And you know how Ash and I roll. I know I can count on her, and she on me. We love you, but you're the wild card here and you bet your ass you don't get to disagree with us, or you're on your own." Lori took her eyes off the freeway momentarily to stare at Kenzie. "So I'll ask you - and this will be the only time – what do you think your odds will be surviving without us?"

Kenzie began to blink rapidly, her eyes glossy with tears. Lori smiled tightly, and focused on the road ahead once again. *Was I wrong in inviting her to come along?* Lori thought. *I knew she would be a pain here and there, but...seems early for the resistance. Or am I overreacting under stress? Shit, let her take her jabs and bitch and moan, and just plow on ahead. And we couldn't just up and leave without her – her heart would have broken and we would be burdened under a crippling cloud of guilt.* Lori felt her heart soften and lighten.

She sighed, and said, "Now don't cry, Kenz. We're all under a lot

119

of stress – I feel I'm at the breaking point at any given moment. But we can't squabble at the minutia, okay? Now more than ever, we can't argue just to argue – our lives may very well depend on it."

Kenzie nodded, and wiped at her eyes and nose.

"Well guys," Gabe said quietly from behind her. "If that's the bridge y'all are talking about? The point is, at this time…moot."

Lori flicked her eyes to the left, and flinched. *Well, we won't be travelling over* that.

Out over the Columbia, the center section of the bridge where the truss should be was missing. Twisted girders waved at either end of the empty space, and it was possible she could see some black scorching on the concrete supports, but other than that it was as if it had been plucked out by a giant hand and carted away. She couldn't see any wreckage in the river, but honestly didn't want to spend too much time searching for signs of it. *I mean, if it's gone, it has to be down there, right?*

They shot by the exit ramp and then under the crossing that lead to the bridge. Lori noticed for the first time the words 'Journey Through Time' painted on the sandy-colored concrete of the overpass, and the wheat motifs on the arched railing.

Is this how it's going to be from now on? Mysteries with no solution, and noticing the mundane touches we've overlooked before?

"Well, looks like fate has out-voted me too," Kenzie muttered, and began to cry again.

* * *

She thought she might relax a bit once they were past Arlington, where the rocky cliffs paralleling the freeway fell back into steep slopes of scrub and dirt, but she didn't feel any less claustrophobic. She expected to be shot at, frankly, and waited for a window to explode into the little crumbles of safety glass you always see littering the ground after a traffic accident. Or just to hear the twang of bullet on metal, or the *pow!* of a tire blown out. Were those columns of rock basalt, like back home in Spokane? Surely the ice age floods scoured down through the Columbia River Valley too? Anyway, they looked like they would make a great vantage point for a sniper of sorts. But the steep hillside could provide cover as well, and make it easier for someone to run down and check out whatever spoils they may have just won. Not for the first time did she wonder if she would ever experience the feeling of relaxation again.

Would there be much point in ambushing anyone along these empty stretches, though? she wondered. *For sure in towns, wait until someone comes in and just take what they have. But out here?* She honestly didn't know if things were at that point yet. *I mean, looked like there was something shady going on in The Dalles, and there was the minor problem of a section of a bridge that was missing, but everyone thinks this is going to just burn itself out eventually. Just stay home and the dead will finally stay dead and we can get back to normal.* The problem, though, was the people that were going to up the ante and try to take advantage of a disaster. Loosen up the lug nuts a bit and it won't take long for the wheels to fly off the luxury car of civilization. The first world has finally found a *really* big problem, by golly. Were there sheltered or nomadic tribes out there that will be untouched by all this? *I hope so.*

"Someone stopped up there," Kenzie said.

Lori squinted, and up to the left a car had pulled over. Not wrecked, no skid marks leading up to a distressed vehicle. It was just a Mustang that had pulled over as if to watch the river roll on past. Lori felt her senses elevate, could see the wind farm in the distance, the blades on the turbines still spinning. As they shot past the car, a lone figure sat on the hood, shoulders hunched, and a body lay in front of the Mustang, a tangled heap made up of a blue dress, black

121

hair, and blood. The person on the hood of the car never acknowledged their passing.

"He look like he was armed?" Lori asked. "Or talking into a radio or anything?"

"Not that I saw," Ashley answered, and Gabe grunted in agreement.

"Just looked like he was done with it all," he said. "Defeated."

Lori sighed quietly, came close to saying, "Aren't we all?" but pressed her lips together in a determined grimace. *Like hell. I will fight my way home, and I'll make it there – we will make it there - even if I gotta crawl.*

The wind turbines caught her eye again, and the heartbreaking glimpse of normal life she avoided at the falls grabbed her by the neck and she let out a small gasp, then covered it by clearing her throat. The dread could smother you at times, and she fought to surface from its depths. *Like being strangled slowly, while a songbird is chirping it's merry ass off,* she thought bleakly. She shook her head, inhaled through her mouth and then exhaled forcefully through her nose. *We. Will. Make it.* Home, *damn it all.*

Fortunately, she only had to endure seeing the turbines for a few miles, and then they were behind them, along with the cliffs, and the freeway diverged away from the river. *And now it starts to get dreary and dull,* Lori thought. Drab scrub and brush, with unimaginative-looking farmlands. *Give me the Palouse in the spring, with its rolling green hills and chocolate-colored earth tilled up in neat, mesmerizing lanes.*

Finally, the exit for 82 West (Hermiston/Umatilla) came into view, and she smiled. *82 west? But I'm heading east! Madness!* Actually, she would at last be heading north, and soon over into Washington. It was, what? About eight or nine miles to the border? Not too far. She guided the old Forrester over the curving ramp that crossed over 84, and soon they were heading north.

And into trouble.

* * *

Signs of...skirmishes began to show on the highway and the surrounding fields. She could easily maneuver the Subaru around them – stalled cars or collisions, all windows smashed and tires flat. Bullet holes would dot the sides of some of them as if they were back-country speed limit signs used for target practice. Occasionally, pools of maroon blood would paint the cement roadway near these piles of violence, but she could see no bodies that must have been involved.

Lori glanced over to the opposite side of the highway and could see the same shenanigans going on over there. They passed one of their landmarks, what they always called 'the gravel pit', the road curving to the north signaling for them that they would soon cross over the Columbia. Lori hit the brakes as the random spots of broken cars turned into a minefield of them.

"Shit!" she yelped.

They stared with astonishment at the tangled wreckage strewn across both sides of the highway, their breathing hitched and rapid as if they had sprinted into the carnage and not driven. Cars, trucks and farm equipment blocked their view of the bridges ahead. *Is that a freakin' combine? How in the hell...turn around! Go back and cross at Portland. We saw less of this nonsense back in the city. These people are insane out here!* But her gut told her nowhere was safe now, and no matter how they approached Washington, there was a whole lot of empty space between here and home.

She eased the car forward, and ignored the sharp hiss of breath from Kenzie.

"Well this is scary," Ashley said, and Kenzie gave a sharp bark of a laugh.

"Let's just see if there's any way through this," Lori answered as she maneuvered the Subaru past a tractor that looked like it had tried to mate with a pickup. Something writhed listlessly in the twisted mess, but she could not see what it was. Kenzie let out a low groan.

"Got something to say, Kenz?" Lori said between clenched teeth.

"I'm just trying to not throw up right now," Kenzie replied. "Leave me alone."

"Well, roll the window down if you're going puke. Just don't pull a Sam on us and get grabbed by something."

"Jesus, you're cold."

"And serious."

She was able to squeeze the car through the mangled debris field – there was always just enough room, and she began to feel as if they were following a path of sorts.

"This seems…off, don't you think?" Ashley remarked.

"Off?" Kenzie asked.

"Like we're being lead somewhere," Gabe said, and Ashley hummed in agreement.

"Yeah, my neck hairs are at attention," Lori muttered. "I do not like this."

She began to wonder if she should just back them out of this, when the whir of the passenger-side window being rolled down startled her. *Oh Kenzie, now is not a good time…* She could hear a faint tinkle of metal on pavement punctuated by the coughs and dry heaves of Kenzie. A flicker of movement in the rear view mirror caught her eye and she saw a hunched shape reaching for the car, then there was a sharp bang on the hood and a dead man in coveralls sporting a mangled nose was staring at her through the windshield. They all screamed as she goosed the accelerator, and the man's face left a rancid smear across her side window as they shot past.

"Roll the fucking window up, Kenzie!" she shouted. "Now!"

A hand was in the car for a moment, scratched along the back passenger-side door and was gone. They all started screaming for the window to be rolled up as Kenzie mashed the control, and it was an eternity before the glass thumped up into the top of the door frame.

"I recommend you don't do that again," Ashley muttered, and Lori gave a shaky laugh, then jumped at another thump on the side of the car. She fought the urge to stop the car, and then a figure lurched in front of them, reaching out.

"Don't you dare stop," Ashley growled, and Lori actually goosed the accelerator, clipped the hip of the man outside causing him to spin and drop out of sight. The left end of the car lifted and dropped, and they all hissed in sympathy.

"Well, that was my first hit and run," Lori said quietly.

"Uh, doesn't look like it will be your last," said Gabe.

They had made a turn past a tower of storage pods and a gang of the dead were waiting for them in what appeared to be a cul-de-sac created by semis, tractors and any heavy machinery that could block access to the bridge beyond. Lori hit the brakes.

"What the *fuck*," Gabe breathed. "Seriously, what is the point to all of this? Are they that fucking bored out here? I swear to *God*, white people, man…"

"I mean, is this some sort of choke-point, or whatever?" Lori said. She wished she had paid more attention to her boyfriend and all his tactical-talk nonsense. "I would think someone would be shooting at us by now or something, right? Why on this side of the river if not to take our stuff?"

"I've said it before, and I'll say it again," Gabe laughed. "Farmers are fucking weird, man."

"Jesus, look," Ashley blurted. "They're all chained up – chained to the wreckage."

About a dozen people had been milling around in the dead end, and were now shuffling towards the Subaru. Some were drawn up short by chains looped around their waists, and yet they still strained to reach them. Others had more of a lead, and grasped at the car. One woman in tattered pajamas batted dully at the door handle next to Lori. She would look up, as if expecting instructions on how to operate the latch, then back down to her hands. Lori double-checked the locks were engaged.

What is going on in that brain? Lori wondered. *Is it all about taking a bite out of me? The prime motivation as far as we know, I guess, but shit – there must be more firing away up in there. She seems to remember door handles!*

"Is there a gap up there to the left?" Kenzie asked, her voice thick. "Can we get out of here? Please?"

Oh God, please do not puke, Lori thought. *That is all we need.* She tromped on the accelerator and shot towards the gap in the wreckage, knocked down three of the dead, clipped the cab of a semi and then they were through, off the side of the highway and into the median. They all cheered as they plowed through the brush and up to the south-bound side when the tires blew out, dropping the front end of the Subaru into the edge of the pavement of the highway. The engine roared as they were all thrown forward and the back end fishtailed, generating a huge plume of dust until Lori jerked her foot off the gas.

The rage of the engine settled down to an uneven revving, with occasional hiccups, like a toddler after throwing a tantrum. Lori gently turned the key in the ignition, and the engine rattled to a stop. They listened to the metal pop and tick as it cooled.

"God damn it," Lori said quietly.

A window whirred down, and Kenzie leaned out, finally emptying the contents of her stomach.

* * *

"Yeah, both tires are flat," Gabe sighed. "Looks like there is some sort of spike-strip under there." He straightened and ran a hand through his thick hair. "I do believe we were set up for this."

Lori massaged her temples, and tried to take deep, calming breaths. *What a dumb-ass I was,* she thought miserably. *Seriously, you felt that this was all wrong, but you just charged ahead because you were afraid of a little puke?*

"I'm sorry," she said with a tremor in her voice. "I'm really sorry."

"What?" her sister asked. "How is this your fault? You couldn't have known there was a trap set up here."

"I should have thought it through," Lori answered. "Shouldn't have been so impulsive and seen that we were being guided right to this end."

"Hey, we *all* wanted out of there," Gabe offered.

Lori shook her head. "I should have stopped before we headed in there. Jesus! I was stupid."

"Hey, don't go there," Ashley snapped. "Seriously. We all were along for the ride. We didn't realize it was a trap until we were too far into it. We can't have you lose the momentum now. We already have one – " She stopped and lowered her voice, her eyes flicking over to Kenzie who stood alone up on the highway. "We have to accept what happened and figure out what we're gonna do now."

Lori nodded her head, but she still felt deflated and wrung out.

"What I would like to know is, where's the welcoming committee?" Gabe asked, and Ashley hummed in agreement. "I mean, they set this elaborate bullshit up. They got us. Then where they at?"

"Kenzie," Lori asked, and received no reply. "Kenzie!" she repeated, louder.

"What?"

"What do you see?"

"Pardon?"

127

"How's it looking on that side? Can you see the bridges?"

"Yeah."

Jesus, Lori thought and pinched the bridge of her nose, took a deep breath. *Ask specific questions to get specific answers…*

"How far away are they, can you tell?"

Kenzie was quite for a moment, and then answered, "Maybe a quarter of a mile?"

"And are they blocked? Like, completely?"

"I think so? I mean, the right one has a pile-up blocking my view, and the left one…like there's a cement mixer sideways across the road. Hard to see past that."

Left is southbound, right is north, I'm guessing she means, Lori thought.

"Okay. Thank you. See anyone moving around up there?"

"No."

"Is there a lot of wreckage up there? Like, all the way up to the bridges?"

"Um…no, not really. Not like what we just went through, anyways. Just looks more concentrated up nearer the bridges. The left side looks like it would have been better to drive on than the right, I think."

"Thank you."

"Yep."

Okay. So, whoever constructed this playground doesn't seem to want to hang out here anymore – or they have other problems now. Lori kicked the toe of a hiking boot into the dirt. *We can probably use the jack here – seems stable. But – we only have one spare.* She looked up. "See any cars with good tires on them?" she asked.

"Um," Ashley answered, and all of their heads swiveled in search of tires that might be of use. Gabe stepped onto the highway and towards the wreckage they had just exited.

"Jesus Christ!" Lori blurted. "Don't go in there!"

Ashley tugged on the back of his shirt. "What the hell?" she asked. "Why would you even try that?"

"They're all chained up," Gabe answered. "Not like they're gonna be chasin' me."

"First rule we talked about before we headed out today – always remember *Sam*," Lori recited. "Don't assume anything about them, and stay clear whenever you can. Just because they aren't going to be coughing in your face doesn't mean you can only get the fever from them biting you. Who knows what might fling from their fingers as they're reaching for you?"

Gabe's shoulders and head dropped dramatically, and Lori was convinced she could see his eyes roll through the back of his head.

"Think about it, genius," Ashley chided. "Did you see any compact SUVs while were driving through all that? Maybe back father, but any of those tractor tires gonna fit on our little Subaru? Think we might have a problem bolting them on? Think those semi's tires will be a bit tight?"

Gabe shook his head and chuckled. "Fine, we can backtrack on this side."

And so they did, Lori reaching in the back to grab the rifle. She looked at the arranged piles of backpacks and duffle bags, thought about her rule that if they left the car, they didn't leave anything in it to be stolen, but felt comfortable that they wouldn't stray too far from it to worry about that.

Ashley and Gabe headed south, Kenzie and Lori north towards the bridges. *Dang, it would be nice to have walkie-talkies right now*, Lori thought. *Good old-fashioned 10-4 good buddy toy walkie-talkies.* She shook her head. *What we thought were useless and given away when we got too old to enjoy them! Now our phones are useless, but some cheap slabs of plastic and some 9-volts would be handy as hell right now.*

None of the cars they came across had any tires in decent shape.

All – *all of them!* – had either been slashed or shot out. *These bastards were methodical!* As she and Kenzie neared the bridges, they had to decide which side to explore, since the median dropped towards the river and the highway began to elevate. They bore left, the southbound side, since it looked more navigable. It soon became clear that even if they found any suitable tires, there would be no driving across any of the bridges. On their side, there was not one cement truck, but *two* of them, with flattened tires blocking the bridge. Lumpy concrete surrounded the vehicles, and Lori guessed that at least one of them was as full as it could be with the hardened material. *Those aren't going to be moved any time soon,* Lori thought grimly. *And there is no way in hell we are driving into Washington from here…*

They couldn't see much beyond the cement mixers, but it was obvious there was a tangled mess beyond them. On the other side of the highway – the northbound bridge – another pile-up of semis and farm equipment blocked the passage crossing the Columbia.

"Does this mean we have to turn around?" Kenzie asked quietly.

"Maybe."

"All the way back to Eugene?"

"I don't know if we can even get the car rolling again, Kenz."

A faint clinking and rattling from the other side of the cement trucks drifted to their ears, and Lori sighed. Kenzie didn't seem to notice it, or chose to ignore the sounds. That and the shuffling noises.

"Are we going to have to walk from now on?"

"Probably – unless Ash and Gabe find some tires," Lori answered.

"Which way?"

"What?"

"We walking home, or trying to cross the river?"

"Well, we've come to the bridge, so…"

Kenzie just stared blankly her.

"We'll cross that bridge? We've come to it, so we cross it…No? Not funny?"

Kenzie looked doubtfully at the bridge, then back south. "Maybe we can find a car that works?"

"Well, let's go find Ash and Gabe."

* * *

"Nothing," Ashley stated. "These people sure seem to have a thing against tires."

"Also looks like they worked over the gas tanks – can smell it strong, and they're punctured all to hell," Gabe said.

"Wasteful," Ashley muttered irritably.

"They seem intent on just killing any vehicle and leaving it as an obstruction," Lori said.

"Jesus, where are they?" Gabe blurted. "*Seriously* man, sneaky-ass God-damned crackers!"

"Maybe they all got the fever?" Ashely offered. "A lot of the rural folk seemed to think it was a hoax, or that it couldn't touch them – it was a city problem."

"Whatever it is," Lori said, "I do not like hanging here for too much longer. We have to make a decision."

"I say we cross," Ashley stated firmly. "*Technically*, we are closer to home – to Spokane – than back to Eugene."

"Gabe?" Lori asked.

"I never disagree with her," he laughed.

"Kenzie?"

"I…I mean, we know what we went through and it only really got bad until we got here?"

"Known compared to unknown, a valid point," Lori conceded. "Still, what's behind us is unknown *now*. Things can change in a hurry. Looks like the shenanigans going on here have at least died down for *now*. And I still want to go home. I vote we cross."

Kenzie turned her head and looked doubtfully at the bridge, back south, and then north again. "Which bridge?" she asked.

"Well, I've been thinking about it," Lori answered. "I think there is a pedestrian and bikeway on the northbound bridge."

"There is," Ashley affirmed.

"Right. I don't think we can assume it's any more clear than the highway, but I don't know what lies between us and it now – we can't see shit with all the wreckage. I suspect we have some of the fever victims on both bridges too – they seemed to get a kick out of adding them to the party." Lori looked into Kenzie's eyes, and did her best to look honest and not domineering. "Those cement trucks were pretty close to the truss on the southbound bridge, weren't they?"

"Close to the what?"

"The truss – the metal framework thingy on top of the bridge," Ashley answered.

"Oh. Yeah, I guess."

"Right," Lori nodded. "Now, as far as *I* saw, I didn't see any fucking tractors or semis or anything else hanging from them, did you?"

Kenzie snorted. "No. That's stupid."

"Right? So I'm thinking we ought to get a pretty clear view from up there. What do you think?"

"I guess. Yeah, sounds legit. You plan on climbing up there then?"

"I do," Lori said firmly. "But here's the thing – if I get up high enough to see, I am just going to keep going."

Ashley let out a sharp laugh, and Gabe shook his head. Kenzie blinked several times, then said, "You are fucking crazy."

"Undoubtably. But it's going to happen."

"How is that going to do the rest of us any good if you can't tell us what you're seeing from up there?"

Lori pressed her lips together softly in a gentle smile, and just stared at Kenzie.

Ashley laughed again, and Gabe whistled. "Good lord," he muttered. "How did I wind up in the company of two bat-shit crazy chicks?"

Realization dawned in Kenzie's eyes, and transformed into horror. "Oh, *fuck* no!" she yelled. "What the hell is wrong with you – you know I hate heights!"

"We can keep you in the middle of all of us, Kenz – "

"No! No, no fucking *no*, end of *story,* I can't do it!"

"Then what are you going to do?" Lori asked.

Kenzie blinked again, panicky confusion contorting her face as she began to cry. "Why do you fucking hate me? What did I do to make you act so mean to me?"

"Don't say that, Kenzie," Lori said, a tremor in her voice. "I don't hate you – you know that. I'm sorry if you're feeling bullied again and I swear that's not what I'm doing – I don't have it in me right now. I'm tired and scared and just don't want to waste any more time. And I'm more afraid of some dead person biting me than I am treating that bridge truss like it's a set of monkey bars."

"I can't climb up there!"

"It's kind of an easy slope up – look, I don't intend to try and walk across them. One gust of wind and I'm history, right? But if we can just – "

"No!" Kenzie shouted, then turned to Ashley and Gabe as she wiped away the tears on her face. "Are you two going to enable her on this? Just cave like we always do and let her have her way?"

"I'm not telling anyone what to do – "

"Shut up! Just shut up. Let them answer."

The group was quiet for a while as they let their ears lose the ringing of Kenzie's rant, and Lori listened to the wind blow through the weeds, dirt and machinery. The soft clink of metal and the distant rush of the Columbia was almost soothing.

"I mean, I don't want to get bit or anything," Gabe said quietly.

Kenzie's arm rose in the air and dropped down to slap her thighs as she snorted. "We don't even know if there are any dead people on the bridges," she scoffed. "And she can't even be bothered to go up and look, then come back and let us know."

"Why don't *you* go up and take a look around, and then *you* come back down and tell us?" Ashley said with sugar in her voice. "Oh, wait…"

"I don't even want to go over the stinking - " Kenzie caught herself, and her mouth snapped shut.

"Ah, so it's a matter of *direction*?" Gabe asked. "I get it. But you don't. We have had one direction in mind the whole time, but you think it's always open for debate? We're going to Spokane, baby. The only thing up for debate is whether you're coming with."

Kenzie squeezed her eyes together, and balled her fists so tight her arms shook. Lori sighed, a bit surprised anger hadn't risen in her like a cobra, ready to strike. Right now, she only felt sorry for Kenzie. But she was done wasting any more time.

"Alright then," she said. "Kenzie, let's divide up supplies for you – you can have a quarter of the food, and I'll let you have the Buck knife. We're going to leave the gas cans I guess – maybe you can find a working car and come back for them?" Lori didn't bother to look for a reaction, she just turned and strode to the back of the Subaru and popped open the back hatch.

* * *

She'll follow. She'll follow. She'll follow. The words repeated in Lori's head as she slid along the dun-colored steel. Slide hands forward, pull as she lifted her rear across the girder. Rinse, repeat.

Lift left leg over cross brace, slide hands forward, lift ass and scoot along little doggy. Rinse, repeat... *She'll follow...*

Her world right now was a steel beam, surprisingly cold in the bright sunshine. She had a pack hanging in front of her, and the rifle slung across her back. Ashley right behind her, with a pack in front and back. Gabe anchored the trio, and was also burdened with two packs. They left Kenzie with probably a bit more than a quarter of their foodstuffs, plus the promised Buck knife. There were no long goodbyes, hugs or tears. Kenzie seemed too much in shock to try and argue with them. Lori was almost certain her friend's declared fear of heights was just another faux phobia that was designed to make her appear adorable. *But is she really terrified?* Lori thought. *Was there a childhood trauma at the root of it? Or did she just get attention once because she refused to climb on an amusement park ride? And if she is truly afraid – what are we supposed to do?* Guilt pangs began gnawing at her belly, and the thought of her friend lonely and terrified brought tears to her eyes. *Am I just being a bitch? Should we have figured out some other way to cross?* Because they *were* going to cross, and make their best effort to go home. *I love you, Kenzie. But I love my family more...*

She twisted her left leg over another cross-brace, and pushed herself along. The wind blew steadily and would gust on occasion, but on the whole she hadn't felt like she was in danger of being blown off the bridge. On the deck below, the tangled wreckage had thinned out, but the dead were roaming at will with no chains to restrain them. The wall of carnage behind them apparently was able to keep them contained. She estimated there were at least ten to fifteen of the fever victims wandering around below that she had seen so far. Not a mob, she guessed, but she wasn't paying much attention to what was going on underneath her. And she hadn't even spared a glance over to the northbound bridge yet.

"Hold up," she yelled, wanting a breather and a chance to take a look around. She stopped, and felt Ashley's front pack snug up against her briefly, pushing the Springfield into her back. The incline they were inching along didn't look very steep, but it was taking its toll on her arms. *It'll level out here in a bit,* she thought. *Why, we are probably very near the top by now.* She looked up, and recoiled, giving a yelp. The pack hanging from her front tilted to the left, and its weight pulled at her and she began to slide off the girder. She heard Ashley gasp and yell her name as her body twisted around and she hooked her right leg around the cold steel, and for a moment her upper body was angled out over the bridge, the rifle's sling digging into her neck. As her heart hammered between her ears, her mind was screaming, *the fuckers can climb? That is so not fair!*

A small hand grabbed at her wrist and violently tugged her upright onto the girder, and another reached to stop her from over-compensating and diving off to the right into the river between the bridges. Lori's heart swelled with love and gratitude for her little sister. *She may be a shorty, but Jesus she has long arms for her size!*

"Thank you," she managed to wheeze as her lungs worked to draw in the air that fright had exiled.

"What the hell startled you?" Gabe called out.

Lori let her breathing even out, then leveled a finger in front of her. "That guy," she barked.

Her instincts were correct, they had nearly reached the part of the truss where it became horizontal. About ten yards away, a maintenance ladder and platform with safety cage was positioned at that point, and standing on it was a dead man. Lori heard Ashley gasp as she took in a sudden breath.

"How in the *hell* did he get up there?" Ashley asked.

"Right?" Lori said.

The dead man had apparently noticed their little group, and was straining to reach them. His upper body twisted as if trying to throw some momentum into moving, like someone walking through a pool of water, but he clearly wasn't going anywhere. His denim-clad legs were bound to the deck's railings and also to the ladder's safety cage. A hodge-podge of rope, chains and zip-ties kept the guy in place. Lori's mind raced through the logistics of dragging a body up the ladder and could not justify it. Was he infected, and someone made him climb up here to die? Or... did he make the decision for himself? She couldn't see any evidence that he *couldn't* have lashed himself to the mast, so to speak. *Wow. That is some serious dedication to defending the home front*, she thought.

The man had some severe lacerations to his bare arms and his scalp, tufts of hair and skin were missing in raggedy chunks, and there were holes peppered across the shoulders of his white t-shirt. *Birds must have been having fun with him until he rose from the dead... God, are there going to be more of them all the way across this bridge?* Lori shifted her gaze to the other side of the truss. No access ladder on that side. There were cross-braces in the shape of an X that could get them to the other side...maybe. They looked awfully thin – inches wide at best. *I do not like the idea of dragging my hoo-hah across that, and I don't think Gabe's crotch would enjoy it either.* She supposed they might remain balanced lying down and scooting across on their bellies...but they looked so damned *thin*. She remembered how she felt she had been misdirected into a trap down on the highway, and this smelled a lot like that. *Could the supports be weakened and we would drop to our deaths?* She had no clue what tampering of that sort would do to the overall structural integrity of the bridge, but supposed that wasn't a high priority to whoever had set all this nonsense up. *Man, these idiots were ambitious up here! Seriously, were we utterly clueless to these types of shenanigans going on while back in Eugene, thinking everyone was just hunkered down and riding it all out? Or were these fuck-wits just bored and finally found an excuse to exercise the wargames they always wanted to play?* She shook her head. That sort of speculation wasn't helping them in the here and now.

"Guys." she called out. "I think I'm going to have to shoot him."

"Aw, crap," Ashley grumbled.

137

"You have a better idea? Something that doesn't involve getting too close to him?"

"No, not at all– I'm not criticizing your idea. I'm just not happy about it."

"Well, neither am I. This rifle has some recoil to it, I can tell you."

"I'll take your word for it. So how do we keep it from knocking us off our perch here?"

"I don't know. Have to try. Here, I'm going to scootch forward a bit."

Lori slid along the girder until she could lift the rifle's sling over her head and lay it across her legs. She then unzipped a pocket in her pack and pulled one round out. *One at a time,* she thought. *Don't care if I act like a ninny, I don't want to forget any rounds in the chamber. If I miss the first time...well, I will reload until I hit the bastard. In the head, I hope....*

She slid the bolt back, chambered the round, and shot the bolt back into place. "We are now live - or whatever the hell you say when there's a bullet in the damned gun," she informed them. Ashley giggled nervously behind her. "Okay," Lori continued, "Scoot up next to me. Closer. Damn it, closer – I need a cushion."

"That's all I need is that rifle stock going up over your shoulder and smacking me in the face," Ashley muttered.

"It's not going to smack you in the *face*. It'll kick my shoulder good, but hopefully you can absorb some of it, and Gabe behind you."

"What? What if it knocks us all off?"

"Nah. It's physics and shit. We'll be fine."

"I don't know," Gabe joined in. "Kenzie isn't looking so dumb right now..."

"Well, if you want to back out of this, wait until I shoot this guy, okay?"

"Aw, crap," Ashley whimpered.

"I feel so supported right now," Lori said, trying to sound casually confident, but could not keep the tremor out of her voice. Her mouth was dry, and her heart pounded in her ears. *Oh, Jesus...*

She brought the stock up to her cheek, and squinted through the site, her finger on the outside of the trigger guard. She waited until a gust of wind died down, then flicked the safety off and slipped her finger inside the trigger guard. *Relax, don't tense up...* She couldn't remember how she was supposed to breathe. Let it out while shooting? Hold it, then let it out? *Shit...* When she felt she was as steady as she could be, with the dead guy's head squarely in the site, she gently squeezed the trigger and then the rifle boomed and slammed her shoulder and a jet of gore shot out from behind the dead man's head and he rocked back, twisted to the side, and then slowly drooped over forward at the waist and was still, just his arms swaying gently.

Lori carefully lowered the rifle, and drew in a deep breath. "Are we all still here?" she asked.

"Yeah," whispered Ashley.

"Present," Gabe called out.

"Well, looks like I got him," Lori said.

"Yay," Ashley said weakly. "May I go change my shorts now?"

"That wasn't so bad," Gabe said. "I didn't even move. And it took him down without any drama."

"Oh, man – he's dripping stuff out of his *face*," Ashley observed. "Oh, gross..."

"What did you expect?" Gabe asked. "Confetti and glitter?"

"All right," Lori said, removing the spent shell and then slipping the sling back over her head and the rifle across her back. "Let's get a move on. We got a lot of bridge left to cross."

* * *

After edging around the dead guy, and debating whether they should cross over to the other side along a broader cross-beam, they decided to stick to the east side of the truss, hoping if there were other maintenance access ladders they might be able to climb down if the coast were clear. After an agonizing amount of time making it to mid-span, there was another ladder. But the bridge below still crawled with the dead. *How the hell did they round up so many?* Lori wondered. *Is that why we aren't seeing anyone alive – they ignored the risk factor, caught the fever, and are now part of the dead themselves? Probably thought that they were God-chosen and invincible. You heard a lot of that nonsense, that was for sure, while we still had media, social and otherwise...*

They decided to give themselves a rest on the maintenance platform, joking that they would be bow-legged for the rest of their lives. While shaking out her arms and hands and wishing she had brought some gloves, Lori thought she heard a faint cry of despair. She swiveled her head around, trying to locate where it came from. "Did you hear that?" she asked.

"Yeah," chorused Ashley and Gabe, whose heads were turning as well. They heard another, longer cry of anger-tinted anguish. "Aw, shit – over on the other bridge," Ashley gasped, and Lori snapped her head around - then she gasped as well. It was Kenzie.

She had obviously tried to cross in the pedestrian section of the bridge. Lori was astounded that she had made it that far. Quick glances over as they made their way across their bridge had shown that the northbound bridge was just as obstructed - and infected with the dead - as the one below. *She must have crawled, dodged, wriggled past and climbed anything she could,* Lori thought. But now, she appeared trapped between two groups in the pedestrian crossing. She held the Buck knife in her right hand, her backpack in her left, and she slashed and swung and cursed at the dead. And was that a *wound* on her shoulder? *God, let it be a scrape and not a bite...*

"Fuck," Lori muttered, and slipped the .30-06 from her back as she fumbled in the pack for a round. Her hands were shaking and a bullet promptly slipped out and pinged off the deck before dropping forever to the bridge below. "Shit!" she screamed, and fished out another round, chambered it, then fit two more in and slid the bolt home, raised the rifle and sighted at one of the dead. She flicked off the safety, and then...hesitated. *What if I hit her instead? That's a lot farther away than the other guy. Fuck!* She was locked up in indecision, afraid to hit her friend, afraid to not try and shoot. *What if I scare her? She might think someone's shooting at her and try and*

do something stupid like –
Jump off the bridge.

Kenzie had been pushing at overwhelming odds. More of the dead had been closing in from the vehicle lanes, attracted by her screaming, and she was hemmed in on both sides, and a dead woman in hospital scrubs had reached out and dragged a cold and bloodless-looking hand through Kenzie's hair. She let out a shriek, gave one desperate glance across the bridge, and Lori could have sworn she saw Kenzie's heart sink out of sight as her friend's shoulder's sagged, and she turned, dropped the pack, pulled herself up and then rolled over the metal railing and dropped from view.

They never heard a splash. Lori gave a shout of outrage, and shot all three rounds off at the dead. Only one hit a target – the woman in the scrubs, who looked curiously at the massive wound in her arm. "Fuuuuck!" Lori screamed, and hit the railing with a balled up fist. A sob bubbled up from the depths of her soul, and many more followed. Ashley watched her, recognizing the pain that only a sister that has lived with you all her life can identify immediately. And empathize with.

I do not get to feel like this! I don't have the right! Lori's mind raged. *You abandoned her, left her on her own, and now you think you can just feel the sorrow of a lost friendship – feel the loss of life as deeply as you do now?* She screamed so loud her throat burned, and hit the railing again. With the pandemic, gone were the days of pulled pork at Papa's, of Duck's football games and going to Portland for concerts and Powell's Books. Of early morning donut runs to Voodoo, and late nights at the barcades or Max's. But now, all those memories would be tainted with guilt, and feeling like you were the shittiest friend in the world.

"Did you see her?" asked Ashley. Gabe was staring down at the strip of river visible between the two bridges. "Did you see her go by?" Gabe slowly shook his head, and then gave an anemic shrug. Ashley shielded her eyes against the sun and gazed west, to see if she could see anyone in river heading downstream.

"Fuck," Lori repeated quietly, and wiped at her eyes.

"Was…is she a very good swimmer?" Gabe asked.

141

"I mean, she could swim, I know that much," Ashley offered. "The fall isn't *that* far, is it? She could survive it?"

"I guess? But if she hit it wrong, or just gets pulled under? Or hypothermia? Odds aren't good if you ask me – that's a whole lotta river to try and get out of." Gabe shook his head again, and they both looked at Lori warily.

She's gone, Lori thought. *That's that. I let her down – I should have been able to convince her to go with us – shit, we should have all just stopped and smoked a joint to calm her down. You didn't think, you were tired of her shit and just wanted to show her...show her how wrong she always was. And now she's gone. And we have to keep going...*

Lori let out a deep breath. "We need to get going," she said. "But I'm going to tell you two something – I will never hesitate to shoot again."

"I don't know if it would have helped her at all," Ashley said.

"Maybe not. But if anyone – any *thing* – is coming after you guys, I am going to shoot at them. I swear, I will go down with guns blazing. I have *had* it with the world right now."

She made sure the Springfield's chamber was empty, and slung the rifle across her back. "Let's get a move on."

* * *

There was another access ladder where the truss began its downward slope on the north side, but Lori thought there were still too many dead on the bridge. There was another barricade at this end, and they would just have to hope there were no surprises when they got there. She was beginning to feel a bit unbalanced as she headed downhill, and the last leg was made especially uncomfortable when they had to straddle two pipes that ran across the top of frame. Her hands had begun cramping something awful, and her forearms were feeling the strain of not only moving herself forward, but also from keeping her somewhat upright. Her thighs were numb, her feet tingly from the lack of circulation, and she wondered if she would ever be able to walk again. *Don't be a baby,* she thought. *Just keep swimming, just keep swimming...*

There was a dump truck among other smaller vehicles blocking this end of the bridge, but mercifully free of the dead on the other side of them. Lori resisted the urge to hasten their pace, and only dropped off the truss onto concrete where the angle leveled out once more. She immediately sagged to her knees, and both Ashley and Gabe looked like they felt their legs were composed of jelly. *Jesus, I feel like I am* still *straddling the metal beam,* she thought bleakly. *How long is that gonna last? It's like a lost limb, only it's a phantom girder...* She pushed herself up to her feet, and leaned against the barrier.

"That was fun" Ashley remarked dryly.

"Never imagined doing that when I woke up this morning," Gabe laughed. "Holy *shit.*"

"Well, we made it across," Ashley said. "And where do we go from here? Just follow the highway? I don't like the idea of being easy pickins for any road-warrior wannabes."

"I was thinking about that as we were crossing," Lori answered. "I could see it from up there – let's just head up the road a ways and see if it's what I thought it was."

The highway began to head uphill, and they avoided random cars that had been shot to hell, but one caught Ashley's eye and she cautiously approached it. "God damn it," growled Lori.

"Just chill," Ashley drawled. "Something's different about this one." She pulled a bandana from her pack and tied it around her face – it had come in handy once before, and the fumes from the car were a bit ripe. She bent closer, recoiled and retched, but was clearly excited about something. "Gabe!" she yelled. "Come here."

"No thanks," he replied.

"Just come here – I need a towel from the pack on your back."

"A towel?" Gabe asked. "You guys seriously brought towels with you?" He edged closer as he fished a small hand towel out of the backpack, then tossed it to her.

"You never leave home without a towel, Gabe."

"God damn it," Lori repeated.

Ashley used the cloth to yank on the door handle. A man's body

143

spilled out, and a shiny revolver skittered across the concrete.

"Aw, yeah," Ashley said, and picked up the gun with the towel and wrapped it carefully in terrycloth.

"Hold on, hold on, hold on," Lori scolded as she approached Ashley. "Let's make sure the hammer isn't cocked – looks like a single-action." She bent over and stared at the firearm. "Okay," she grunted. "Wrap it up carefully for now - do not snag the hammer and cock it. Here..." She fumbled in her pack for a gallon-sized plastic storage bag.

"Jesus," Gabe snorted. "Are we carrying your whole God damned kitchen with us?"

"Let's keep it in that until we can clean it up."

"Bring the sink too?" Gabe asked. "How 'bout some dishwashing liquid?"

Ashley tucked the gun in the bag, then pressed the seal shut, and tucked it into her front pack. "Now *I* have a gun," she said. "Ho-ho-ho."

Lori smiled grimly. "Doesn't look like it helped him much."

"I think he shot himself with it," Ashley said. "Got a big hole in his head. Someone else in the car too."

"Yeah, I can smell them," Gabe said. "Can we go now?"

They continued on up the grade until Lori steered them to the median. They had reached a point where the highway turned into an overpass again, and down below railroad tracks stretched out to the east.

"Come here, Gabe," Lori ordered. "I need to look in *your* pack, I think."

"Jesus," he shook his head. "You got one of those pump-car thingys in there?"

"Ah, shoot. Forgot to pack that." Lori dug in his pack, gave a triumphant gasp, and pulled out an ancient spiral bound book.

"Oh, shit," Ashley laughed. "I can't believe you held on to it - if we make it home using that, dad will never let us hear the end of it."

"Good ol' Thomas Brothers," Lori said, and flipped open the Washington/Oregon map book. "Look," she said, holding it up for them to see. "Railroad tracks are marked."

"Nice," Gabe breathed. "You think we can follow them all the way to Spokane?"

Lori nodded. "These things were pretty detailed."

"Well, if it keeps us away from the bad guys, I'm all for it," Ashley said.

"Let's get to it, then," Lori said. "We got a lot of steps ahead of us."

They secured their packs, the map book now within easy reach. Before they began the descent down to the tracks, Lori turned and stared at the river with a frown of sorrow. She studied it momentarily. "So long Kenzie," she whispered. "I am so sorry – I wish we had done better by you." The pain of loss tried to bubble up and overwhelm her again, but she grimaced and forcibly controlled herself. There was no time for that. Pure survival instinct needed to have the upper hand now.

She turned, and began the trek down to the bright rails below, two shining parallel lines that converged to a point in the east, like an arrow pointing towards home.

145

Cothrom Ceartas

I find an unpretentious beauty in locks. A simple, binary mechanism with a function of either/or. Locked, unlocked. Stay away, enter. A lock doesn't pretend to be anything else – there are no half-measures for a lock. Any symbolism that is projected upon them is caused by our own guilts and fears.

Most locks I can grasp and coax open with a gentle whisper, but not this one. Cold hard iron, and the hasp just as cold. So cold it will burn me. Being constructed in adherence to ancient superstitions and not diluted into steel, it is not at fault for its rude form. Its functionality is the same, but it is also unwittingly being used as a message - much like the horseshoe above the door.

She is upset with me again, and I honestly do not know why. Here's the thing of it – if I truly wonder at her reasoning, I will figure it out. But like most fae, I will become bored or distracted and lose interest. I simply do not care enough to ponder such things at length.

I know how that sounds to your mortal ears, and it's not meant to be casually cruel or dismissive. I have lived among you for many, *many* revolutions of your world around your star. I gave up cruelty when I realized my participation is not needed in what you excel in amongst yourselves. What you perceive as my arrogance no doubt makes you bristle and fume, and it does not trouble me because I am incapable of feeling troubled at your concerns. I understand them clinically, and perhaps that is enough. Believe it or not, I can feel admiration for you at times, and that can surprise me.

The iron lock is a message, more than likely symbolizing a broken promise. Knocking, calling, waiting will prove fruitless. She is upset, and so be it. I would think she should know by now I never break a promise. It just might take me longer than she likes to have it fulfilled.

It seems I will have to go see the troll first.

* * *

He lives under the Monroe Street bridge, but you'll never see him there, unless he wants you to. Like most trolls these days, he doesn't want you to. Trolls are bullies, and bullies are cowards. All it takes is one Billy goat to destroy your reputation, and they hide forever after. Yes, he is the troll of legend. Like most stories and fables, there is only a kernel of truth at the heart of them. But he *did* get defeated by a mere goat, and the shame of it drove him across an ocean and a continent, finally going to ground in Spokane. I suppose it's not any more unusual than an elf living here, and to the troll's credit, it is a very handsome bridge that he chose. More than likely you have no idea how many of the fae actually live among you. Some even by choice.

His lair exists in the fae realm and your world simultaneously. Technically, visiting him violates the terms of my exile. But my visits fulfill the terms of my punishment – I never really make social calls, it's all strictly for matters at hand. His lair isn't exactly the radiance of a sidhe. But, it isn't protected by iron, and so I enter to find him hunched over his computer, grimly poking away at his keyboard.

"Hello P.K.," I say.

147

He grunts, his thick, gnarled fingers tapping with a delicate fury, and pretends to ignore me.

"Trip, trap, trip, trap," I offer, and his shoulders rise past his misshapen ears as he leans toward his monitor, a hint of steam venting from his smashed nostrils.

"And who are we offending today?" I ask. "Left, right, or those on the fence?"

"Sod off, you elvish twat," he grumbles, but his attack on the keys begins to falter.

"I will, gladly, if you can help me acquire something."

He straightens in frustration, black, beady eyes drilling into my sea-foam green. "You know, mate," he growls, "you only seem ta wander in here when Siobhan's pissed at ya."

"Your point?" I ask.

He begins a soliloquy of swearing so vile the plastic shell of his computer softens and starts to melt, his skin glows a dull red, white-hot cracks forming in the elephantine folds of his skin. I suspect the reality of spacetime and faerealm are in danger of fusing into an impossibility so dense it will sink the heavens to depths from which it can never escape. I let him continue. It doesn't bother me. I rarely find anything loathsome or ugly, but often find beauty in small things, and the troll's profanity has the purity of music.

Eventually he winds down without causing anything to burst into flame, his skin cooling to its normal ash-gray hue, and stares at me, looking both sullen and embarrassed. We play this game on each visit, and I encourage his tantrum before we proceed with business. I believe it clears his mind.

"Whadja do to get her pissed at ya this time?" he asks.

"Who can say?"

"I bloody well think *she* might have a word or two to say about it."

I pretend to think it over. "She can't still be upset about her toes?" I ask.

"Of course she's still pissed about her bloody toes, you poncy git! People usually don't forgive and forget when they lose digits, especially ones that tend ta keep 'em upright!"

"But I gave her shoes - elvish construction, mind you, the finest –
that maintain perfect balance for her."

"Jayjus, mate, people - women, *especially* women - like their
toes! Women like paintin' 'em and shit. Puttin' rings on 'em and the
like. Blazin' hell's bells, you've been around 'em far longer than *I*
have, why don't you know these things? Keen intellectual elves my
arse. You can understand the songs of fern and pine, but know fook-
all about human nature."

"I am an elf. I don't need to know 'fuck-all' about human nature."

"Then I reckon you're *never* going home, mate."

I pause for an appropriate amount of time, then say quietly, "I
warned her not to dance with them."

"And how do you think she could have resisted that?" he answers
just as soft, despite his voice's tendency to sound like an avalanche.

"I had no choice. I am here to serve them, give them what they
ask. That is my sentence."

"Ya didn't have to let her know you were bloody fae, and could
give her passage to the sidhe."

"I am here to serve them, give them what they ask."

"Oh, aye, off you go sweetheart, just don't be gone so long you
dance your bleedin' toes off. You *knew*."

I stare at him for what was probably an uncomfortable amount of
time. "It could have been far worse. She could have aged tremendously."

"Aye. Good thing she got back in time before the unimaginative
oafs declared her legally dead, yeah?"

I sweep my left hand in the direction the river should be, and
point my right to the bridge above. He snorted.

"That's the trouble with you elves. You live too long, and expect
others ta see it all from your lofty perspective. I doubt it's water under the bridge ta her."

"Regardless," I say, "she has let me visit many times after she set
up shop again – with my help, mind you. My thought is that something else has her upset with me."

"When's the last time ya seen her?"

I pretend to calculate. "Three-hundred and eighty-two days, I believe."

He whistles. "A wee bit over a human year? Well goodness me, ain't it obvious? You're practically smotherin' the gal with attention. Better back off, son. Don't want ta appear too clingy."

I pretend offense. "We are not in a relationship – despite the legends of her people, the elves do not have strong desires of the flesh - at least not of human flesh."

"Well, with talk as sweet as that, she'll come 'round, you silver-tongued bastard."

"I don't need her to – "

"Christ on a skateboard, man! It ain't about desires of the flesh, it's about the decency of friendship. Maybe try popping by just to say 'hi' now and again, instead of only when you want somethin', d'ya think?"

I look at him thoughtfully. "A troll lecturing me on decency," I remark. "I thank you for the thrill of a surprise, P.K., truly."

"Quit calling me that," he mutters. "You've used it too long, the world will begin ta think it's my true-born name, and it will have power over me."

This was true. Names have power, and no one should ever know your real name. In fact, you should change your alias often. The troll taps half-heartedly on his keyboard, then asks, "What didja want from her, anyway?"

"I was hoping for a few drops of *lacrimacorpus dissolvens,* if you must know."

"Why don't you just fetch some from the source?"

"I may be quick of foot, but Pennsylvania is a bit too far to travel for me at the moment."

"Who said anything about Pennsylvania? We got one right here."

I actually blink several times.

"I'm sorry, what did you say?" I ask, even though my hearing is, of course, impeccable.

"We got one of the buggers here – out at the Rocks of Sharon. You didn't know?"

Now I actually do feel a thrill of surprise run up my spine. I never understand the resentment humans can feel when they've been informed of something they were ignorant of. I suppose an elf never feels foolish, so the act of learning something new is a precious gift to us. Not that I would let the troll know this. I will continue to let him feel a bit superior in the moment. Which of course he finds great delight in. He lets out a series of great, booming laughs.

"Oh, this is lovely! The by-my-lord-know-it-all-elf-king ain't got a clue we got us a squonk right in our very own garden!"

It would be pointless to remark that I am not, and never was, a king. So I settle for yellowing my eyes, shifting the shape of my pupils into horizontal bars as hair shoots out of my chin, and I bleat loudly. This, of course, makes him laugh harder, believing he has reduced me to taking a cheap shot. It will make him charitable later. I wait for his laughs to dwindle away into chuckles, and then to a wide grin as he shakes his head.

"I gotta tell you mate, that made my day."

"I live to serve."

"That you do, mate, that you do. Any idea if you'll ever be allowed to return to the land of fae?"

"I will know when the binding-runes disappear from my back, and that is the fact of it."

"Must stick in ya craw to have such pure skin disfigured so."

I shrug. He stares at me for a while, then frowns. "How d'ya think that little bastard made it all the way 'cross the country to park it out at the Rocks of Sharon?"

"I imagine it could be much like a bedbug. Perhaps accidental, but a fortuitous move to new territory if it is thriving."

"Yeah, they ain't the brightest of beasties. Couldn't have been a purposeful journey." He cocked his head. "The next few nights ought to be good trackin' – moon's big and bright. Shine those drops and puddles up real good for ya."

I smile politely, and neglect to mention I would have no need of the moon's light.

151

"You need to be careful with it, mate," he adds. "Those tears are downright infectious. You don't want ta be a blubberin' mess for days."

"I appreciate your concern," I say, although I feel nothing of the sort. "But we elves are immune. As you like to point out, we don't have an overabundance of empathy to feed from."

He actually looks embarrassed, but then says, "Well mate, maybe the day you learn some feelings those nasty runes will disappear from your back."

I smile. "Perhaps. Now, despite believing you are playing the next fiddler in line, I did have reason to call upon you tonight."

His wire-brushed eyebrows raise in surprise. "Oh, aye? And what might a miserable twat like myself have to offer ya?"

"Your skill at that charming device that drinks up all your attention."

And I explain what I need. He looks shocked, and rather disappointed in me.

"Never sussed you as a blackmailer, mate."

"I am not blackmailing anyone. I live to serve."

"I just…it don't figure that it's your line of work, yeah?"

"True, this is new to me as well. I'm not sure how I could have become involved – people like this certainly don't believe in our kind. Perhaps we are entering a new age indeed. Regardless, help was asked of me, so I live to serve."

"Yeah but – listen, I ain't going ta lose any of my beauty sleep over this, it's all a load of bollocks if you ask me and I could give two shits about politicians – but is blackmailing someone agreeable ta the terms of those runes on your back?"

He genuinely seems concerned about this. I wish I could say I was touched.

"Nothing is excluded, except extreme physical harm and kidnapping. I am to learn from the good and the bad, it seems."

"Jaysus, mate. You've been at it how long? A few millennia, as far as I know. And some think that's just a drop in the river. Christ, how long does it take an elf to learn something?"

It's hard to explain the notion of time, or lack of it, to anyone other than an elf. We don't perceive time as anything other than the moment of now. All that you see as dim past is now to us. I understand that a journey to Pennsylvania will happen now, and it will also coincide with a now elsewhere and I cannot be in two places at once – I am not that race of elf. So it can be hard to relate to your perception of time's direction. I have made progress on the matter, attempting to relay tales in a linear fashion. And it is true - I have been in your world a very long time to your mortal eyes. But what I perceive are events that have occurred. It is not time that erodes the rock, but the waves that batter it. And perhaps I have not been battered enough yet.

And so if I can't explain, I will change the subject.

"If it helps, this isn't blackmail. The information is to be used in hopes of sabotage, it appears. All's fair, they say, in love and politics."

He snorts. "Maybe that'll give you an inklin' of the joy I get pokin' at 'em online. Anyway, what's the squonk's tears got ta do with it all?"

"And that is my own affair," I answer, and he shrugs.

"I believe something of far more interest to you is your payment," I state, and pluck a flat stone from the air and toss it lightly to him. He catches it, the sound of rocks clacking together echo in his cavern lair. He eyes the object suspiciously, turning it over.

"What's this?" he asks.

"A wishing stone."

His eyes widen. "You bloody liar!"

"I don't lie. I just might not tell all of the truth."

"No fooking way!"

"Note it's size, now. It won't bring you anything bigger than itself. I trust you can make use of it, though."

His grin breaks across his face like a fault line. "How many has it got? Three? Wishes? Ain't that always the way of it? Three of 'em?"

"Do you know, I haven't the faintest idea? I'm sure it has a bottom, but it might take some time to reach it. You may actually want to put some thought into a few of them."

He holds the stone flat on his palm, and brings it eye level. "Bring me my favorite bite ta eat," he whispers. A small, yellow sponged cake wrapped in clear plastic materializes on the stone, and he roars with delight, tipping the cake off of the stone and into his mouth, plastic and all, and the sticky-sweet filling of the cake drools out of the corner of his mouth as he chews with enthusiastic ferocity. He repeats the command twenty-seven times, then changes to small bags of crisps with unnatural hues, and bottles of a liquid that looks as if it could just as well cool the engines of automobiles as quench your thirst.

"Remember," I say gently, "it *does* have a bottom."

He drags the back of a hand across his lips, the sound of a concrete block skating on asphalt. "I'm going ta have some fun finding it, I can tell you that, mate."

As he offers me a lazy grin, I reach up again and bring fingers and thumb together to pinch at the air. A smooth, sharp arrowhead balances on the tips of my fingers. It is so black it threatens to swallow all of the light surrounding it. "And this," I say, "is for Siobhan."

He swallows, the sound of gravel trickling through a clay pipe. "That," he growls, "could fetch me a pretty purse from the right folk."

I pretend not to hear that remark, and reach out with my left hand to snatch a small, white velvet bag. I drop the arrowhead in it, and pull on the silver ties to seal the opening. "When you give it to her, tell her she is not to handle it with bare skin – she would be lucky if it only cuts her. She can only handle it with iron tongs, or the bag. Volume seven of *Magical Curiosities and Curses* by Yeats will inform her of the chemistry she will need." I snap my fingers to draw his attention away from the bag to me. "You will *tell* her this, when you *give* it to her."

He blinks at me stupidly. Apparently I am not making my point, so my eyes redden, my ears sharpen, and if the arrowhead appeared to try and suck in all of the light, I actually *do*, and I finally see the fear in his eyes.

"Let me be perfectly clear," I say, my voice so cold that bare skin would stick and fuse to it - even that of trolls. "If I hear of anyone becoming elf-shot, all of those involved in the transaction will only have room for the pain they feel as they die, and none for regrets." I offer a grin, but it is pure wickedness. "And then I might never return home. How could you live with that knowledge, P.K.?"

The light in his lair gutters back to life, and my features soften back to perfection. I can tell I have made my point. "The arrowhead is for Siobhan," I stress, but gently now. "She is the only person I trust to use it for healing, and nothing else. When you give it to her, you will tell her what I have said, and the safety measures needed. Especially those. We are clear on this, yes?"

He nods vigorously. "Yes," he whispers hoarsely.

"Very good. And please tell her one more thing," I say, then pause for a moment to add a bit of weight. "Tell her that I wish I was a better friend."

I am almost certain that I mean it.

* * *

A common misconception about squonks is that they are defenseless. This may be true in that they are not sharp of tooth and claw, but the poison of the wrong berry or mushroom wields no slashing blades either. This is not to say that any encounter with the squonk has been fatal, at least immediately. They are thought to be shy and retiring, but that is nonsense. When you are in their environment, you are on their stage and have no idea you are part of the performance. It makes little sense that a creature would exist only to wallow in the misery of its ugly countenance.

Why one would be out in the rugged Rocks of Sharon is a mystery that more than likely won't be solved – asking the squonk itself would prove fruitless, since it would be as ignorant of its situation as the rest of us. The creature prefers the moist hemlock forests of northern Pennsylvania. I suspect I know why the squonk has thrived in its current location, since it feeds off the emotions of people. Particularly pity, but fear, revulsion, anger, sorrow and joy can sustain it as well. The Rocks of Sharon can elicit most of these. Its natural beauty to the human eye brings the joy: craggy granitic monoliths jutting skywards, and a wide eagle's-eye view of the Palouse, along with the enjoyment of nature and adrenaline rush of the climbers. Its steep trails no doubt generate a flood of endorphins to those addicted to them, and misery to those not fit of form. Downhill can be hard for those with problems of the knee, and I imagine sharp twinges are like shots of whiskey to the squonk.

The terrain is not one you would want to traverse at night, unless you have my eyesight. I move perfectly well, and of course make no exertion across the rocky ground and steep paths. The squonk is a very old-fashioned creature, and so I drop all charms on my clothing that cause it to appear more agreeable to a modern eye. The soft, dusky-gray doe skin of my cloak, leggings and jerkin are as supple and clean as when I first donned them, the mahogany color of my boots and quiver still rich and deep. The braided silver stitching glows as if it has an internal light in the moonshine, and to mortal eyes I must be quite a sight, my hood covering my ash-white hair, my bow nocked with an arrow as I move quickly and confidently up the hill. I ignore all curious wildlife. Most scatter from my path, but a mountain lion follows me until it has second thoughts.

I can smell the creature before I see its sign – bright, shining drops and puddles of tears. Now, this is a curious fact no one on this world may know: once you've seen the tears, the squonk knows you are in its presence, even if you are as stealthy and silent as I am. I slow to a walk, and soon I hear a faint sobbing.

"Who is there?" I call softly, and the sobbing stops.

"Ah, my ears trick me tonight," I say, and pretend to move along. "I only wish to catch snipe to feed my hungry babes, but my worries transform themselves into phantom sounds in these woods."

Yes, I know - any self-respecting hunter would not prattle on so. We are not working with the keenest of minds when dealing with squonks, but we are in a play of sorts. The worst of melodrama, to be sure, but to catch the creature one finds sinking to its level is the quickest course.

The pitiful cries return, and I act as if I intend to ignore them, and the sobbing grows a bit more forceful, so I stop in sudden exasperation.

"I ask again, who is there? Friend, are you in need of aid? You need not hide from me." The sounds halt once more.

"You add more sadness to that which I bear, friend. I am not without pity to those in need, even though my five hungry, motherless children weigh heavy on my thoughts day and night. If you seek no solution to your woes from me, I wish you best fortune and I shall not trouble you further."

Undoubtably sensing no such emotions from me confuses the squonk, and it wails in frustration.

"Friend! I ask for a final time, how may I help you?"

"You ain't no friend," a timid and moist voice answers. "No one ain't never been my friend."

"Ah, friend – friend! My heart lightens at our discourse. I feel we could become fast-friends, best of friends, comrades, brothers – *brothers*, my friend – just think of it! All our woes behind us as we face the world's troubles with locked arms and heads down to bowl them over!"

"I ain't never had no friend, and you won't be neither," the squonk laments. "If you lay eyes on me, you'll be revolted and run away. Or laugh, that's what you'll do. You'll laugh and point and make fun of me."

"Oh, unkind my friend. Unkind! The world is cruel and callous to me and my five hungry babes, I would not multiply it's malice by treating you so low and hideous. Even though life has dealt me poor hands in the game of fate, I myself deal squarely and cheerfully. I know your appearance will lift my soul that it might join in song with the music of the spheres."

You wouldn't be wrong to ask why I just don't shoot the creature – I know exactly where it is, even hidden by foliage. And I answer that it would do no good – my arrow would simply pass through it and the beast would escape. You might also ask why don't I just collect its shed tears and be done with it, and truly it is a matter of potency, and their efficacy later.

The squonk stirs in the brush, still not understanding why its pitiful cries appear to leave me unmoved, even though I am adamant in my declarations of friendship and love.

157

"You'll just be like all of 'em," the squonk blubbers. "Get a gander and you'll be gone, sorry you ever seen me."

"Oh friend, my eyes never regret what is offered to them, only the sights unseen they had a chance to behold."

"You'll be sorry, and I'll be sadder because you all lie and say you'll be my friend and then you ain't never."

The squonk was desperate, and decided it had to play its ace. The leaves rustle as it shuffles out of the brush.

Its loose skin, dotted with mangy lumps and bumps, hangs in uneven folds across its misshapen frame. It wipes its long, wrinkled nose with a red rag that is caught on a tooth that looks in danger of tipping out of its lower jaw, the lip hanging loose in a perpetual droop. Its gnarled ears can't decide if they would flop loose against the scabrous skull, or pull back in imitation of canine dismay. And its eyes are huge, black and perpetually wet.

It is a thing of beauty, for it meets its design so well.

"And there you are!" I say with enthusiasm. "It is a pleasure and honor to meet you plain and unhidden!"

"You're a liar. You think I'm disgusting."

"I most certainly do not, friend! Can't we agree that a companion is a most agreeable thing, and two on a journey in these rough woods bodes better than a solitary trek?"

"I ain't no good at fightin', mister," the squonk mutters. "I will only cause you misery."

"On the contrary, friend! You give me the will to fight with the strength of a hundred knights! For the beauty of friendship warms the blood and thus the heart."

"Ain't no thing of beauty about me," it sobs.

"And I am here to change that low opinion you hold to yourself, friend, for I have never met a creature I have not loved."

As brainless a beast as a squonk is, it no doubt feels itself superior in intellect to the clearly blind dolt before it. The creature moves into an unobstructed patch of moonlight to give me a closer look. Surely now, I will see it plain and feel revulsion and pity.

But I pour out a soliloquy on friendship and beauty with such eloquence that tears begin to ooze from its very skin, and as it wails in frustration I use the distraction to bring forth the sack and the beast is at the bottom of it, the opening sealed, the container across my back, and I'm running down the hill before it knows it has been trapped.

It bounces in the sack for several hundred of my strides, then mutters, "You bastard."

"Any major dude with half a heart surely will tell you my friend," I answer, knowing full well pop-culture references will be meaningless to it.

It swears at me, and then begins to sob and cry again. I have nothing left to say, and wait for it to quiet as it surely will, because another little known fact of the squonk is that its ugly exterior is not its true state of being. It is a liquid that is its standard form, and contained unto itself in the sack, it will dissolve into bubbles and tears.

As I race out of the Rocks of Sharon, and through the valley of Spokane, the squonk's pitiful cries become fewer, more muted, until all that is left is a gentle gurgling and sloshing. If you feel that the creature has been treated unfairly, know that it is unharmed. Yes, I will keep a few small drops of it for my own ends, and it shall remain contained as a gift. Perhaps it will find itself used until it has evaporated away. Or perhaps, like water, it will find its way out or in. Either way, it is of no concern to me. I have an errand.

* * *

People tend to like me, even if they don't think they do. People who meet me for the first time want to like me very much, even if they don't understand why (I have met sociopaths that my charms are lost on, and it is diverting to frustrate them when they learn they can't dominate me. Psychopaths even more so).

And so I tend to get into places others cannot. Yes, I do have elvish tricks to play, and illusions to distract and misdirect. I always have the proper papers, credentials – at least as far as anyone knows. But by and large the natural attraction you humans have to elvish charm gets me where I want to go without having to rely on magics.

I am able to move down the hallway to the senator's green room largely unmolested. The badge at the end of the lanyard has been

159

scrutinized by security several times since I've drawn near the theater, passed barricades and entered the building. I always pass with crisp, curt nods. I can look important, harmless or even famous depending on my needs. And I will be forgotten if I want to be, which is most of the time. I knock on the room's door, and it is yanked open by a harassed and exhausted blonde woman as she berates someone at the other end of a headset.

"He said he wanted the *red* tie with the goddamn *blue* stripes – the *thin* blue stripes, not the wide-ass ones with silver trim. What? Because he says the flag pin stands out better on that one, and what's it to you? Do your goddamn job and get him the right tie!"

She looks up at me and immediately her eyes soften, and I can feel relief radiate from her. "Please just get him the correct tie. It's important to him, and we're all on the same team, right? Atta girl. See you in a bit."

She tips the mic away from her mouth and smiles at me, honest, open and warm. "You have no idea how happy I am to see you, sir."

"I have a little idea, I think," I say lightly, and she giggles uncontrollably. I can tell she is almost appalled at herself for not having the icy demeanor she believes she always has, but she convinces herself she is just stressed and a little harmlessly awkward flirting never hurt anyone.

I pull a thumb drive out of the left pocket of my overcoat, and extend it to her. She inhales in a sharp gasp, and stares at the device as if it were an artifact from the tomb of Christ. Tears glisten in her eyes.

"Does…did you get what we needed?" she asks.

"I did. Name, address, phone number. Hospital records. All that you asked for."

She exhales in ecstasy, her knees sag slightly. "I honest-to-God could kiss you right now," she breathes.

"Why, Annie," I chide, "I may not be able to handle that! I might walk right in front of a bus in a delirious daydream, and that would be the end of me!"

"Oh don't even say that!" she shouts, then looks around, embarrassed. She takes the thumb drive, her fingers lingering on mine, then sighs and tucks it away. "And you're sure there is...no payment? Absolutely none?"

"I live to serve," I say simply.

She wrinkles her nose and tips her head. "Well, I'll consider it a donation to the campaign."

"Certainly," I say. "Now, I am going to need the card back – part of our deal."

"Oh! Yes, of course – I'll just go get it for you."

Before she can turn to go, I touch her shoulder lightly. "Annie. I have to get it in person. From him. He has to transfer it back to me."

"Oh, really?" She looks doubtful. "He's getting in some last minute prepping for the debate."

"I understand. However...the terms of our deal have been stated, and will be abided, yes?"

She grimaces. "It's just that...you know, I had to gloss over the...he's not one to believe in ancient...things, you know? He is a Godly man, and..." She trails off, her eyes pleading her case.

"Of course. And that makes no difference to me." I smile, and I can feel her heart flutter. "I promise I won't bother him with any mystic nonsense. But, for this to work, he needs to give me the card back."

The last of her defenses weaken and break, and she nods firmly. "I'm sure he would like to meet you anyway," she says brightly, and leads me to a side room.

"Atta girl," I remark, and she giggles.

In the side room, several men are grouped around a tall man at a podium. I wonder briefly if it was his demand for the prop, or if one of his assistants thought it was needed for accuracy's sake. The lesser men all turn and stare at me as we enter, a serious and intense group that lack the looks, charisma or strength that their boss exudes, but they seek power nonetheless. They are lackeys that once snatched armbands and other shiny bits of metal tossed to them, now they grab at recognition, pretending their prejudices are ideals worth fighting dirty for. It is their job to protect their leader from the small irritations of life, and they all are desperate to prove their worth with scowls and frowns.

"Sorry to interrupt, sir," Annie says timidly. "But this is the man that I told you about, and he has...delivered for us."

"Annie," a balding comb-over sighs with barely restrained contempt, "we are in the home stretch here, sweetie and – "

I stride confidently forward. I have my role to play as well. I appear to be dressed in an overcoat, with a knit cap to hide the tips of my ears but also to show I don't plan on staying long – I am a busy man too.

"I won't take up but a moment of your time, and then I'll be out of your *hair*," I say jovially as I stare at the man's shiny forehead (again, sociopaths can be a pleasant diversion). "Annie has some information that will help you tonight. I suggest you not waste her time and figure out how to blend it into the night's debate."

And I am done with him, and now only deal with the senator, who is a textbook example of slightly graying temples, granite jaw and steely blue eyes that can pretend tenderness. For my part, I exude confidence and professionalism - for all he knows he is in the presence of an ex-Navy SEAL that has gone into the business of political consulting, with arcane abilities to dig up the dirt no one else can. I extend my right hand and he reaches out automatically to grasp it. My grip is firm, but not overbearing, which allows him to think that he might just have an edge if push came to shove. He smiles.

"Ah! Mr...?" He lets the question of my name hang between us.

"Better if you don't know sir," I say with a smile and jerk of my head. He nods as if he understands completely. "I won't take up any more of your time, I just wanted to wish you fortune, and ask for my card back."

He looks puzzled momentarily, and I am about to remind him it is in his shirt pocket, above his heart, when his eyes clear and he grins. "Ah yes," he says, and reaches in to pluck it forth. "I forgot about your rather unusual rule." I shrug with a roll of my eyes as if to suggest these rules are beyond us, but we have to abide by them so what are you gonna do? I take the card with my left hand and tuck it away.

"Again, I hope I have helped," I say. "I suppose this wraps up a tough campaign for you. Good night sir."

"Thank you for your contribution," he replies. I turn to face the scowls of his entourage, and notice the balding one is hunched over a laptop with Annie, both of them grinning like devils. She is done with me, even if she doesn't know it, so I slip out of the room silently without goodbyes.

I move down the hallway and across the building, lift my lanyard with my credentials to a curious security guard, and I see her standing in the hall texting. She looks crisp and trim in her business suit, the pants hiding the artificial leg she refuses to use as a prop tonight. Her long and arrow-straight black hair is tucked behind her ears as her dark eyes reflect the phone's screen. I sense she is taking a break from her own entourage, not needing any more affirmation of who she is other than what she already knows. I am reluctant to intrude.

"I would wish you luck tonight, but I have a feeling the senator is the one who needs it the most," I say as I tuck a glove onto my right hand, looking as if I am on the move and have no desire to linger other than to pass on my best wishes. She looks up, puzzled, but then grins of course. People want to like me when they see me.

"Why thank you. I look forward to a spirited debate," she says, then cocks her head. "Have we met?"

"Possibly," I say and extend my left hand and she extends hers.

"Ah, a fellow leftie," she laughs as we shake.

"Oh, I give both of my hands equal time and do not play favorites. But offering a gloved one feels rude to me."

"I suppose so," she says. "Are you leaving? You won't be in the audience?"

"I will be watching for sure," I say, and smile warmly. "I would like to offer a bit of advice, and I apologize because I am certain by now you are rather weary of it being given to you – wanted or unwanted."

She smiles, and tilts her head, waiting.

"I believe your opponent will dance rather clumsily tonight, and that may shock you. Remember that he is acting in desperation, and that your grace in the presence of fire will win the day for you again. I know this."

163

Her deep brown eyes study me for a while. "Thank you for the head's up," she finally says, and gives my hand a squeeze before letting go.

"If I could vote for you, I would," I say, and I am almost certain that I mean it.

* * *

I decided to stay and watch the debate from the shadows in the back of the hall, and it didn't take the senator very long to use the information I provided for him. As the matters of disclosure and transparency are brought up, he tries to deflect from himself in what he no doubt feels will be a double-dose of shame that his voter base will find fault with.

"Tell me, Ms. Martinez – since we are talking about honesty and integrity – does your wife know about the child you gave up for adoption, and how his family is trying to reach out to you for your medical history?"

She blinks rapidly several times, stunned at his audacity, stunned at his inept intrusion into her life, stunned at just how low a human being could descend to keep a seat of power. You might wish that I felt a tug of shame for my part in this, and of course I will disappoint you – I can find beauty in the mean and cruel as much as with the selfless and caring. There is a purity in winning at any cost, when the resolution in your favor means more than the lives of others or what's best for your country. There is no subterfuge in that, which is why I am fascinated by those that can decide to be blind enough to excuse it.

The moderators are baffled, looking at each other as if they had reached the edge of the world and were uncertain of what they were seeing. This was an abyss unknown. As a moderator begins to stammer out a mild rebuke, the senator's opponent raises a finger in reply.

"I will answer his question," she says, her posture forged in steel. "I must admit I'm a bit surprised at his bravery in bringing this up himself instead of leaking it to the press. Bravo, senator. I'm sure you are justifiably proud of yourself."

She smiles tightly. "I think there is a big difference between fiscal transparency and our personal lives. I, for one, would never bring up rumors of multiple infidelities, feeling it has no bearing on what is being debated tonight. But here we are, with my past brought forth inelegantly. Yes, of course my wife knows I gave a child up for adoption before enlisting in the Army. I would think I should be given *some* points for deciding to bring him to term, and letting a loving family be blessed by him. I don't think I would have been a very good mother at that time, and I stand by my decision. You seem to hint that I am not cooperating with his family, and while I have not spoken with them personally, I am supplying them with any information I can. If I thought that skipping this debate to sit face-to-face with them would help this family's son, I would do it in a heartbeat – I would find that much more enriching to my life, I can tell you. After this election, I would like to meet with them if they so desire. But here's the thing, senator – you just brought them into this. An innocent family that was, until now, anonymous. I can't imagine they will have much rest, and while I implore those in the press and the trolls online not to discover who they are and make their lives a living hell, I am not foolish enough to believe that will happen. Again, bravo senator. Take a bow."

It is the senator's turn to blink several times, and before any moderator can formulate a question, the man bursts into tears. He grips the podium so hard his arms shake, and great, heaving sobs shudder up and out of him. He tries to harness the anger he feels at his loss of control, to beat and dominate his tears like he has every opponent in life, but there is no defeating them as they overwhelm and drown the fury, and he surrenders to his crying, draping himself over the podium as his back convulses. His lackeys hang back, uncertain and confused, now fearful to be seen near him. No one seems to know what to do, until his wife rushes up to him, and then Annie, and they rub his back as he blubbers and wails, then slips off the support he had clung to and curls into himself on the stage floor.

165

If it were possible, I imagine he would cry even stronger if he knew that this will last for several days.

His opponent looks doubtfully around the auditorium, not sure if this is a new debate tactic or if she is just witnessing a mental breakdown. The audience begins to murmur in amazement, so only I can hear her say to herself, "Was it something I said?"

* * *

As I exit out into the crisp fall night, I reach in and take the card out of my pocket. The size of an average business card, it has a pearlescent, shimmering quality to it, with the words, 'Ask for help and I will find You' etched across it. You'll be able to read it, no matter your native tongue. I toss it, and it blows up and away, out to seek another who might be in despair, or overwhelmed, or victimized. If you come across it, it helps to be attuned to the fae in a way you don't understand, but there are no strings attached. I will help anyone who presumes to ask sincerely.

I did stretch the truth in telling Annie that I needed to get the card back directly from the senator. Technically, it is she that asked for my help, not him. And she received what was asked of me. All I really needed to do was shake his hand. I will have to keep a glove on my right hand for several more trips of the hour-hand across a clockface before the squonk's tears lose their potency.

Now, if you feel that I cheated on my promise of aid in sabotaging the senator's image, recall that I helped Annie. And do you really feel pity for Annie since she is surely affected? Recall what form of help she requested. And I fulfilled that need. I just went further in helping the senator to gain a bit of empathy, for the squonk will never leave him completely. Now, you may think that is a very rich thing coming from me - to impose empathy on someone since I seem to lack a significant amount of it myself. You surely know my answer if you were to ask if I care. While I can admire the beauty of the powerfully cruel, there is even more beauty in seeing them get their fair justice.

I move through the streets of Spokane without notice until I desire it. I find myself heading west on First Avenue until I come upon a small shop, old fashioned of door and dressing. The multi-paned shop window has green vines painted throughout, with the words, 'Siobhan's Apothecary' in bold, shining gold. Under that, in smaller font, there is 'Dealing in Spices and Herbs and Strange Wine, with Some Very Nice Tea.' The cold iron lock is now gone, along with the horseshoe above the door. She appears to have forgiven me. I can hear her above in her apartment, humming to herself as she settles in for the evening, and I smile, and then move along. I will visit soon enough, and – but I stop, and turn back. There is no time but the present, and I have nothing that needs my attention elsewhere.

I grasp the small brass knob of the door, and whisper quietly to it. I hear a small click, and then a louder one from the deadbolt above. Come in, they say to me.

Long Forgotten Blue

R ed.
The color beat down upon him as if angry that he liked blue better. So angry, in fact, that it could not allow the memory of blue, let alone any other color.

Ah well. Green had been lost to his memory for some time now, so it really wasn't a surprise that blue would be next. Still, he felt a pang of regret – no, way more than that, damn it. *Loss*. A boundless horizon of empty loss that seemed to fill him until it spilled out of his ears, his desiccated nostrils, past his mummified lips, even slipping out under his fingernails and crawling under the lids of his eyes to dampen and cake his cheeks. Blue was his favorite color! Blue was royal. Blue was the oceans, and rivers and lakes of old. Blue was cool midnight and electric gemstones.

Red could go right back to the hell it fled from because your eyes could be baby blue and --

Ah. *That* was it. It was his *eyes*. His eyelids, precisely. He had passed out again and the late afternoon sun was baking him, drying him out, his body's precious water evaporating from him in a desperate offering to The Mother.

The Mother could give a damn about him, he knew. The Mother only wanted to pressure cook herself, burn out humanity like a fever sweating out a virus, and start over. The funny thing was it had been *his* idea long ago – offer up the old guilty ones to The Mother. It had been their fault that Mother was in the state she was in. Trouble was, if you lived long enough, you ended up being one of the guilty too. And why not? He could still recall the days when cars ran across The Mother. They were less numerous than in the days before he was born, but he clearly remembered when there were more of them than bikes.

Funny, he had a bike that was blue when he was a kid. He had loved that shade of blue – it was his favorite above all. It almost hurt his eyes to look at it, and he was told some pools of water used to look like that.

He wished he could remember it. But red wouldn't let him.

Abruptly, red was gone. Well, not gone, but an after-image that cooled and shrank and the temperature drop on his skin was considerable and he almost gasped, but only managed a dry groan. Small dirty fingers explored his face, and tried to pry open an eyelid. He groaned again, and that earned him a slap, and red was back and then he was kicked viciously in the ribs.

The boy was checking to see if he was dead yet. The little bastard. Not that he blamed him at all – the boy would want to go below and get out of the heat. But he was supposed to watch the sacrifice until it gave up its water to The Mother, and not let any animals in to hurry things up. Even if it was only crows. No blood was to be spilled on the rooftop – that would have been an offering to the God of greed and would insult The Mother. Once the sacrifice was dead, then let the animals eat. But the water belonged to Mother. Maybe she would give it back one day…

That was the idea, anyway. Not that he believed in The Mother – not as some conscious entity, eager to take revenge or embrace the offer of sacrifice. But hell, it was a convenient way to get rid of the old and useless – or just rivals that could be blamed for the days of old. Like his father. He had been the first offering to her. Seemed like a good idea at the time. Until *you* grow old and everyone begins to resent the air *you* breathe, or the water you take away from them…

Hadn't it all started as a joke? Well, it hadn't been very funny to his *father*. Still, everyone but the old boy had seemed to enjoy the sight of him splayed out on the roof of the arc, skin baking a swollen

169

red in the harsh noon sun while he cursed at them for being ingrates and leeches. He had known what was best for them, saved their asses, and here they were executing him with some hippy-dippy Gaia nonsense.

Yes. The new-age angle was a nice touch, and that had probably hurt more than broiling on the hot arco roof. That the self-sustaining colony started to decline after a mere decade of shutting out the rest of the world owed more to cost-cutting of its budget than the abrupt and catastrophic climate change. You could only blame the criminal neglect of the carbon build-up, the loss of permafrost and the release of methane (and ancient pathogens!) into an ailing atmosphere for so long before resenting reclamation filters that clogged with mold, tepid air circulation, and piss-poor solar cells. So getting the pampered occupants (who had expected to live in comfort as the rest of the world gasped for water) to fall for some old-timey woo was pretty easy when they were afraid. Once people were scared of the dark again, burnt offerings were easy in the daylight.

All too easy.

The red cooled to purple again and he flinched, knowing the boy was over him once more. He could hear him muttering incoherently, grunting, spitting out anger manufactured from years knowing only resentment of those who had come before him.

The filthy little fingers that smelled of cooked rat pinched and picked at his eyelids, and then a searing pain in his right eye – amazing that he could feel such an escalation of pain! – as a dull knife dug through his eyelid, rooting behind his eyeball as it was dug out from his skull and he was reminded of carving pumpkins as a child – a rich person's memory – and sawing off the hat to get to the guts of seeds to scoop them out. He might have laughed if he could remember how.

The boy gave satisfied, guttural chuckles and slapped him hard across the face. He barked something sounding like an order, and slapped him again, then tried to pry open his left eye.

He knew this boy would go through this someday as well. He knew it with a ferocious certainty. Maybe 30 years from now, maybe 20 – hell, maybe far sooner than that, even. This boy would be offered up on the roof as well. He would be beaten today, and made to watch over many sacrifices to The Mother until he learned his lesson. But he would wind up an offering just the same.

But his children wouldn't, surely. If he ever had any.

He was slapped again, and somehow he managed to open his one crusted and swollen eye. The boy chuckled, an out of focus smear, grimy fingers dangling and swinging a bloodshot orb in front of his eye.

What an odd thing to see. The boy giggled and his rotten breath blew against the sphere. And then he recognized it - there! *There* it was!

Blue.

That was blue! He could remember it, and a grateful joy filled his chest, spilling up and out of his throat in a convulsive sob.

Blue, goddamnit.

All ill-feelings he had for the boy were gone. He wanted to thank him, and his lips quivered and his throat clenched but he managed to wheeze out the words, "Thank you. *Thank* you."

Of course they sounded nothing like that, and the boy struck him again.

Still. He had seen it one last time.

Blue.

The Dolittle Curse

The sasquatch was making good time on the Centennial Trail. Striding confidently along the pavement, he didn't worry about leaving footprints behind. When traveling across terrain that was unforgiving in hiding his tracks, however, he would strap carved planks to his feet - evidence of obvious fakery. They hurt his dogs something fierce, though, and were obnoxious in the amount of noise they produced when banging against rocks. Now, they spooned against each other in his backpack, clanking softly together in muted protest against their disuse.

That was a sasquatch gift – being able to understand *everything*. Even pieces of old, dead wood. Dead things tended to complain an awful lot.

To say that he was in a good mood would be wholly inaccurate. Possibly, he was not as annoyed as he usually was at any given moment. He might have, once in his very long life, been within spitting distance of true happiness, but had returned to his senses before succumbing to such madness. He had chalked up the close call as being caused by the stench of pot, combined with the delicious expression of fear the startled hippie had worn. Scaring hippies had been as close to having a hobby as he ever had. No one ever believed them. But these days, it seemed the whole damned state smoked weed – even so-called "respectable" folk. It just wasn't the same anymore.

"Hey handsome," the coyote yipped. "Where you off to in such a hurry?"

And it was gone. He once again was fully satisfied in his commitment to a grim life.

The sasquatch's eyes searched the path for a rock to throw at her. Moonlight was daylight to him, even in the satellite's thinnest sliver of waning light. But no rocks were within easy reach, and he didn't want to waste time by straying from his steady pace.

He grunted, and tried to ignore her.

"Aw, come on," she teased, trotting along just out of reach. "Don't you get lonely? Why are *all* of you so shy? Don't you want friends?"

"You want to be someone's dog, you know who to go to," he grumbled. "They'll coo and squeal over any flea-bitten cur."

That was a sasquatch gift – being able to talk to *everything*.

She laughed. "I don't look good on a leash."

"Who does?" he muttered.

"Hey!" said the squirrel. "Where're we going? Huh? Food, food, food? Heading to some food?"

"Fuck," grumbled the sasquatch.

The coyote giggled, and so did the squirrel, although he suspected the witless rodent only did so to fit in.

That was a sasquatch gift – *everybody* wanted to be friends. If he weren't here, the coyote would have snapped up the squirrel in a heartbeat. The thought of it made his belly rumble, but he wanted to be in and out of Peaceful Valley before dawn. He might crash in Downriver park for the day, and sleep soundly without worry. That was a sasquatch gift – when they slept, they were never found. His uncle once joked that for a people who slept so soundly, they sure were a grumpy lot. That was the day his uncle was banished. Sasquatches did not tolerate jokes.

"What ya got in the pack?" asked the squirrel. "Something to eat? Food? Food? I like chips. Chips. Ya got chips in there?"

"He doesn't have food in there," laughed the coyote. "Can't you smell? It's just two stinky pieces of wood." The fake-feet in his pack ceased their rattling, insulted into silence.

"What d'ya need 'em for?" asked the squirrel.

"Because they help turn me from sasquatch into bigfoot."

"But you *already* have such big feet," said the squirrel, astonished at his ignorance.

"The better to squash you with if you don't shut up," he snarled.

"Harsh," scolded the crow as she wheeled around his head. "Harsh, harsh, harsh!"

"Oh, go back to your murder!" he snapped, and made a determined swing at the bird, but she flew just out of reach. "A crow should have better sense than to be out after dark."

"I'm safe with you," she cackled. And it was true. All of them were safe near him. Not *from* him, but he would not slow down, continuing on towards Peaceful Valley to steal back the damage his uncle had caused.

His idiot uncle. Who knew that banishment could cause such trouble? But, one joke is one too many, and you had to nip that nonsense in the bud.

As he slipped into the neighborhood, his trio of followers fell into their own habits of stealth – even the squirrel, who only quieted for mimicry's sake. Dogs called out greetings, and he could smell cats – they were indeed curious, but were far too cool to try talking to him. For cats, it was appearances sake above all else.

He targeted a tiny, single-story building under the Maple Street bridge, and with a single stride he climbed the weedy grade up to the house. As he passed a window lit by a bouncing screensaver, he knew the house's lone occupant had fallen asleep while arguing on a skeptic's forum. WokeAF69 had been bragging he had rock-solid evidence that would prove once and for all the existence of bigfoot.

Not for long, you don't, he thought, and his hairy knuckle's polite knock took the back door off its hinges. WokeAF69 jerked from sleep with a startled yelp, dumping a bag of corn chips to the floor. Two steps, and the sasquatch had the man's cell phone crushed, a laptop broke in half. Moving to the kitchen, he yanked off the freezer door, snatching a frozen glass vial from under a bag of peas. And that

was a gift of the sasquatch, knowing *any* move you would make
before you made it.

WokeAf69 trembled as the sasquatch moved back to the man,
bent down, and shook the frosty-white tube in the man's face.
"I recommend," he growled, "you give this up. I could take you
out, but that's too much trouble." He could taste the man's fear,
excitement, and bitter tang of disappointment. "If you're a laughing
stock, that actually helps. Tabloids love a 'bigfoot love-slave' story."
He wrapped a thumb and forefinger around the man's throat. "So,
sing any song you like, but come looking for us again and...." He
gave a gentle squeeze that bulged WokeAF69's eyes.

He grabbed the bag of chips, was out the door and back to the
street before the man could start crying, protesting that he had earned
the evidence and it wasn't *fair*.

"Harsh," called out the crow.

"Chips!" the squirrel gushed.

The sasquatch tossed down the chips, and the rodent squealed
with delight as it darted into the bag. He slammed his mighty foot
down, chips and squirrel guts exploding from under his heel.

"Shit! What did you do that for?" yipped the coyote.

"I saved you the trouble of hunting him down," he grunted.
"Didn't he die happy?"

"Yeah, but..." She didn't know what else to say. Already the crow
was spiraling down to get at the chips. The coyote trotted along,
looking up at him.

"I don't understand you," she whined. "You have a gift, and you
just –"

"A *gift?*" he growled. "You think knowing everything is a *gift?*"
He drew his arm back and whipped the vial out into the dark. Only
he could hear the tiny splash it made in the river, and it said, "I'll
keep your secret..."

You would like to keep my bones covered, he thought. You could
trust water to want one thing – to drown the world.

"You know what I wish?" said the coyote. "I hope someday no
one cares if you guys are real or not. Maybe then you'll *really* feel
cursed."

175

"I would love the chance to find that out," he replied, but the coyote had stopped following him. He knew she would turn, look back at the smear of squirrel and chips, that she would growl and run to it, the crow would caw and lift up into the night, a chip in its beak.

He had a lot of ground to cover if he wanted to get back up to Colville, and he picked up his pace.

Behind him, the coyote growled.

I Was Told There Would Be Jetpacks

He was restless – he was always restless these days. Too damn many people were restless, that was certain. But that didn't mean you just went back to normal and did whatever the hell you wanted. He was convinced that was why his wife was in the hospital now. Some young *punk* – and he immediately shut down that train of thought, refusing to succumb to the mindset of a bitter old man. It could be some *old* punk – more than likely *was* someone of his age, or not much younger. They were stubbornly suspicious of change, to the point of fanaticism it seemed – an anti-revolutionary fervor, viva la status quo!

Still, when seeing the cavalier attitude of gathered youth, crowds of them flowing and mingling and uncaring, remarking that they weren't worried or just didn't care – they were young and didn't think Covid was a big deal, at least to them – it was easy to feel resentful and angry. And to blame them. And had he been more socially conscious when he had been their age? Would he have done the same? Well, no he wouldn't have because he hadn't been much of a partier back in the day. Still, he had felt the invincibility of youth, and could not imagine his own death.

He sure could now, though.

So he had allowed his restlessness to drive him out to the Bowl and Pitcher. The trail there was easier on his knees, yet you felt you were far away from the city. Early in the morning, any time of the year, he and his wife loved to stand on the bridge that stretched across the river and just listen to the water. She would tip her head back, eyes closed, her lips content to shape a soft smile. Her long hair – once a rich blonde and now a blinding white – would curl and wave around her head as her face caught the rays of the sun. Or, if in winter, snowflakes on her tongue.

He leaned on the railing, his head drooping over to look below him. The water speeding underneath the suspension bridge gave the illusion he was standing on the fantail of a ship as it churned through the ocean, making him feel that he was on a voyage into the unknown. His sunglasses would periodically mist over from his breath, his mask directing the airflow up to them, then clear as he inhaled, his lungs creating a rapid ebbing and flowing of fog. *Foolish, wearing your mask out here alone*, he thought. But he refused to remove it. *Stubborn old goat.* His wife would have insisted he keep it on, along with the battered fishing hat fending off sun-grown carcinoma from the glossy dome of his head, and the windbreaker to keep the chill off his bones. The jacket now lay draped over the bridge railing as the sun was higher.

Well, she had always kept her mask on, and look where that got her. And of course he had an immediate pang of guilt for thinking that. *She was careful, and she still got sick. And you didn't, and for some reason you blame yourself, and she would call you a big giant idiot for feeling that way, but there we have it.* At least she was off the ventilator now. But he still had no idea when he could see her again. Or touch her. He wanted desperately to be able to curl up next to her in bed again, the ritual of their bodies molded together, one of her ankles hooked over his, his hand cupping her breast, their breath joining together, rhythmic and whole.

A tear dropped onto his sunglasses, drawing a track through the condensation as it rolled across the lens, and he squeezed his eyes tight. *No pity-partying, you old bastard*, he thought. You've had a good life, and if it ended now you could still claim it was a happy one. There are people out there protesting to be able to have a life as easy and privileged as yours. To be able to take it for granted, even.

Isn't that what everyone deserved? Trouble was, there was a substantial amount of the population that just didn't want what *they* deserved, they wanted what *you* deserved as well. And that was the crux of it. There seemed to be a deep and inherent need for people to feel superior over someone else. That need bred the notion that if you were superior, then you could justify just about anything.

He used to think that people would want to know the truth of things, no matter what. Youthful idealization, sure. But didn't that make sense? But he now knew people only wanted to believe in what they *wanted* to be true. They probably hadn't changed, had always been like that. It was just easier for people that thought the same to find each other these days, and easier to ramp each other up, feed on each other's indignation and anger. There was a lot of anger out there.

Not that a lot of it wasn't justified, truly. Hell, *he* wanted to hurl a brick through a window these days, get in the face of authority and scream until his lungs scorched his throat. And that would never be satisfying, because it would have to erase his privileged apathy all these years. Oh, you could talk the talk, *believe* the talk, treat everyone as you wanted to be treated, acknowledge the injustices done to people of color or gender or identity, and yet he had never been active, never been vocal, never even protested against the war, or Tricky Dick. And now he feared he was too tired to make amends, and that in turn wanted to make him hurl a brick, to scream his guts loose.

But here he was on this bridge, alone, and right now he only wanted to kiss his wife and he was afraid he would never get the chance again. *Foolish. She is getting better.* But the doom in the pit of his stomach held the ankles of his better nature, and would not let it take flight.

How did we wind up here? he wondered. Where half the population is at odds with the other half, people are still starving and old enemies seem to be rising from their graves to plague us once more. *Hell, they were never gone, I guess.* But it was hard to quiet the astonished and angry child in him that expected the utopian dreams of his youth to be realized now. *I was told there would be*

179

jetpacks. I was told we would have flying cars. I was told there would be racial harmony. I was told no one would starve anymore. And then he felt more guilt for listing the whizz-bang over the social justice. *Is that where your priorities have truly been all these years, you miserable old nerd?* He did not regret a dime spent on exploration, of going to the moon, on to Mars and out of the solar system. *Curiosity* - knowledge - *needed to be fed, along with our bellies. We need to understand how* small *we are to the universe. Because, by God, thinking we're the center of it all sure as hell hasn't helped us much - or the only home we have.* And yet, those philosophical luxuries meant less than nothing to a child dying of starvation, he knew. The problem of dreaming big often came at the sacrifice of others.

He sighed, the lens of his sunglasses fogging over again. *We know enough about our place in the cosmos to treat each other better – to make amends and give everyone an equal share.* Perhaps it was time for him to dream of things closer to home, and let go the dogmas of the quiet past. *You are* not *too old to change. You are* not *too old to help those that haven't benefited from privilege that you've enjoyed all your life.* He wanted to be a better, more caring person. To be able to make a difference in lives less fortunate than his, and not end his days playing the bitter dirge of the old dead gods, sighing still for the things that might not be. He just wanted the chance to have his wife with him when he did. It was selfish, of course. But the ache of loss in him was his world right now.

A low buzzing registered in his ears. It had been growing for some time, and finally had made itself known over the roar of the river. He held still. *Murder hornet! Took you long enough to show up.* And he chuckled. *It's funny how everyone expects the year to just get worse, not better. Come on old man – dream bigger!* He imagined an advance scout for a fleet of saucers, scanning his body, and then blasting him and the bridge with a pyrotechnic death-ray, cauterizing their shadows into the basalt cliffs, clouds of steam billowing up from where the river used to be. Now *that* was a way to go out…

He opened his eyes and looked up. The condensation on his sunglasses had cleared, and he was mildly disappointed to see that it was only a drone. The machine hung in the air about four feet away from him, staring. *What in the Sam Hill?*

It seemed to be a cross between Ed-209 and the Central Scrutinizer. It could have looked menacing, but what looked like a loudspeaker on top made it look a little dorky instead. *Gotta work on your appearance, son*, he thought.

The droned bobbed up and down. He straightened, and waved at it. "Hello?" he said, annoyed. *Just leave me be, whoever you are. I was content to wallow in my misery. Alone.*

The drone drifted up, then pointed down, dropped to his level, and repeated the gesture. *Oh, for the love of Mike, just leave me alone.* What the hell was it doing out here? Probably getting one of those scenic-vista shots that is supposed to wow you on the local news. Look at the beauty of our backyard! As if we were unaware of it. *Am I spoiling the shot?* he wondered. *Does it want me to leave?* Anger bubbled up in him, stubborn and defiant. *To hell with you, I was here first.* He looked around, trying to locate the operator, but couldn't see anyone, glare from the morning sun obscuring anyone on the rocks above. He imagined an impatient young guy, thinking he was just doing his job and had to get his beauty shot, and this old man was in the way. Well, too bad.

The drone flashed and blinked lights at him, and continued its bobbing and dipping, as if it were some tropical bird dancing its come-hither ritual. It only served to irritate him further.

"You're not my type," he shouted over the roar of the water. "Leave me alone!"

The drone zoomed closer, causing him to take an involuntary step back. *Stupid, jumpy old man. Stand your ground!* But it was hard to not feel uneasy. Someone, somewhere, was controlling this machine, and they were probably enjoying their harassment of him, getting a giggle out of messing with some old dude, no doubt. Well, hell. Maybe they had their prejudices of the old like he did with the young. It was a battle as old as time, of course. But the combatants sure did shift sides over the years, didn't they? And not a one of them ever saw it coming.

The drone swooped in an arc before him, left and right, as if it were a pendulum, then began its bobbing again.

"You're boring me," he murmured.

The drone leveled out, then crept closer. He stood still.

"Do it!" crackled out of the loudspeaker.

He frowned. Do what? What does it want me to do?

The drone bobbed up, then dove down. Bobbed up, dove.

"Do it! Do it! Do it!"

He shrugged, palms up. "I don't know what you want. I don't *get* it."

The machine tipped its nose to the river again. "Do it!"

It's just a recording, he thought. *It's playing a message. What the hell is it meant for? What could it be trying to provoke –*

And then he knew. The shock of it, that cold realization that made you feel like your body was contracting into your gut, made him step back and a hard anger settled over him. *They want me to jump off the bridge!*

The rational part of his brain tried to convince him that it was nonsense, that surely no one would be that callous and twisted. *Oh, so there's no video out there of two teens laughing at and taunting a black man as he drowned? If two monsters could do* that, *it is surely within the realms of possibility that someone would try to convince a lonely old man to jump in the river. And record it for their amusement…*

"Do it!" the drone ordered, and repeated the command in brainless repetition.

Screw you, he thought. *Enough of this.* He turned, and swatted the air with his left hand – the universal old-man wave of dismissal. The drone continued to blast out its message, and he scooped up his jacket from the railing, shook it out as if he were ready to don it, and then in one smooth motion he cast it like a fishing net and it sailed out and snagged two of the rotors of the drone and the machine tipped drunkenly on its side, the change in pitch of the rotors sounded like a startled cat, and it dropped out of sight.

He blinked, and a rush of elation surged through him – something he hadn't felt in…well, a *very* long time. He was convinced he would miss the drone, that it would dodge away and continue its taunting, and he would be out a jacket. Which would have been no big deal, but it was the gesture that was the point. He thought that it would have been a momentary shock to the operator, giving them a shot of adrenaline as they jerked away from his jacket, and that would be that. Well, they were probably pretty shocked *now*, it was safe to say...

He leaned over the railing, and might have caught a glimpse of his jacket being dragged under the churning water, sliding around a rock and then gone for good. Huh. *That was probably a pretty expensive toy,* he thought. *Someone is pretty darned mad right now.* Interestingly, he was not apprehensive, not afraid that someone would come running up ready to beat an old man senseless. He calmly removed his sunglasses and tucked them in his shirt pocket, then removed his hat and mask and tucked them under his belt, pulling his shirt over them.

Probably best if you just got moving. He turned, and began to walk across the bridge to the trail head that lead to the parking lot above. *You just littered,* he thought, and felt a pang of regret. *Even if you had missed the drone, your jacket was going into the river, and that was thoughtless. Enough crap in it already. Stupid old man – think!* But he continued to replay the glory of it, seeing the drone tip on its side and drop, and a grin spread across his face. He felt *energized.* He had made a *stand.* It was a pretty pathetic one, in the grand scheme of things. But hell, baby steps, right?

As he reached the edge of the parking lot, an agitated man in a faded Iron Maiden t-shirt and clutching a controller came huffing down from the rocky columns to the north. "Hey!" he yelled.

And here we go...

The man, who appeared to be in his late thirties, ran up to him. "Hey!" he shouted again. "Did you see some old guy in a hat? Had a mask on?"

He paused, as if considering the question. "Oh," he said slowly. "Oh, yes. Yes I did. Thought it was a bit strange, having a mask on out here."

183

The drone operator stared at him for a second, then tipped his head back and forth in impatience. "So where did you see him?"

Again he paused. "Well, let's see. Oh. It was on the steps going up to the trail on the other side of the river? Seemed to be in a hurry. Didn't even – "

But the operator was tearing off in the direction of the bridge.

Good luck son. He didn't know if he had been recorded. Probably, but he bet it was on a card on the drone, and any footage of him was now being battered and tumbled under the waters of the Spokane River. No matter – he could certainly afford to pay for some idiot's drone if he got identified.

He climbed into his Subaru and turned the ignition over, wondering what he would do with the rest of his day. Was there a protest downtown? It was Sunday, so…maybe?

He continued to replay the take-down of the drone, watching his windbreaker sailing out to intercept the machine.

Soon, he began to imagine the jacket as a brick.

Meanwhile, On a Cul-De-Sac in Rathdrum, Idaho

*N*ot yet, not yet, not yet –
The words rapped out in an endless loop in his head, as annoying as fingers ceaselessly drumming on a desktop. Yet his exhausted brain would not stop generating them any more than it would stop his heart or not allow him to breathe. Will worried that the words would soon be the only thing left flitting through his mind, like a bird trapped in a house, battering itself against windows to try and find a way out.

But... *not yet.*

"What are you up to, Billy?"

Will stiffened, and then sighed inwardly. *Jesus. Would that ever stop being annoying?* he thought. His constant internal chant was distracted into silence – or at least muted for now. *Why can't you just call me Will like everyone else?* Except most everyone else had his or her own nickname too, and more than likely hated it.

"Well, what does it look like I'm doing, Deke?" Will replied calmly, and continued to load supplies into the back of his truck.

"I'd say it looks like you plan on going on your trip," Deke said quietly, in that tone Will assumed was meant to sound patient and reasonable, but always came across as condescending.

"I'd say you hit the nail on the head there, Deke. We are taking a trip." Will tightened up some cords to secure some gas cans, then reached down and grabbed a backpack to stow in the truck's bed.

There were several moments of uncomfortable silence, and then Deke said, "I thought we talked about this already. Decided it was a bad idea."

Will sighed audibly this time, but finally turned to face Deke. He was only mildly surprised to see the man's teenaged children standing behind him. A boy and a girl – the "Spooky Twins," Lori and Ashley used to call them. Both had jet-black hair, ruler straight, that contrasted with their father's wavy dishwater blond locks. The girl's hair fell to her shoulders, the boy's cut crisp and neat above the ears. Both shared the heavy dark lashes that framed their wide, staring eyes that would have given them a look of perpetual astonishment if a sense of detachment weren't so prevalent. Will wasn't surprised to see that each had a gun strapped to their hips. And Deke as well. His own pistol felt extremely heavy on *his* hip right now. *Everybody's packin'*, he thought, and suppressed a grin. That sounded like some sort of rockabilly tune. *Jesus, the thoughts that pop into your head at times like these...*

Will studied Deke silently, and tried not to feel intimidated by the man. *That's what he wants*, he thought. *The stupid sunglasses, always planted on his face.* Dark and impenetrable – *"I can see you but you can't see me!"* Ellie was right – this guy was a master manipulator. Or wanted to be. Tried *desperately* to be. But no matter how hard or how subtle he tried to manipulate you, people usually saw right through him – dark glasses or no.

Ellie says he's a sociopath, Will thought, but wasn't sure he agreed. He thought labels like that were too easily applied. But there sure was something unsettling about the man – no getting around it. Lori agreed with her mother's assessment, but went beyond sociopath to psychopath. Will basically agreed with Ashley's succinct diagnosis of "creepy fucker".

"Well, Deke," Will began, matching Deke's patronizing tone, "what I remember is *you* declaring that going to find my daughters was a bad idea, but everyone else thinking it was none of your business."

Will didn't expect any sort of visible reaction so he wasn't surprised at Deke's seemingly impassive and unflinching demeanor.

The silence stretched, and Will imagined the clacking and whirring sounds of ancient computers inside the man's head as he processed what had been said. And, as more often than not when Deke heard something he didn't like, he pretended not to have heard it at all.

* * *

Ellie was certain her husband didn't realize the danger he was in right now. He usually wasn't so obtuse about people – could read them fairly well. She didn't think he was *blind*, per se, when it came to Deke. It was clear he didn't care for the man, but he believed in giving people the benefit of the doubt. Trouble was, that was a dangerous thing to do these days.

Ellie stood on the porch of her parents' house, almost hidden in the shadows of the early morning. Not like she was trying to be covert – the girl had given her a quick glance, but her twin brother only seemed to be able to focus on the back of his dad's head. Deke, of course, would act as if she wasn't there at all, but she was certain he knew she was on the porch, watching.

Bastard never liked me – not that I give a shit, she thought. The feeling was most definitely mutual. *The son of bitch probably resented the fact he can't add the "ee" sound to the end of my name without sounding like a twat.* She gave a quiet laugh at the thought, and the girl turned her head and stared at Ellie again, longer this time, with those intense eyes. Ellie held her gaze until the girl directed her attention back to her father. *That's right honey,* she thought. *Even with one good eye I can beat your ass in a staring contest.* She might have felt the familiar tug of pity she usually had for the twins if the situation wasn't so damned tense. Ellie resisted the urge to dig a finger up under the patch that covered the hole where her right eye used to be and scratch the hell out of the empty socket. Sometimes it itched so bad it burned, and right now it was on fire. The sensation only increased the thrumming of the live wires that were her nerves and she wanted to fly off the porch, screeching like a banshee, and pistol-whip the living fuck right out of Deke's

187

stupid curly blond head. Instead, she settled for taking a step forward – out of the shadows - and leaning against the porch post. She could feel the cool wood through her denim jacket and corduroy shirt, and it was just another irritation so she pulled away and crossed her arms across her chest.

The girl turned to look at her again. Was that a glimmer of nervousness on that usually vacuous face? Ellie arched her left eyebrow, and the girl jerked her head back to her father again.

Good Lord, can this get any weirder? she wondered. *Why couldn't we have been on the road before the bastard knew what we were up to?*

The security door behind her creaked open, but Ellie kept her focus on her husband and Deke. She heard the door shut with a clang, and her dad was standing next to her, his wizened eyes taking in the scene.

"What's that ass-wipe want?" he asked, a little too loud. As usual.

Both of the twins turned this time and stared, but Deke's attention never wavered from William. Ellie tipped her head towards her father and whispered, "I don't know daddy. But I've got a bad feeling about this. Do you think you could go get the doc? Maybe go back in and head out the back way, though?"

Her father nodded his bushy gray head - hair longer now than she could ever remember it being! – and slipped silently back into the shadows. The door squeaked open, but shut softer this time.

* * *

"So…what?" Deke asked. "You just plan on driving all the way down to…Eugene, was it? Where your girls are?"

Will stopped fiddling with the gear in the back of his truck and turned again to Deke, deciding to give the man his full attention. He stared into the man's black, featureless granny glasses.

"Yeah, Deke. If we can," he stated firmly.

"And what do you think the odds are of being able to do that?" asked Deke.

"No Idea."

"Huh. And the odds of finding your girls, too?"

"No idea, Deke."

"Well I'm not a mathematician, Billy, but I've got to figure the odds are pretty astronomical, wouldn't you say?"

Will studied the man's impassive features, but consciously directed his gaze into the flat lenses that covered Deke's eyes. *You will not intimidate me,* he thought. If he could convey that message through sheer willpower just by staring into the man's sunglasses, he was sure Deke would go away.

He wondered if the man could understand what he and Ellie felt – not knowing for months if their daughters were alive or dead. Or - of all the horrors - undead. The thought made his gut clench in a spasm of fear – a feeling all too familiar for far too long now. How worry, guilt and shame could make you leap from the bed in the middle of the night to pace randomly, anxiously, until you were exhausted enough to crash for a few moments until the unease and distress would dig its way into your spine like the tip of a switchblade and your legs would tremble and shake and bounce you to your feet until all you could do was pace some more and mutter useless promises to a God you weren't sure was listening anyways.

No, he was now certain Deke couldn't feel anything like that. What the man could *actually* feel Will was sure no one would ever know. The man's wife had died several years ago – "accidental overdose of sleeping pills" or some such thing. Will was hazy on the details, and it was not something he thought was any of his business to know too much about. But the cul-de-sac Ellie's parents lived on was rife with suicide and murder gossip, with Ellie's mom firmly in the "it was murder" camp and her dad sided with those that thought "it was suicide to get away from that creepy bastard." Will did feel that the man's reaction to his wife's death felt carefully...*prepared*, for lack of a better word. And he had seemed to enjoy the attention for some time.

Perhaps the man *was* a sociopath, and could never understand the needs of someone else – caring about someone else more than yourself. Will let out an explosive sigh.

"Well Deke, it's like this – I know the odds of finding my

daughters are way higher if I *don't* do anything, wouldn't you say?"

"Unless they're on their way here," Deke replied.

"Then maybe we will run into each other."

Deke smiled, refusing to give that speculation the dignity of a reply.

"Look," Will said, closing his eyes and trying to calm his frayed nerves, to not let his rising irritation with the man show. "We know the...war, battle - *whatever* - in Spokane has run its course. Marty made it as far as Ritzville and seemed to think 395 was doable."

"I'd like to know how he came to that conclusion without heading down it." Deke paused to give that statement some weight, and then added quietly, "And we have heard that the Tri-Cities is hell on earth."

Will's eyes tightened, the lids squeezing in the sudden hot tears that wanted pour out of him. His stomach clenched, his teeth ground against themselves as his heart pounded loudly in his ears. Fury was building in him, swelling, rising with the ever-present panic he had been feeling for so long now. He was a man who kept his temper. He reasoned out problems calmly and sensibly. But right now he was having trouble keeping his right hand from reaching down to grab the pistol that nestled against his hip and fire round after round into Deke's face – right between those blank lenses covering the man's eyes. The idea was as startling to him as it was enticing, and the fact that he wasn't shocked by it – wasn't even ashamed he could think of doing such a thing – was kind of a marvel to him. After all, he had killed the dead and living alike in defense of the neighborhood and the lives that dwelled there. It would be so easy to use the gun as a means to end an argument. And right now the temptation was *massive.*

Will released a shaky breath, drew in another, released. His heart still hammered, but his nerves weren't so jangly and raw. *Losing control will not help anyone,* he thought. *You will not find the girls if you turn into a madman. Let that happen if...if things don't work out.* The idea of letting the demons out, of turning into an insane, gibbering wreck as a consolation prize for when his worst fears were realized helped calm him further. *Not yet, not yet, not yet. Miracles can happen – even in this day and age. You may see your girls again. Not yet, not yet...*

He opened his eyes, the corners of them wet and cold in the morning air. He found his voice.

"I don't expect you can understand, Deke. I don't think you're capable of it – to have empathy for someone else. That's just the way you -"

"I do understand why you want to go, Billy, but you haven't thought –"

"I *have* thought about it – Jesus! I haven't *thought* about anything else!" Will stopped and drew in several deep breaths to control himself. "No," he continued, "it doesn't make sense. It's reckless and foolhardy. But if we can make it down to Eugene, then that's a start. If our daughters aren't there, then you can bet they will have left some sort of message for us."

Deke stared at Will, weighing the impact of what he would say. Gears whirring and relays clacking. "If they were capable of doing that," he finally said.

* * *

Ellie saw William's hands clench into tight, white-knuckled balls. She had never seen her husband so agitated – even during the teenaged years of the girls: two headstrong, smart-mouthed and very sharp girls (*Paybacks are a bitch*, her mom would reply sweetly whenever Ellie complained about her daughters). Ellie found her hand on the grip of her pistol under her arm – she was unaware she had grasped it. The girl was staring at her again. Ellie made no effort to drop her hand from under her jacket, but the girl made no move for the gun on her hip. She just stared. Ellie could see nothing in the girl's face other than that slightly surprised look she always shared with her brother. Perhaps she had imagined the nervous look the girl gave before? If Ellie wasn't so keyed up, she might try a smile of encouragement. But she was certain she could only manage a crooked grimace and who the hell knew how the girl might interpret

191

that?

Ellie flicked her gaze back to her husband, taking in his posture –
a steel cable about to snap. And Deke... Relaxed. Unfazed.
Complacent. So why did he seem more dangerous than her husband?

Ellie was tired of the talking without saying anything. This was a
conversation that had been hashed out over and over already – from
initial possibilities and probabilities to serious discussions of if the
trip was even feasible. In the end, the neighborhood had decided if
they wanted to go, then it was their call. Brutal honesty dictated that
no one thought they had a very good chance of finding their
daughters, but best of luck to them. Except for Deke, who seemed to
think it was his duty to quash the idea completely. And the fucker did
not seem to get the idea he had no say in the matter. He could argue
about valuable resources and duty to the community, but Ellie knew
it was just about Deke not getting his way, and that the man could
not stand it.

And here they were, talking it over yet again. Her husband could
labor a point to death – often times not content to finally win an
argument when it was conceded but to continue on and list his
validities until you just wanted to punch him. Ellie remembered
Ashley several years ago, treading dangerously close to disrespect
blurting out, "Just stop *talking!*" Ellie wanted to scream this to her
husband now. *Enough with the forced politeness. Just stop talking!*

* * *

Will could taste copper in his mouth, and realized he had bit his
tongue. But the sharp pain brought clarity of mind. *Enough.* The idea
that Deke was baiting him – possibly trying to provoke a dangerous
response from him helped to calm him more than any meditation - or
Ellie's soothing touch - could. *He would love an excuse to shoot me,*
he realized. Will worked the stiffness out of his jaw, and managed a
polite smile.

"Well Deke, it's been nice chatting with you," he said. "But we
want to get on the road. So if you would be so kind as to piss off and
leave us be, I would appreciate it."

Deke responded with his impassive stare for a moment, then with a move as smooth as a drape billowing in an open window, drew his gun and shot Will above his right knee.

* * *

The casualness of it was what shocked Ellie. No warning – no telegraphing of the punch – just a quick reach as if he had an itch to scratch on his leg, then gun in hand and *boom!* Her mouth hung open for far too long, then Ellie screamed in fury, and she pulled out her own gun tucked up under her arm.

* * *

The pain was not as immediate as the surprise of it. *Holy shit*, he thought. *He didn't need an excuse!* Then a white-hot poker jabbed its way into his thigh and his leg crumpled, dropping him to the cement of the driveway. He slapped his hand against the side of his truck to keep himself from lying down completely, and looked up at Deke, too shocked and outraged to sputter any of the indignities he felt. He heard Ellie scream, and he flinched.

"I'm sorry, Billy," Deke said, shrugging his shoulders unapologetically. After all, his hand had been forced. "Looks like you won't be driving anywhere in your condition."

The impassive and neutral expression behind the sunglasses enraged Will, and he pushed off the truck, shifting his weight to his left arm as his right hand flapped around, feeling for the gun on his hip.

Deke raised his gun again and said, "Now Billy, this doesn't have to go any further. Patty will get you fixed up –" And then the man's forehead exploded, a squib of blood and brains pattering down on Will as he watched Deke drop lifeless to the driveway. Behind him stood the man's daughter, gun still raised, and a look of apology on her face.

"He shouldn't have done that," she stammered. "I don't know why he did that, but he *shouldn't* have." Her brother stared at her,

193

eyes wider than ever, mouth open.

So that's what they look like when they're actually surprised, thought Will. Laughter began to pant and hiss its way past his teeth. *You and me both, kid. You and me both.*

* * *

Ellie came so very close to shooting the girl that she was certain she had done it - and was shocked not to feel the recoil of the firearm and hear the bark of the shot. Still, she continued to train the gun on the girl, her trigger finger stiff and locked and she was afraid she would never straighten it again. The girl – *Jesus, what the fuck was her name?* – was saying something to William. Ellie's legs finally found a way to move her forward, to her husband, when Doctor Patrick shot up the driveway, her long copper ponytail swishing in the sunlight that had finally crawled up over the horizon, deciding at last to make it a proper day. Ellie's father trailed behind, puffing and wheezing. The doctor knelt by William, her med-kit slung off her shoulder to land in the stream of blood that ran from Deke's head.

"Aw, shit, Will," Ellie heard her mutter. "What sort of trouble did you get into now?"

* * *

Will gasped out a chuckle, and began to shake. Nausea began to simmer in his stomach.

"Just having a friendly little chat, Doc," he muttered.

He couldn't think of anything wittier to say. Weren't you supposed to have some sort of clever quip in a situation like this? Take the cigar from between your clenched teeth and jam it into the wound to seal it off, then hop up and shrug it off with only a mild grimace? Instead, he knew he was going into shock. Cold sweat crept down his neck, and a shiver swept across the backs of his arms.

He saw Ellie running down the drive towards him, her right arm stiff and angled away from her, clutching her 9 mm in a death grip. In a heartbeat, she knelt down by him and he leaned gratefully into her.

"Let's get you lying down, Will," Doctor Patrick said, and Ellie shifted back to use her lap as a pillow, but the doc motioned her to let his head rest on the concrete so his feet would be elevated above his head by the slope of the driveway. Ellie shrugged off her jacket and tucked it gently under his head.

Will watched the doc's tanned arms explore his leg, then turned his head and stared into the blank eyes of Deke, the man's sunglasses knocked askew. It seemed so wrong – he remembered a movie when he was a kid – *Westworld* – and the poster for the movie had half of Yul Brynner's face missing, with just machinery underneath. That was what he expected to see under the ruin of Deke's head. Not mere blood, tissue and brains. It seemed the damndest thing to expect…

Ellie's dad moved cautiously up to Deke's daughter, who had finally lowered her gun, but still gripped it tightly.

"Hey honey," his father-in-law said in soothing tones, "how about we secure your weapon? Huh? Yeah? There we go. Good girl. Good girl."

The girl looked into the old man's eyes.

"He shouldn't have done that," she stated again.

"I know honey. I know. But he did, and you were very brave to…do what you did"

Holy shit, thought Will. *Who knew the cranky old goat had a gentle streak to him?*

"Why don't we move outta here, huh? Let the doc take things from here? You too, son?" The old man spread his arms to gather up the twins and herd them into the house. They turned meekly away, but then the boy twisted back and gave the body of his father a vicious kick.

* * *

Ellie bent over and gave her husband a long deep kiss. He shivered again, tried to smile and raised an arm up half-heartedly. He released a shaky gasp, and tears began to flow from the corners of his eyes.

"We can't go now," he muttered. We can't *go*." A sob burst out of him, and he gritted his teeth and his face twisted into a mask of rage. A growl of fury huffed in his throat.

"I know, baby," Ellie said, and the tears began to run from her now, little drops splashing onto her husband. "When your leg's better, we will. *We will.*"

William nodded his head in jerks, his body shaking. He panted, short little gasps that seemed to have a rhythm to them. Ellie could have sworn it sounded like *not yet, not yet, not yet...*"

The Lure of Tall Bridges After Midnight

W hat's that tapping?" the girl asks.
    We sit on the wide bridge railing, the sturdy concrete leaching the girl's body heat from her. The early morning air is cold as well, and she is miserable and trembling. Her stretched nerves no doubt add to the quick spasms that shake her thin frame. Fog had formed just after midnight, adding intimacy to such an open and public space, but obscuring the falls of the Spokane river – for *her*, anyway. And it is probably just as well. The girl is terrified, but does her best not to show it. Compared to the power the water likes to exhibit in the spring, it is a mere trickle in the fall. Still, it could be daunting enough to dissuade someone that was contemplating jumping. Or a lure to those more serious to the task. I knew how serious the girl was about it. But did she know?

"What's that tapping?" she asks again. "Is that you? If it is, quit it. Sounds like some Morris code shit, or something."

"Does it?" I ask. "I apologize. It might be something I do if I were nervous."

"What do *you* have to be nervous about?" she sneers, or does her best to. She is betrayed by a bout of shuddering.

"I am sitting near someone who is considering jumping into the river below. Don't you think that should make me nervous?"

"You don't seem the nervous type," she says, then adds in a whisper, "Besides, why should you care?"

197

I remain silent to her question. It's probably best not to inform her that I really *don't* care, so to speak. But it is in my best interests to try and help her.

We have been here for over an hour, and that is only after I convinced her to sit and not stand on the railing. That had been a considerable task in and of itself. You may very well ask why I don't just snatch her and be done with it, but that is ridiculous and will only exacerbate her problems. She will see me as another authority figure she wants nothing to do with. Not that it would trouble me, but I am here to help her find her way, and not just off the bridge.

The dark below our feet shifts with fog and rushing water, although I doubt she sees it. Strange enough, I can feel its pull, and wonder briefly if she is fae and effecting my perception. Nonsense. She is a human girl. The dark seems to be holding secrets this morning, and not many secrets are kept from me. Interesting.

"It's 'Morse' by the way," I finally answer.

"What?"

"Morse code, not 'Morris' code."

She rolls her eyes and curls a lip as her head waggles in contempt. "I'll sleep better knowing *that*," she mutters.

"Let us hope so."

She lets out a disgusted sigh. "Why are you bothering me?"

"Because you asked me to."

"The hell I did!"

"What's written on the card in your back pocket?"

She stiffens, and now actually turns her head to me. She is very young. Far too young to entertain any notion of her life ending, much less believe in it. Her eyes are a golden blue, almost green, and faint freckles explode across her face like the shadow of fireworks against her dusky skin. Her chocolate black hair is creeping back, driving away the teal and purple coloring that had disguised it.

She shakes her head. "This is bullshit," she mutters. "Seriously? You some *angel* or something?"

I laugh. "Hardly."

"Then what the hell?"

"I am what you have wished was real, and perhaps always knew in your heart, is."

Now she laughs. "Great. So I'm crazy. I've always been told that, now I know."

"You know *better*."

"I don't know *anything*," she says, and her voice cracks, and not due to the cold.

We sit near a pavilion, a bison skull eavesdropping on our conversation. It strains to see us, but its eye sockets look perpetually down to the river with an expression as if it has dropped something that is gone for good, but it's still in the confused moment of unacceptance.

We sit in silence, the muted rush of the river below, and the occasional car on the bridge. They don't see us, because I don't want them to.

"Seriously!" she barks. "*Dude* – enough with the tapping!"

"I apologize," I say. But my fingernails remain active against the concrete.

"I am reminded – you would see it as so many years ago as to be unimaginable – of another girl I met on a bridge," I offer. "She, too, thought her life was over."

The girl rolls her eyes again, and sighs heavily. "This where you start throwing Jesus in my face?"

"I never had a chance to meet him, so I never proselytize for those I cannot vouch for personally," I assure her. "This girl," I continue, "was despondent at not being able to call unicorns again."

"You gotta be kidding me."

"Not at all. They are as real as you or I."

"I have my doubts about *you*," she mutters.

"You don't. Or I wouldn't be here."

She snorts.

"And so this girl was ready to jump from the bridge to the river below. It wasn't as high as *this* bridge to be sure, but she could not swim and so would drown. She had been raped, and despaired that since she had lost her virginity she could no longer call to the unicorn. I convinced her that her virtue did not reside in an insignificant scrap of flesh, and should mean nothing to a unicorn, or anyone."

"So she didn't jump?"

"She did not. She lived to be a grandmother, happy as was possible in those days."

"And did she still meet with unicorns?"

"Oh, heavens no. Unicorns are fickle and worthless beasts. Vainglorious and condemnatory. Ask yourself, would you want the companionship of something that thought so low of you for not being a virgin? In a case of *rape*, no less? She was far better off without their company."

She actually laughs, an honest outburst that takes her by surprise.

"Take all unicorns and compress them to weigh on a scale, and the combined weight of their worth does not equal the measure of yours," I tell her. I am almost certain that I mean it.

"Wow, you really hate unicorns," she laughs.

"I hate no *one*, or no *thing*. That is just the fact of it. Unicorns are unfit even to keep lawns mowed."

"I bet their horns would dig gouges into the turf," she laughs.

"I had not thought of it, but yes, I suppose they would at that."

I smile, and I can tell the idea of amusing me pleases her. While most humans are charmed by elvish folk, most of your kind are pleased to have a joke laughed at, that you brightened someone's day with a witty remark. I sometimes wonder if that is ultimately how you decide to tolerate each other. I think she wonders that as well, and is weighing those precious little moments against all the ones that make life intolerable. She frowns, and grows silent again. I am certain most people in her life, at best, are too preoccupied with their own troubles to care about her wit, much less be entertained by it. And those left over are only concerned of what else they can take from her, since charm and wit have no value to them. I am also certain she does not want to jump, but the impulsiveness of youth can be a dangerous thing at times.

I can tell she wants to chastise me again with my constant finger tapping, but has lost the energy to complain about it. She understands nervous twitches, after all.

"Have you not grown tired of sitting here?" I ask. "You are awfully cold."

"Why aren't you?" she asks, through chattering teeth.

I shrug. "I don't get cold. Or hot. My kind isn't bothered by temperature."

"Are you," she begins, and falters. "Are you really...?"

"Yes," I say, and remove the charms from my clothing that make them appear modern. "I am an elf. I would offer you my cloak, but I fear you are too proud to take it."

"Are there a lot of you? Here?"

"I am the only elf in Spokane, but we are rare enough in your world. Most elves are content to stay in the faerealm, but there are many fae on Earth, blended in so as not to be noticed. You no doubt have met many in your short life and have not known it. Or, to be more precise, did not know it *consciously*."

"So why are *you* here?"

"In Spokane? It is as good a place as any, truly. I have lived elsewhere, and will again. I am content where I am for now."

"No, why are you *here*, in our world?"

My attempt at dodging the question having failed, I am forced into honesty.

"I am exiled here, banished from the faerealm until I have served my sentence."

Her eyes widen. "No shit?"

I nod.

"So...what did you do to get stuck here?"

"It is a complicated matter, and my own," I answer.

"And so the card I found...do you do this to keep occupied? Help people, I mean?"

"Truly, it is part of my sentence as well."

She frowns, then growls in disgust. Even the bison skull seems disappointed in me.

"So...you're just like some sort of fucking social worker?" she snaps at me.

"I assure you, I am far from being a social worker."

"But this is your fucking *job*, you prick?"

201

"I don't *have* to help people if I don't want to. But I will never return to the land of fae if I don't, that is certain."

"Oh, keep the worthless street-kid from jumping off a bridge to get brownie points, is that all?"

"Well, it is best not to insult a brownie," I say, but the joke is lost on her.

"Just another creeper looking for something from me," she sneers. "Should have been able to tell by your fidgety fingers – all the worst pervs have some sort of creepy habit."

"If you are looking for validation from a stranger, I can only offer that it would remain a far more interesting world with you in it, rather than not. If you are looking for acts generated from the goodness of hearts, look to your own first, girl, and then expect it from others."

"Oh, fuck *you*. What do you know about my life? What I've gone through?"

"I know that you do not want to jump."

She laughs. "Do you?"

"I do. And I can prove it to you," I answer, and then shove her off the bridge to the river.

She is so shocked she doesn't even scream as she plunges into the black mist below.

"Oh, *no*," the bison skull remarks.

* * *

Footfalls tap their way towards me from out of the fog, the tempo increasing the closer they come. They have an urgent, musical rhythm, generated by someone who has learned grace from dancing with the sidhe for many of her years. Siobhan will move with an elvish fluidity until the grave halts her. She does not dance for pleasure any longer, because she cannot stop dancing at all now. It can be a mesmerizing event, watching her move about her shop, even to an ancient elf. However, being that I tend to find beauty in aspects of the mundane, perhaps my opinion cannot be trusted.

She is near breathless as she reaches my side, not from the running, but shock having drawn her breath away.

"Did she *jump?*" she gasps, and peers over the railing to the void below.

"Not at all," I say. "I pushed her."

Her head snaps around, her French braid - auburn with threads of silver – snaps like a whip at me. Her tawny eyes are wide and full of disbelief. She is nearing 60 years of age, but appears to be shy of 40. Dancing with the sidhe usually takes its toll on people, but Siobhan was able to drink in that energy – even if she did lose her toes in the bargain.

"You *what?*" she shouts, her breath puffing into its own fog, and it is lovely to see it mingle, mix and then become absorbed into the surrounding mist.

"I had to convince her that she wanted to live far more than to take an early exit from life," I explain.

"By pushing her off the *bridge?*"

"I understand that many of those that survive an intentional fall from a great height instantly regret the choice they made as they plummet. I feel that experience is the best form of enlightenment."

Her mouth works, yet no sounds issue. She feels this is a new low for me, I can tell. The urge to push me from the bridge radiates from her like an oncoming stormfront. Finally her eyes flutter and close tight. She takes a deep breath, opens her eyes and stares me down.

"Are we so beneath you that you value a tough-love lesson over our lives? Do you think *enlightenment* made her happy as she died? *Shit* – she may *not* be dead yet - I am such an idiot!" Her hand darts to a pocket in her deep green overcoat, and plucks out a phone. My gloved hand reaches out to stay hers.

"Listen," I say.

The sound of rocks crashing against each other float up from below, growing stronger until a twisted stone of a hand grasps the railing, chips of concrete crushing out from under it, and then a rough blanket, trussed up into the shape of a sack, is slung up and over onto the sidewalk. A quiet cry of pain is muffled by the makeshift bag.

Siobhan releases a disgusted sigh, and a distorted boulder of a head peeks over the railing and cracks open a smile as it spies her.

"Hullo, luv," the troll says.

Delicate steam vents from Siobhan's nostrils, and she shakes her head with anger.

"I must say I am disappointed in you, P.K. – playing along with his cruel games."

The troll actually looks wounded. "What are ya pissed at me for? I caught her, didn't I?"

"I understand *him*," she says, and jabs a finger at me. "He probably finds 'beauty' in her terror, the twisted bastard. But you? I thought the fish you liked to fry are bigger - not scared, defeated little girls."

The troll rests his chin in a pout on the railing. "Now, look. There I was, minding myself and my business, trying to watch some vintage Bowie on YouTube when I hears this tappin', tappin', tappin'. All subtle and quiet like, but it's driving me mad. It just don't stop. But after a bit, I suss it as a message, and then I pays attention to it. Cuttin' to the chase scene, luv, what would you have me do? Let the child drop into the river and over the falls?"

Her face softens, and she moves to him, lays her hands on the sides of his face, and kisses him lightly on the forehead. "I forget sometimes you are one of his tough love cases. Tell me, P.K.," she whispers, and taps gently on his rocky exterior, "did his transformation of your skin make you feel *enlightened?*"

"Don't know about that," the troll mutters, and glares at me side-eyed. "But sunlight don't kill me now. Not like I'm apt to partake of it. But I could if I wanted ta."

"May I remind you," I say, "that there was a time you would have eaten that girl for dinner instead of saving her, so perhaps there *was* a bit of enlightenment for you. Regardless, *I* did not pick this bridge, the *girl* did. I hardly see why I am a villain in this."

"Villain might be a bit strong, mate. Arsehole might fit ya, though." Siobhan chuckles at the troll's low wit.

"Well, I am here to learn, and I learn from the best. You are the best asshole I know, P.K." I finally swing my legs around to stand on the sidewalk.

The troll roars with laughter. "I do believe I hit 'im right in 'is pride!"

The troll likes to believe his insults have an effect on me, and I tend to indulge him from time to time. It makes him easier to deal with.

"You fuckers gonna let me out of here?" the girl yells from inside the blanket. "Or are you gonna keep jackin' off out there?"

Both Siobhan and the troll have the decency to look ashamed that they had forgotten her. I, of course, had not. I could tell she would need fresh air soon. But, since I apparently have a certain reputation to maintain, I felt she could decide on her own when containment would grow too stuffy.

"Ah," the troll says. "I best be moving on, then. The poor child don't need to set eyes upon my ugly mug. Nice to see ya again, Siobhan." He stares at me momentarily. "Always a pleasure, you elvish twat." His fist opens, and the blanket unfolds like a seed pod as he drops from view. The girl is huddled around herself, and she gulps in the frigid morning air in ragged gasps. Her eyes snap and blink rapidly as they dart a look at Siobhan, and then target me. She lets out a long, angry scream.

"And people wonder why I have trust issues!"

"You should always have trust issues, girl," I offer. "Always."

"Especially with him," Siobhan says, and the girl looks back to her.

"Who the hell are you, now? Who caught me in the blanket?"

"My name is Siobhan. I own a shop over on First."

"That one with the green vines painted all over it?"

"Indeed."

"That your name on it, then? Siobhan's Apothecary?"

"Yes."

"Always wondered how you pronounced it. Sha-von. Sha-*von*. Huh."

"You were always welcome to come in and ask."

The girl shakes her head. "Most shop owners just run you off, don't want to know you exist, much less see you."

"Only if you're there to rob me."

"I'm not on that level yet."

"Well, let's make sure we keep it that way. What's your name, by the way?"

The girl's lips press together, and she stares at her feet.

"Good instincts," I tell her. "Names have power over you, true ones. Never give it freely."

"We can come up with a new one for you," Siobhan suggests.

"What's all this 'we' crap all of a sudden?" the girl snorts.

"Whether you like it or not, it is a 'we' now," I inform her.

"Is that so?" she practically spits. "I've got news for you, fairy-boy, I don't have to – "

"Let me give you some news, girl," I interrupt, and she falls silent, her eyes sullen. "None of us are as free as we wish to be. You think that running from family woes and living on the street will bring you less trouble? An uncle that gets too familiar, and the frustration that your drug addict of a mother ignores his 'fidgety-fingers' is intolerable, yes. That your father won't let you live with him and his new family because you 'just don't fit in' is wounding to the core, yes. You survived a summer on the streets, yet cruel weather is closing in, and the people surrounding you will grow just as cruel. The world will eat you alive, and you know this. That's why you came to be on this bridge now. If you had jumped, the splash you might have made in the river would have been a far bigger one than the news of your death. It is a sad fact, but you would have been mourned momentarily, and then people move on. They still have their own troubles."

Siobhan opens her mouth to protest, but I glare at her, and she just fumes silently.

"Let me be clear – *you* asked for help when my card found you. *We* are here to help. You will accept it. I know this because the card tells me so. *We* are what you have wished and fantasized for - those from the land of the fae living, breathing, and real. It is not some young adult fantasy novel. No Tolkien, Lewis or Martin. *We* are more than likely a disappointment, and so be it. But let go the troubles of your old life – don't worry, there are always new ones to take their place – and move on to your new one. You have a chance to make a significant and meaningful splash now."

The girl blinks at me, opens her mouth, then shuts it.

Siobhan clears her throat, and then remarks quietly, "To be clear, *I'm* not from the faerealm, I just visited for a while."

"And now she is forever stuck with my company," I say with a grin, but I suspect it is not a reassuring one.

"Don't worry," Siobhan mutters to the girl. "He doesn't visit all that often. I hadn't seen him in over a year, and then he shows up tonight – last night, actually. Anyway, I can tell he was getting bored with me, and then he got this *look* and says he has a new client to help. It's the quickest turnaround he's ever had, apparently. And he actually invited me to accompany him, so that was a first. I'm sorry I wasn't able to stop him from pushing you off the bridge – honestly, whoever would have expected that?"

The girl actually giggles, and Siobhan's relieved smile is as glorious as a sunrise after a long night.

"Let's start with getting you warm," Siobhan suggests, and wraps the blanket around the girl. "I can make some hot cocoa, and we can talk."

"Put some Jack in it, and you have a deal."

Siobhan laughs. "Yeah, no. Besides, all I really have is wine and it wouldn't compliment the cocoa very well."

The girl pretends disappointment. She won't let go of the street immediately, of course, and will always be slow to trust. That is a good thing, and her spirit will be an asset.

I know I will not be invited back to Siobhan's, and understand. I think we all have had enough of my company for the night. I turn to the river, and peer down into the black mist.

I realize there is something dark coming, something that I don't understand. It gives me a sense of time, oddly enough, of the future. And that notion is new and startling to me. I wish I could say it is thrilling, but it has made me uneasy. The abstract idea of time is twisting its tendrils through me, but I don't think that is what will

207

remove the binding runes from my back. I feel half-certain that I pushed the girl out into the void to act as a sacrifice to the dark, but dismiss the fanciful speculation as being too long in the company of you superstitious lot. Again, a glimpse of the idea of passing time. Strange indeed.

"I will need my card back," I say, and extend my hand without looking at them. I am fascinated by the fog as it moves in the dark. The girl places the card gently in my hand, and I tuck it away.

"You both be careful now," I say to them. "One can never tell who is out and about at these hours."

"You're not going to walk back with us?" the girl asks.

I laugh. "I would feel sorry for anyone who crosses Siobhan." And this is true. She learned more than dancing from the sidhe. Still, First Street is not far away. And I can move very quickly. I will follow them with my ears until her shop door closes.

"Alright," the girl says. She pauses. "Take it easy, then"

She will never thank me, I know. And in truth, I am not in need of thanks. Nor deserving of them, I suppose.

"Always," I answer. "Inform me when you choose an alias. I can't keep calling you 'girl', can I?" She giggles.

They turn to head south, and they are several paces away, then Siobhan returns to me, the music of her steps delightful to hear. She places a hand on my arm.

"Are you okay?" she asks.

I do my best to look amused as I turn to her. "Why, of course," I answer. "When am I ever not?"

She gives me a small smile, and her head performs a quick bob. She pats my arm, and turns back to the girl as they head home in the dark.

I study the dark until I hear a door close and latch over on First Street.

My eyes can see the approach of dawn in the east, even if it is some time away. I discover I am looking forward to the sunrise. I can already anticipate it in my mind, but perhaps I will describe it to the bison skull. I hop onto the railing and let my legs dangle over the river once more. I can't resist the notion I am taunting something below. Fishing for trouble, with my legs as bait. Nonsense. I shake my head. I reach towards my pocket to release the card again, send it out to search for those that could use my help, but my hand retreats from the task. I have never been reluctant to set it out again, yet now have an idiotic fear for its safety. It has been with me since my earliest days, not always in a business card form, of course. I have the odd notion that it is my one true friend. A constant companion, at least. I swear on your gods, this night has been a strange one.

The sun eventually arrives to brighten up the day as more cars, and then pedestrians, begin their travels across the bridge. I can hear the troll snoring in his lair. The sun is muted and pale, but begins its job of burning away the fog. It does so gently, giving the fog a chance to be both canvas and paint. Crepuscular rays are distinguished by the shadows that lie between, and they both shift and dance with the movement of trees, cars and people. Eventually it loans a steady warmth to the bridge, and the pavilion where I sit.

"Ah," the bison skull says. "That feels good."

"I imagine it does," I answer.

"That was a long night."

"Yes," I whisper. "Yes it was."

209

To Bed: 11:30

I was in our backyard, kicking around some clods of dirt when it occurred to me that over the fence and down the hill was a pool. I couldn't see over the massive barrier of unfinished wood, but I *knew* that pool was down there, and very likely empty of dirt clods. That this pool belonged to the infamous Fishcorns - a family known for producing a healthy stock of bullies - either didn't occur to me or my six year-old brain was incapable of seeing that far into the future. All I knew was it was time to start blindly lobbing hunks of grass-tangled mother earth over that fence and into what was surely the clean and clear waters below. My first few shots missed apparently, not even the sound of a disappointing empty thud to hear. Undeterred, I grabbed a fist-sized hunk of dirt, bent so far back my hand grazed the pile of earth that was my ammo dump, and heaved it in a perfect arc up and over the fence. I was rewarded with a distant splash and felt a thrill of victory run through me.

Until I heard the irritated shouts.

Four boys – all several years older than me – boiled up over the fence like ants out of their kicked nest. I was dumbstruck and terrified at their anger, not comprehending much more than "Hey, kid!" shouted at me.

What cut through their yelling was my mother's shrill, "You leave him alone right now! What's wrong with you? He's so much smaller than all of you!"

Their heads turned to her in stony insolence, lips curled and eyes squinting, ready to dish it right back to her. No one can be as righteous as a kid who feels he has the moral high ground. But their eyes widened and their jaws dropped along with the color in their faces. One last synchronized turn of the heads to me, and then they sank from view, without further protest.

I turned to my mother, grateful to her for coming to my rescue. As she began to ask me what on earth could have caused them to gang up on me, she glanced at her right hand, stared at it for a moment, and then began to laugh. She had been inside peeling potatoes, and still had the knife in her hand as she shook it at my tormentors. She found that so funny she never asked me what had happened, and I never offered. If she had caught me throwing the dirt clods over the fence, I would have been in trouble, probably spanked and then marched down and forced to apologize and clean their pool.

I personally had little trouble with the Fishcorns after that, though.

* * *

My mom more than likely would never have considered herself a feminist, although I believe she was one before the description and idea was coined. She could be ironic about her femininity at times, fully aware she was no dainty flower.

I believe she probably thought of feminism as bra-burning, leg and armpit-hair displays of man hating fury – seeing as it was distorted in those early days by those who felt threatened by it, both male and female. The truth is she never even considered that she should defer to a man's judgment, keep her opinion to herself, or to

211

let my dad be the 'decision maker' of the family. In short, she was not going to be told what to do, think or say by anyone. This in a time when advertisements and articles were lecturing women about how to please their man. Or at least about how not to piss him off.

My earliest memory – one that I trust, anyway – is of it being easier to crawl rather than walk. Walking was new and a little dangerous. Every once in a while if felt nice to drop on all fours and scoot across the floor. I remember doing this in the dining room, my hands and knees squeaking across the cheap tiles towards a distorted rectangle of sunlight that made me squint against its glare. This memory doesn't have my mom in it directly, just a sense of her, a presence. She was not far away, probably getting dinner ready.

I've been accused of being a momma's boy all my life, and I ceased trying to dismiss that accusation long ago. If, by being a momma's boy, that meant I shared her distaste of crowds, fake people, real but *way* too happy people, full of themselves people, full of shit people, and people who look like they're full of shit because…well, they *look* like it, then yeah I plead guilty.

My mom could be domineering and controlling, prone to bad moods and had a mean streak that would surface occasionally. Yet she was caring and could be gentle, and never once did I feel unloved. While *she* could bully, she could not stand the trait in others. I believe she was aware of this complexity of self, and at times be apologetic. She never took herself seriously, could be self-deprecating, and if she helped you get into a bit of trouble, would own up to it.

* * *

It had been the summer of *Star Wars*, the movie that was an atom bomb in the nerd world – even non-nerds could enjoy it as a guilty pleasure. This is the only movie that I can recall my mom seeing twice in a theater, and when it hit premium movie channels years later, she could be caught watching it with an embarrassed grin.

As a red-blooded, pimple-garnished nerd who's heart leapt into love at first sight of the *Millennium Falcon* and was already experimenting in stop motion with the family's super-8 mm camera, by golly I was going to make my own *Star Wars*. I built an elaborate backdrop of a star-scape with a frame jutting out at the top corners supporting a rig that could be adjusted incrementally frame by frame to give the illusion of zooming starships - a poor-boy's motion control. Sadly, they jerked oddly across the movie frame, orchestrated exactly like you would expect from an impatient teenager. Undeterred, I decided I had better get some test footage of explosions.

I settled on a combination of model rocket engine and flash-bulb filament – a lot of smoke and pretty sparkles, all set off by a transformer from a model railroad. I pried the propellant out of its housing, wrapped in the silver threads from a flash-bulb, and tied the concoction up with wire and suspended it from my framework.

I should probably point out that my movie set was located in the front living room of our house. Maybe because I gave my mom the role of cameraman, she allowed me to fire off said model rocket engine inside the house. Neither of us consulted dad in the matter.

I laid out a heavy canvas tarp under the future explosion to protect the white shag carpet underneath – never let it be said I was not thinking of safety, after all – and began to lecture my mom about what would happen.

"There's going to be a bright flash with some smoke, but don't worry," I told her.

She nodded her head with a business-like professionalism. "Okay."

"The engine is just going to flash, but it's not going to go anywhere since it's out of its housing, so don't worry."

Nod. "Okay."

"So just keep filming until it's out, okay?"

"Yep," she replied crisply.

The first two attempts were duds, with the filaments flaring a dull red. I carefully re-wired the setup, and instructed my mom to start filming again. I flipped the lever on the transformer, and with a mighty whoosh the engine lit and sparkles exploded like a miniature fireworks display. Smoke began to fill every square inch of the house, and the traitorous smoke detector blared out in alarm.

213

Well, that's more smoke than I thought there would be, I thought as I watched the engine burn through its support wire and drop onto the tarp, proceed to burn right through *that* and into the carpet below. Naturally, that started a fire.

Holy shit!

I started to stomp on the flames.

"Mom, we've got a fire," I reported.

"What?" she asked.

"We've got a fire," I repeated, voice shaking.

"But you said keep filming," she said. "No matter what."

"That's okay." I assured her as my right foot was a piston trying to snuff out the fire. "We may need some water, though."

My dad entered, stage left, with a look of confused anger on his face. "What the hell is going on?" he bellowed.

"We're doing explosion tests," my mom offered brightly.

"Exploding what?" he asked as he watched me trying to extinguish the flames.

"Rocket engines!" my mom answered.

"In the *house?*"

Mom helpfully pointed to my background of stars. "This is where the set is."

Thankfully, the fire began to die out, and I felt it was safe enough to leave and get some water to pour over it. My dad, still looking as if he was in over his head, went down the hall to pry the battery out of the smoke detector.

My mom and I pulled the tarp back and drizzled water over the glowing chunk of propellant, which looked like a tiny meteorite that had punched through the carpet to lodge itself into the hardwood flooring below.

While my dad had a lot to say about the general stupidity of it all, my mom never remarked on it without laughing. She was complicit, after all.

And she got the shot. Even dad agreed it looked pretty spectacular on film.

* * *

We can wonder what paths our lives might have taken if only events had occurred differently – what might my dad have done if he had completed high school, and had been able to go on to college? If my mom's fiancé hadn't cheated on her, and so ending their impending marriage and helping her to decide Bradford, Pennsylvania, was just a bit too small for her tastes now and it was time to head west, young woman. So my sister and I are lucky she and a friend did just that, meeting my father in San Diego. He had joined the Navy.

It's not like she had severed ties with her past – we visited Pennsylvania as often as we could – but it was now kept at a distance. She may have missed her family fiercely, and didn't care for the crowded bigger city life over the lush green hills and hollows of home, but it was away from wagging tongues and snide comments soaked with baited beer-breath. While she was prideful, she also may have thought that moving away was better than punching smart-asses in the face for the foreseeable future. Not that she wouldn't have minded having a valid excuse to do so, I suppose.

* * *

It's not a leap of imagination to see that I received my love of story-telling from her – any mundane event from the daily grind could be clay to be shaped and molded into a story if it had made her laugh, or pissed her off. And if she embellished it, at least she was consistent, and no doubt truly believed her version. You wouldn't dare tell her she was wrong.

Once I had decided I was going to Speedy Mart – the 60s incarnation of 711 – and took a roundabout route through the canyon, fully aware I wasn't supposed to go to either place. My brilliant plan was to wind up at our usual hangout, a mini-gully where we would ride bikes and have rock-fights, innocently proclaiming I had been up there all along. Naturally, I was caught coming back from the mini-mart and my plan collapsed, was spanked and grounded for two weeks. She loved to tell that story, and always started it with, "Well, he ran *away*." Well, *no*. I just wanted to go to Speedy Mart.

215

In kindergarten, apparently I had given my teacher the impression that my dad was black. No doubt noticing my pasty complexion was a little confusing to her, so when she finally met my father at a school function, they decided that since my dad was so tan from construction work, I thought he was a black man. When my dad got home, he tucked a thumb into his waistband to tug down his pants far enough to display that his skin was, indeed, as white as mine.

I remember being a bit bewildered that they thought they had to prove this to me, and I had no memory of stating that my dad was black. While I was still pretty ignorant of race relations, I did understand that some of my friends had darker skin than mine, but my dad was not like them. What I think must have happened, since it was 1966, the description 'colored' was still in use, and by golly my dad was colored and I mentioned it, not knowing what it meant.

My mom loved to end the story, "And do you *know*, Chuck had to pull down his waistband to prove to Bobby that he had white skin!" While it's sad to look back and think that it was something they felt they had to prove to me, I suppose it made a better punchline for her. Because stories were to be entertaining, and have a funny ending. And boy, did she have a lot.

When we would go back to Pennsylvania for a visit, there was nothing better than when my mom and her brothers would reminisce, laughing so hard in recounting their tales that they could become incoherent. There are plenty that will be lost forever, but I have a crazy-quilt memory of 'member-the-time-whens punching the air of my grandparent's kitchen, the flak of each one still hanging above the table as new stories poured out. That time when their oldest brother kept her and her other brother pinned down in a ditch because they had teased him mercilessly for so long he grabbed a rifle, taking shots at them each time they poked a head up. That time they gave a hated neighbor a loaded cigar, and when it went boom it blew up so strong it tipped his rocking chair - and him - over backwards and off his porch. That time they had been out skiing through the woods, the whole group of kids had ran over the oil pumper that been squatting down doing his business, making him fall right *into* his business. That time my mom had been out hunting, and a bear fell out of a tree right in front of her, scaring them both. That time my mom punched a future opera singer in the face because she had stomped on her hand while they were climbing a playground slide. Because of *course* the girl did it on purpose.

* * *

How many memories pile up over the years? It's not like layers of sediment, where the oldest are damn near unreachable without massive drilling platforms. Some are as close and bright as the day we lived them – at least, we think they are. I believe we misremember a lot, even though we are convinced our perspectives are the truth.

I find the human mind fascinating. The ability to recall so many memories. Some that have been forgotten for many years only to be brought forth because of some trigger. Smell can really do that to me, but there are countless associations that make a long-dead memory flash into the light, and for the most part it thrills me because I am lucky and privileged enough not to have had any major trauma in my life, I suppose. Painful memories I tend to not forget. Ever. I have a memory of betrayal where the person involved has been gone a long time, and those who didn't believe me no doubt have forgotten it. I guess I justify letting it be as not worth 'stirring the pot'. And it makes me who I am, and in the grand design, people have suffered worse by far.

And so how many memories pile up over the years? I don't know if it has ever been, or can be, quantified. We do know they blur and merge and change, and maybe they have to. Perhaps the brain is juggling and shifting them over the years to keep us sane. We aren't compartmentalized like a hard drive, right? So they can pile up, and some of us can recall things sharper than others – but are they ever really gone? And when a mind begins to malfunction, I can't believe those memories are lost for good. Are they just sealed off? Losing the ability to communicate isn't the same thing as not remembering words, is it? Not recognizing a loved one doesn't mean the memory of them is gone, right? Maybe it becomes inaccessible, but it might still be there. Or perhaps it's remembered, and just not understood anymore.

217

* * *

"Bob," my sister asked me over the phone, "has mom sounded…quieter when you've talked to her? Less talkative?" My parents had moved to Idaho in the late 80s, and Kari and our first daughter moved up to Eastern Washington in the early 90s. We lived fairly close, but with two daughters now and our own house to take care of, it could make it hard for us to see my parents as much as we had throughout the year. So we talked on the phone a lot. And now that my sister mentioned it, my mom *did* sound uncharacteristically quiet on the phone lately.

So I called them and asked what was up. "Well," my dad said, "we think your mom probably had a stroke. Not a big one."

Crap. As much as I suspected (her mom had had one several years earlier, and ultimately passed away from it). At first, she just didn't participate in conversations as much as she used to. She was still able to converse well enough, but if you hadn't known her you may have thought that she was just a thoughtful and quiet person. She did go to therapy for a while, but ultimately I think it became too frustrating for her. So there was a steady decline in her ability to communicate over the years, and ultimately in cognition. When it was apparent it was dangerous for her to be left alone – my dad did have to sleep, after all – the difficult decision that my father made to put her in a nursing home was done after Mother's Day in 1999. While it was fairly traumatic for her at first, she did get used to it. When we would visit and it was time to leave, the nurses would distract her by saying, "Oh, Joyce – we need your help over here!" The take-charge instinct to help and fix things was still there, and she would charge off to see what needed to be taken care of.

If it seems I'm reluctant to go into too much detail at this time in her life, well – guilty. How can a mind go from a sharp and insightful instrument to a dull and confused jumble of emotions? This was a woman who you could not win an argument with (something our oldest daughter inherited, alas). She could shift gears so fast – hell, it didn't matter if what she was saying was relevant. She made you think it was, and she won most of the time. And on the rare occasion where she couldn't out-argue you, be prepared for the silent treatment for a day or two. This was a woman who most people liked, even if she didn't like them. Animals loved her – a dolphin at Sea-World was absolutely entranced with her once (she claimed it was her nasal twang that attracted it – they spoke the same language). This was the only woman that my paternal grandfather had any real respect for. I guess when you can't dominate someone like you're used to, that is an impressive thing.

So yeah, it's hard to write about a dynamic force of nature having the wind taken from her sails. And yet, during this time, you could still see her in there, trying to pluck the checkbook out of my dad's pocket when he would lean in for a kiss. Still playing with her granddaughters – a simple game of dropping a penny through the lattice work of a patio table, but it was clear she enjoyed the interaction.

Her mom kept a journal over the years – you can't call it a diary. It was more of a terse recounting of the day's events, notation of the weather and judgement-free. My mom took up the task late in life, and as far as I can make out, the last entry is December 24th, 1998. Most entries are as short and to the point as her mother's were, but soon they became routine declarations of bedtime and yard work. Many were "Played on the computer" (solitaire, no doubt) or "played in the yard". Gone were the "Clyde and Donna came over for dinner" or "took Bobby out for his birthday" recounting and the day's temperature. It appears she lost her place in the spiral notebook she wrote in, because she has some December notations before October ones, and the last page, with a notation of *Dec 12 Wanted Cleared youre to bed 11:30* is at the top of the page. I'm thinking it's "watered cleaned yard" since she clearly was fixating on yardwork in most of her later entries – although the likelihood of her watering the yard in December is probably nil. Her journal entries clearly have become a route task by now, and in fact her last one was telling in its repetitiveness:

Dec 24 The Cleared by the
To bed 11:30 The bed 11:30
To bed 11:30 To bed 11:30
To bed 11:30 To bed 11:30
To bed 11:30 To bed 11:30

I wonder if she knew she was not writing what she wanted to, but couldn't make her hand guide the pen to the words she meant? Was it frustrating? Above the last entry, there is something scribbled out – and that small section is in pencil, where her last entry is back to pen. I suppose it is pointless to try and decipher what state her wounded mind was working in. All we know is that it was betraying her, and in several months she would be in a nursing home for almost three years.

* * *

My dad called us and told us that this would probably be her last night, and that we should probably come over to see her. The last several years had seen her steadily decline, of course, but she still seemed alert, enjoyed our company when we visited, even if it was to just to smile with us and watch TV. I'm not certain if it was ever explained to me why her last few days were so sudden, and she was *not* alert, and she was *not* smiling when we went to see her. I didn't want my daughters to go in, but Kari overruled me and they got to say goodbye. I took them back home, had Kari call my boss and tell him I would not be in the next day, and drove back to be with my dad. We sat with her, took turns swabbing her lips to give her some moisture, and at one point we were kicked out as the nurses wanted to change her and give her some pain medication. We sat out in the waiting room and we both dozed, and then I apparently fell asleep and dad woke me up saying she had passed. He was with her alone, leaving me to sleep, and I suppose that was a fitting thing after 43 years of marriage. I went in, gave her a final kiss goodbye, and we went back to my dad's house to get some sleep.

I woke with a terrific headache, and had it throughout the day. We met with the funeral home to make arrangements – there was to be no funeral per her wishes. She thought they were barbaric. So she was cremated, and later buried in Spirit Lake (she was later moved to Hayden where she rests next to my dad's second wife, and where he will be buried).

As I was heading back home into Washington, my dad asked me to return a DVD player he had bought at Circuit City. The damn thing was defective – every movie looked washed out. When I went in, a manager was called and the eye-rolling and bluffing began. "Why isn't your dad returning it himself?" I was asked. "Because my mom – his *wife* – died today and he just doesn't have it in him to deal with this," I answered. Well *that* shut them up. They quietly gave me the refund. I couldn't help but think my mom had my back one last time.

* * *

Her dad died in 1982. Her mom in 1992. And she died in 2002. I don't know if there's any cosmic significance to that ten year cycle, but it sure is interesting to me. That her dad was known to his grand-kids as "Bum Bum" and she was known as "Bing" to her own proba-bly tickled her to no end. Both monikers were chosen by each's first grandchild, and I guess we have to wonder what the hell is up with the weird nicknames in the family, but I think we've established the human mind sure can be a mystery.

I hate that she's missed out on the last nineteen years of my daughter's lives. I think she would be proud as hell of them. They have a lot of her in them – not being afraid to pick up and move across the country, to begin with. My oldest won a bar fight in Dub-lin. My youngest traveled to Thailand on her own, lived there for quite some time and they both have been to South America. They have their grandmother's bold sense, and while I am not a spiritual person, she surely lives on in them. I think most parents – if they're decent - want their children to have a better life than they did. For them to be better human beings than they were (my dad rose from

221

being born in a dugout in Montana in the middle of the Great Depression, and not turning into the ill-tempered and arrogant person his father was – but perhaps that is a tale for another time). You don't want them to make the mistakes you did, and you can only hope to help lay a foundation for a better future you may never see. I think my mom did that.

There will be a time when none of us are remembered – at this point, I am not confident that the human race will escape its cradle and outlive the expansion of the star that gave us life, much less another 200 – 300 years (I hope I'm wrong – and I hope *you* think I'm wrong). But we don't have to be remembered to make a positive impact on the world. The atoms of kindness can build an impressive edifice, if we try. It need not be named after us.

Okay, look - I don't like ending this with a bittersweet rumination on the mysteries and fragility of life, and how we all contribute to the circle of it. *She* wouldn't have liked it – she would want you to laugh.

* * *

It was the mid-80s, and she had just arrived home from work, jubilant and laughing, declaring, "There *is* a God – there *is* a God!" She worked for an OBGYN east of Mission Valley, and had been driving home, wearing her spotless-white nursing uniform, steering her enormous Cadillac along 94 on the final leg of the journey. She was a careful and lawful driver for the most part, but would not be bullied of course. As she was cruising past the onramp from Campo Road, a guy in a Honda (one of those "wind-up jobbers", she described) was straining the guts out of his engine to fly onto the freeway. She accelerated to let him drop in behind her, but he was having none of that. It was imperative that he get in front of her, and he laid on the horn and gestured at her with a specific finger.

This did not sit well with mom. She decided to keep at a steady pace, and the man was forced to drop in behind her, honking, screaming, flipping the bird. Once on a level grade, his little car could pick up the momentum it needed to pass her, and he did so, honking, screaming, flipping the bird. She just shook her head sadly, and continued on as he dropped in front of her, turning back with his trifecta of gestures. She rolled her eyes and they continued on as such until she dutifully signaled that she was exiting onto Sweetwater Springs Boulevard, where he shot over and took the exit as well. Much honking, screaming and flipping of birds ensued. He made the poor decision to take the left turn lane towards the east end of Campo Road, where she took the right on to Sweetwater Springs. Undeterred, he cut across in front of her and jammed on his brakes, blocking her. Honking. Screaming. Bird-flipping. She sighed and shook her head, waiting for him to move. And he eventually did, driving forward but gesturing back at her forcefully with his middle-finger - and then promptly slammed into the back of a pickup truck.

She sat there momentarily, astonished as a "big, brawny guy" climbed out of the truck looking none too happy. My mom wondered if she should get out and be a witness, describing the guy's erratic and unhinged behavior. She settled for just leaving, not knowing how nuts the guy really was. As she accelerated away from her stop, the guy blinked at her owlishly as she drove past, and she smiled sweetly, extending her middle finger.

That was my mom, Joyce Marie Brown/Jenson. And I bet that guy never forgot her.

www.ingramcontent.com/pod-product-compliance
Lightning Source LLC
Chambersburg PA
CBHW050929120626
46552CB00001B/110